PRAISE FOR CHASING VEGA

"Jessica Ramirez is a kickass cop with a strong moral compass and the grit to prove she belongs with the big boys. I can't wait to see what she does next."

"A gripping page turner that is brimming with spot-on descriptions and characters that leave a mark on your memory. Chasing Vega is unputdownable."

"Superstar protagonist Detective Jessica Ramirez is resilient and tenacious when it comes to seeking justice. Adding a Latin spice female heroine to the equation leaves the reader hungry and wanting to dive in for more. Chasing Vega...a new thrilling meaning to my law enforcement motto 'Stay Safe!'"

D1518442

"An exciting debut thriller to kick off a series sure to please, anchored by the fierce Jessica Ramirez and her intriguing partner Allie. Looking forward to more from this author!"

"There was enough suspense that I kept turning the pages well into the night – I kept saying "just one more chapter"... Fans of crime/detective fiction or thrillers will love this book."

"Jessica and her partner Alexandra struggle with not only the issues before them but also the decision of who they are and where they fit in the world. I was quickly wrapped up in the story and couldn't put it down."

"A wonderful thriller - Highly recommend it to readers who are interested in plot driven books that keep you on your toes."

CHASING VEGA

TERRY SHEPHERD

Ramirez & Clark
PUBLISHERS

For Judy

FOR INSIDERS

PROLOGUE

North of Flagstaff, Arizona

The man with the teardrop tattoo sat, paralyzed, on the shale outcropping, five hundred fifty-seven feet above the churning Colorado River. He was incapacitated, barely able to breathe. Unable to move, he could feel her hand holding onto his neck, just five fingers keeping him from falling headlong into oblivion.

The woman turned his head to meet her iron gaze. His eyelids started to droop as the oxygen in his bloodstream began to deplete.

She slapped his face with her free hand.

"What is it like to look into a person's innocent blue eyes, and then strangle her until they roll back into her head? Did she scream when she realized what you were doing? How hard did she struggle?"

His body was no longer under his control. He could still hear, see and feel. He could not move. He wanted to scream but his vocal cords felt frozen.

Her voice dripped with contempt.

"What was it like to pervert the system to escape the justice you so richly deserve?"

Her intentions were clear to him now. The woman was going to kill him.

"Listen up, scumbag. Can you hear me?"

He could. His arms and legs felt like rubber. The calloused paws that had closed like a vise around two innocent necks were useless. His lungs were shutting down. His heart raced in a vain attempt to get oxygen to his brain. The pain was beyond anything he had ever experienced. There was nothing he could do about it.

The full moon and the cloudless sky above the Grand Canyon gave its walls a dark, gothic feel. The woman's voice was now a whisper.

"Alton James Mahoney," she said. "I sentence you to death for the murders of Mary Jane Alexander and Norma Lee Christopher."

The soft hand behind Alton James Mahoney's neck pushed him gently forward. The man with the teardrop tattoo tumbled, silently, into the dark abyss.

ONE

The First Day - Paloma, Illinois

"Police!"

Detective Jessica Ramirez could hear Lou Harrison's bellow from the back porch of the meth house on Maryland street. The sound of a battering ram smashing the front door followed. She imagined the portly Field Training Officer that the older cops called "Kojak" handed that task off to Officer Chuck Butler. This would be the newly minted rookie's first take down.

The distinctive sound of AR15 gunfire erupted in the house.

Jess didn't wait for her senior officer to make the call.

"4-David-15, shots fired at 595 Maryland street. Requesting backup."

She could hear dispatch's confirmation in the tiny earpiece that cops lovingly call, "a roach."

Beneath the kevlar vest that protected Jessica's torso, a female voice whispered from an open line on her cell phone.

"Interesting sound effects. Ours or theirs?"

It was her sometime partner, Officer Alexandra Clark.

"No talking, Ali. You can only listen in if you keep your mouth shut."

"I'm close by. Need some help until the boys arrive?"

"I got this, girlfriend. Now keep quiet or I'll have Siri hang up on you."

"Be careful, Jess. This should be a SWAT operation. It smells like Captain Batavia is putting you in harm's way again."

"Then I'll bust some ass and make him regret the decision."

Jess kicked in the back door, charging into what had once been a kitchen.

The place was deserted, not a stick of furniture, no lights, no other sounds. The Latina held a Glock 45 in the ready position against her chest, briefly clicking the barrel mounted LED on and off as she scanned the front room from cover behind the thin kitchen wall.

The roach came to life. "2-Boston-10. Shots fired at 595 Maryland. Probably multiple subjects with semi-autos. Outside requesting backup."

The boys had bailed on her. She was alone in the house with the bad guys. Time to get out and wait for reinforcements.

Jess sensed movement behind her. Then came the strike to the back of her head. And darkness.

1,637 MILES SOUTHWEST OF PALOMA, Illinois, the man who called himself Michael Allen was scanning a street corner in downtown Phoenix, Arizona. The tall redheaded woman he was looking for appeared, right on schedule.

She wore skinny dress pants that were one size too small for her ample hips. A flouncy top that accentuated her charms was wrapped in a red, fitted blazer. Her brown hair was piled at the peak of her head in a barely contained topknot. Large-rimmed hipster glasses balanced above her eyebrows. Nude pumps completed the ensemble below. A necklace with a pair of ivory dice danced, guiding the eyes in the direction most men eventually go. Whatever it was that encircled her left ring finger was definitely not matrimonial.

Michael Allen smiled, typing two words into the encrypted messenger on his cell phone.

"Target acquired."

THE CONCUSSION TURNED out to be minor. But that didn't stop the spinning sensation Jessica Ramirez felt as she fought her way back to consciousness.

She recognized the basement from her youth. Gone were the Mexican murals on the walls, the bean bag chairs, the television and the ping pong table. The distinctive smell of geraniums confirmed that this place was now a meth lab. Propane tanks, boxes of pseudoephedrine, coffee filters, frying pans and an array of bottles and tubing were arranged on a long workbench. A gaping hole in the foundation revealed a tunnel that Jess concluded surfaced beyond the property line, where she had seen a tool shed and a gleaming Camaro in another dilapidated driveway.

A pair of strong arms held hers behind her, pinning her shoulders against the back of a metal folding chair. The roach and the radio were gone. Her two Glocks, the one she kept on her belt and her ankle holstered backup lay on a workbench. Thankfully, they didn't take the vest and didn't know about the cellphone inside of it.

She considered the man who stood in front of her. Tall, around six feet, very thin, with the facial markings of someone who used a little too much of his own product. He held the AR15 rifle loosely in his right hand. The butt of the gun must have been what put her to sleep.

"A beautiful place you have here," Jess said. "I remember playing Monopoly in this basement when I was a kid."

"Do you need another nap?" the man said, massaging the stock of his AR15. "Ricardo, cuff her arms behind that chair. Time to relocate."

Ricardo.

Jess realized that the short fireplug with the muscular arms was a low-level gang banger she knew from the barrio.

The recognition was mutual.

"Making a young boy an accessory to the assault of a police officer. You're full of bad decisions today, pendejo. Give it up before my partners bust in and cap your skinny ass."

"Shut up, Jessi," Ricardo whispered. "He's a user and the fix is wearing off."

The addict pulled Jess' service weapon off of the work bench. He forced her mouth open with one hand and put the barrel of the Glock inside of it with the other. "I say we kill her with her own gun and wrap her cold fingers around the grip to make it look like suicide."

Jess could taste the sting of the petroleum solvent she used to keep the weapon lubricated and clean.

"Let's see what the wall looks like with her brains all over it."

Jess bit down on the gun barrel, her eyes blazing.

"Do it, shithead. I dare you."

"HAVE WE MET BEFORE?" he asked.

She scoffed. "You're seriously opening with your weakest material?"

"Setting low expectations allows me to exceed them later on."

"I see." She knew the type well. Six-foot-two. Expensive haircut. Tanned. Probably a college football star with an ego that matched muscles that rippled beneath his Armani suit.

"I'm due back at work and don't have time for this so my expectations are that you'll give it up and try your act out on someone older and more needy."

"To be totally honest, I thought you were a model with the Austin Agency. My sister works there. She described you. Carrie Underwood's face, Kate Hudson's smile and Jessica Simpson's curves that tongue-tie the photogs. I'd recognize you anywhere."

"That's some of the best patronizing bullshit I've heard. You've earned a modicum of information. I work at April's Boutique."

He looked hurt.

"It's a truthful assessment. April's eh? Maybe it was you who helped me. I'm a dunce when it comes to gifts for women and that place has never let me down."

"For your wife?" His type always had a wife.

He chuckled. "I wish. I love the institution but never found the right partner. I shop at April's for Mom. Since Dad died, I've tried to be an especially attentive son."

It was the right answer but she was still wary.

"What did you get her?"

She saw his eyes scan her body. It was a sensation that at once pleased and disgusted her.

"That necklace. She loves the game Yahtzee. You recommended the dice."

The dice. April didn't carry that item. Clearly this guy was lying.

An idea was beginning to form in her head. She would play the game a little longer.

"I thought they were cute, too." She twisted the small ivories between her thumb and index finger. "One of the regulars said they bring good fortune."

"They certainly worked today," Michael said. "And I think my sister would agree that you are definitely model material."

She had a caustic answer locked and loaded, but this man wasn't going to give her time to fire it.

"Was it tough for you in college? I mean the thing where men discount a woman's intellect just because she's attractive? I hate that."

"You're really working hard on this, aren't you? That's a guy thing. Everybody does it."

"Nope." He was emphatic. "It only happens to the really beautiful ones. I never joined a frat in school for that reason. Objectification drives me crazy."

He had a point.

"Well, I can't say I totally agree with that. Women enjoy being appreciated for our brains." She twirled a lock of her hair with her little finger. "But it's nice to know that the trouble we take to look presentable is noticed."

"Exactly! Now you are totally channeling my mother. Dad used to bring her flowers out of the blue, for no special reason. He'd just say, 'you were on my mind today, love, and I wanted you to know how much I appreciate you.'"

"Nobody behaves that way anymore. And it certainly was not the case in the household where I grew up. The world would be a better place if people were more appreciative."

"He was my role model. Mom always used to tell us that on the day they met, he said, 'Something tells me this is a moment I'll never forget.'"

His line touched a corner of her heart she thought had died long ago. Was he still lying or was this the truth?

"Did you say he passed away?"

"Three years ago. Two tours in Vietnam. The Agent Orange ultimately got him. I still come home and expect to see him at the front door."

"You're definitely persistent," she said. "But I've had it with men for the time being."

"Look, I'm sorry to have taken up so much of your time and I hope you'll forgive that stupid stuff I said about the modeling thing. You really are the entire package. Thanks for helping me make the

April's connection. Mom will love that I met someone else who believes in good luck."

"How do you know I'm not a lesbian?"

She loved tossing that one in the direction of would-be suitors. The question knocked him back a step. But she could see him recover.

"My gay-dar says otherwise. But if that's true, it's just another fascinating conversation topic."

"You're not going to leave me alone until you get something, are you?"

She could see that the word *something* raised his blood pressure in an embarrassing place. He was fighting to get back some control of the conversation.

"You know what?"

Here's where he tries to close the sale, she thought.

"I'm feeling serendipity. I have a sixth sense about this. If it's not too forward, I'd love the opportunity to try and change your attitude."

He was definitely different than her current dating pool. Very different. She felt an odd combination of fatigue and excitement. What could it hurt to give this guy a try?

"I'll tell you what," she said. "Come by at 5:45 on Wednesday, I might have a couple of ideas for your mom. I'll give you a shot at being your authentic self over coffee after."

"Let's make it dinner. It's almost the end of the month and if I don't burn some money at the Century Club, they take it out of my account anyway. 5:45, it is."

"Please prove to me that you're not a total idiot." She proffered a hand. "I'm Ann. Ann Blakely."

He took it. She made sure that her handshake was solid; board-room masculine in its firm grip.

"I accept the challenge," he answered. "I'm Michael Allen."

"See you soon, Michael Allen."

She turned, crossing with the light in the direction of April's Boutique.

MICHAEL ALLEN SMILED. Things were going exactly as planned. He had one more thing to say to her, waiting a beat to make sure the last line had impact.

"Something tells me this is a moment I'll never forget."

TWO

Paloma

"Killing a cop puts us all away for life, gringo," Ricardo said.

Jess could feel the addict's hand shaking. The Glock rattled against her teeth. She was losing patience with these two.

"Shoot me," she said, "and you two will never walk out of here alive."

Her taunt seemed to have no effect on the man with the AR.

"What have we got to lose, Ricardo? She's got a make on all of us. It's only a matter of time before a long burn in the joint."

"That meth you're hooked on is frying your brain, pendejo," Ricardo said. "Let's just leave her here and blow. She's got brothers outside and an army on the way."

His boss could still count, Jess thought. The addict pulled the weapon out of her mouth and put it on the workbench.

"Give it up guys," she said. "Ricardo is right. Turn me loose. Give me the weapons and let's all leave in one piece."

She could sense that the meth in the gun-toter's system was dissipating. He needed a refill. It wasn't helping his mood.

"Uncuff her right arm," he commanded.

Ricardo obliged, holding Jess's left arm tightly in two thick fists. His boss grabbed Jess's wrist, turning it upward. He produced a Border Guard hunting knife. With slow precision, he cut a thin incision from just below Jess's elbow to an inch above her wrist.

"Deep enough to do the job but slow enough so you won't bleed out until you feel the burn. Lock her back up, Ricardo."

Rivulets of crimson bubbled up from the wound, dripping into a puddle on the cement floor. Jess tried to guess how many stitches it would take to plug the leak and thought about how the scar would be one more trophy she could display to any man who tried to tell her that police work was, "no place for girls."

"Assaulting a police officer," she said. "That's it. Uncuff me and watch how this bleeding woman kicks your skinny ass."

The addict shoved the hunting knife in his belt and pointed the AR in the direction of a shelf that hung on the wall right above the chair where Jess was cuffed. On it were two large containers of highly flammable acetone.

"We walk. You die."

He fired twice, one for each can. The hot lead was enough to penetrate the aluminum and ignite the contents. A jet of blue shot across the room like a flame thrower.

"Typical. Another stupid junky thinking with his balls instead of his brain."

She turned to Ricardo. The face she had known since he was a five-year-old looked too young and too scared. Perhaps there was hope for him.

"Do the right thing," she whispered. "Cut me loose."

He dropped the cuff keys into Jess's open palms and put her radio out of the addict's sight behind the rear leg of the chair.

"Adios, hermanita," Ricardo said. "Saludas a tu madre."

Jess smiled to herself. "I own these guys. Never let the bastards see you sweat."

She could see that Ricardo was doing the sweating, some uncomfortable thoughts painting his young face with concern.

"The money!" he said. "It's upstairs in the back bedroom!"

The look on the addict's face told Jess that the boss had not thought about that when he blew holes in the acetone.

Flames enveloped the workbench. They danced across the dry floor joists consuming them like a hungry runner guzzles water after a 10K.

Ricardo went for the tunnel. The addict went for the money.

By the time the two had cleared the basement, Jess was out of the cuffs. She grabbed her Glock and bounded up the stairs, the flames chasing her in search of oxygen. Fire vomited out of the basement door, starting to chew up the first-floor drywall. No time to think about a bandage for the arm. The blood loss was making her lightheaded. Time to bail.

"2-Boston-10 and all units. 4-David-15 is coming out the front door now. One of the perps is headed out the back. The other will be exiting any second. Alert the fire department and get back here to help me bag these bad boys before this place goes up."

Dispatch repeated the particulars. The firefighters would be here in five minutes. Jess wasn't sure the house would last that long.

She remembered the cell phone.

"Still with me, girlfriend?"

Ali was.

"You sure know how to play nice with boys. Did you really dare that guy to 'pull the trigger'?"

"I like troubled souls," Jess said. "That's why I put up with you for so long."

"How bad did they hurt you?"

"I won't be donating blood anytime soon."

"Need some help?"

"Not unless you're O-Positive. I have things under control. Gotta go."

Jess disconnected the call.

She stumbled out of the front door, coughing, bleeding and attempting to aim her weapon at whatever might follow.

She tried to focus. The tunnel vision that fighter pilots get when they pull G's was another indicator of blood loss. It was like looking backwards through a telescope.

Sirens sang in the distance.

Jess's head was throbbing with each heartbeat. She switched the Glock to her right hand, putting pressure on her wound with her left. One could live without breathing for five minutes. You could bleed to death in two.

Kojak lumbered up the berm just as the addict burst out of the doorway. He held the AR in his right hand, a briefcase in his left.

The perp fired the weapon, nailing Kojak gut-center.

The FTO's Kevlar vest did its job. Jess deduced that Kojak would survive, but the impact was like getting hit with a baseball bat.

The FTO fell backwards, clearing the field of view for Jess to fire. She commanded her arms to raise the Glock. They wouldn't respond.

A gunshot erupted from across the street. The .223 caliber round hit the addict squarely between the eyes. Jess heard Ali's familiar voice on the radio.

"4-David-15 from 10-Mary-12. You're all clear, girlfriend. Get the hell away from that fire pit."

Another blast echoed from the back yard, followed by the explosive report of Butler's 12 gauge.

"One down in the shed."

Jess said a silent prayer that Ricardo would survive the day. She turned her fury in the direction of the rifle fire.

"I could have handled this, Alexandra."

"I'm surprised you are still standing. Get off that hill and find some place to collapse until the medics get here."

"You always want the limelight."

"You couldn't raise that gun, Jessica. I saved your life... again."

Jess's head was spinning. The right leg of her cargo pants was awash in blood.

"What do you say, Kojak? Another second, and I would have neutralized that skinny punk without 'Ego Girl's' intervention."

Harrison was on his feet, breathing hard.

"I think you're out of the fight, JRam. Sit down before you fall down."

Her legs wouldn't move. Her body no longer had enough vital fluid in it to comply with her brain's command. Jess felt her consciousness slipping away.

A snakelike hissing sound emanated from the basement. There was enough propane down there to vaporize the place. Jess could feel Harrison's arms around her waist, pulling her away from the danger.

The two police officers rolled down the berm and onto the asphalt. The tanks ignited. 595 Maryland was pulverized into a tsunami of fire and smoke. The siding on the adjoining houses melted like butter, the particle board beneath bursting into flames. A shockwave shattered windows for a block in every direction.

Jess was drifting toward the darkness. Kojak's 280 pounds were on top of her, pressing her body onto the pavement. Ali's voice seemed to come from far away.

"10-Mary-12. Request EMTs at 595 Maryland Street. Officers down."

Jess was face to face with the burley FTO. He was breathing heavily. The bouquet of an Altoid surrounded her with each exhalation.

"I think they won't be making any more crystal at this address," Harrison wheezed.

"You're invading my personal space, Kojak."

"I just saved your life, JRam. A little gratitude wouldn't hurt."

Jess smiled as unconsciousness enveloped her.

"If you want to make love to me, Lou," she whispered. "At least bring me flowers first."

THREE

Phoenix

Ann Blakely entered the store, exactly fifty-nine minutes after she left it for lunch. The Native American jewelry and new age paraphernalia sold there attracted an eclectic group of regulars, and tourists, drawn to the 1960s neon sign that flashed "April's Boutique" in bright orange cursive out front.

April Williamson stood behind the long glass display case. Ann reckoned her tie-dyed sundress could have been worn at Woodstock. Layers of bracelets, charms, Sedona crystals and gold encircled her wrists and neck. Ann saw her boss checking her watch, returning her gaze to the catalogue she was studying on the counter.

Ann knew the drill. April loved everyone, but where business was concerned, you had to be punctual. It wasn't personal, just a habit perfected over 30 years as a single woman, surviving in the cut-throat world of retail.

Ann replayed the encounter with Michael Allen. Who was this man who wouldn't take "no" for an answer? With so much else on her mind, she could use the distraction. And who knows. This

nicely dressed rich guy might be useful. She felt an unusual physical attraction. But there was something else. Something still foggy
and unclear to the inner radar that had served her so well. She
needed more information. Dinner was low risk. She decided that
she would play the game as it developed.

FOUR

The Second Day - Colorado River - Mile 98

The S-Rig Whitewater Raft, christened "Rosie," was at the mercy of the river. Her E-TEC 30 horsepower outboard was no match for Mother Nature. Paramedic Marty Laurent was having the time of his life.

Holding fast to a safety strap at the prow of the boat, he waved to the raft driver. Kevin Smith was doing his best to manhandle his craft without much effect. Every bone-shattering bounce brought involuntary yells from the fourteen passengers.

"Hey, Marty," Smitty said. "How's the ride up front?"

"It's heaven, Smitty! I love it when grown men scream."

"Hang on to your hat, my friend. This is the roughest river I can remember."

"You know me, Kevin. Turn loose the bull!"

Rosie plunged into the Crystal Rapid, the most challenging mile of whitewater in the Grand Canyon. Her outboard was useless now. The S-Rig spun and twisted amid gushing vortices that slammed against the river bed at 2000 cubic feet per second.

The Crystal tossed the raft into the air like a rag doll. She landed with a pounding thud that hit her passengers like a gut punch. The G forces were particularly potent up front, ripping Marty's hand from his safety strap and firing him forward into the raging maelstrom like a mortar round.

Marty Laurent had known his share of hydraulics, the swirling phenomenon that populated rafters' nightmares, but never the ferocity of the tornado that engulfed him now. The landing that ejected him took his breath away. He had to fight the impulse to inhale.

His leg smashed against something sharp and hard. He knew instantly that he had fractured his right fibula. Marty wondered if his skull might be next. And yet, he felt no pain, the combination of endorphins and shock blocked the nerve impulses... for now.

For the first time in his life, Marty Laurent thought he might die. A strange sensation encircled him. Fear melted into a feeling of peaceful surrender. If this was his time, he could accept it. A lifelong agnostic, Marty wondered what there might be on the other side of the darkness. Was the Crystal his portal into the unknown? He let his body go limp, sacrificing himself to its inexorable power.

And then, as suddenly as the hydraulic swallowed him, it spit him back out into the current. Marty's head broke through the surface. He gulped life-giving oxygen. Marty knew that he had few options. All he could do was ride it out and hope that he wouldn't end up encountering the knife-like outcroppings of the deadly sleeper rocks that hid just beneath the surface.

As he regained his bearings, he could see the collection of boulders known as "The Island" looming ahead. With his remaining strength starting to ebb, he clawed his way toward what looked like the most friendly rock, colliding into a notch carved over time by the relentless force of the river.

Marty saw another raft break free of the upper rapids. The guide swung the outboard around to point the boat toward the battered and bruised body. Marty waved a hand, smiling at the stunned crowd of witnesses, while his shattered leg bounced against the rock in time with the modulating currents.

At least he thought it was the rock. Despite the ever-increasing wave of searing pain that radiated upward from the wound, he sensed his splintered limb was bumping against something soft.

Marty submerged his free arm below the rim of the boulder. He recognized what he found there. As people watched from the raft, he pulled a human body to the surface. Even in death, the corpse revealed a small teardrop tattoo under the right eye.

FIVE

Paloma General Hospital - Room 215

"You should let me prescribe some pain meds for you, Detective. That's a pretty serious scrape."

The surgeon reminded Jess of one of the also-rans on the Bachelorette; attractive, great resume, but a little too focused on his career. She wondered if he was making the same inner observations about her.

"Gotta keep my head clear, doc. I think I'll stick with alternating Motrin and Tylenol."

"You may want a few of these Percs for later, just in case."

He handed Jess the prescription, taking another look at his handiwork.

"Call the duty nurse, if you need anything."

"Thanks very much for that, but I'm sure I'll be ok." Jess considered the gauze that covered the long laceration, carefully taped and wrapped. "Appreciate the needlework."

The doc's voice betrayed exasperation. "What is it with you cops? You come in here broken and near death, we put you back together and you don't give yourselves time to heal before going back out on the streets. The blood loss and laceration are pretty serious injuries, Detective. If I were talking to your boss, I'd recommend a couple of weeks to recover."

There was an unspoken bond between docs and cops. A mutual aid society where officers hung around to make sure potential trouble-maker patients behaved and the physicians didn't rat on the injured who were determined to stay in the game. "Thank you for not saying anything to my boss."

The doc chuckled. "Call us if there's any redness around the stitches. Try not to do anything to wreck my artistry. I took on a lot of student debt to learn how to sew like that. And stay away from the water for a couple of weeks. Those holes in your arm will suck up contaminants in a heartbeat."

"Stay away from the water," Jessica thought. "If he only knew."

SIX

10 Miles North of Flagstaff, Arizona

The Bell 407 life flight jet copter flew a 300-degree heading at 130 knots. On board, Coconino County Sheriff Danny Lopez sat next to Mabel Smith, the life flight trauma nurse. Behind them, newly minted Medical Examiner, Joey Price, was typing notes into a laptop.

The voice of Stephen Morris, Chief National Park Service Ranger for the Grand Canyon District, came through the noise cancelling Bose headsets.

"Three Zero Bravo Four from NPS ground. Can you hear me, Sheriff?"

"We're on our way, Steve. Be there in fifteen."

"Really appreciate this, Sheriff. We're swamped and the word is that you've got two to bring out. One alive and one for the icebox. Are you breaking in your new M.E.? I hear he's one of a kind."

"Dr. Price is with us and he can hear you," Danny said. He looked over his shoulder at the short figure seated behind him. He was not much beyond five feet four inches tall, maybe 150 pounds.

He still had the look of a medical school intern, young, brainy, caffeinated, with bags under his eyes from lack of sleep. His glasses were a bit too big for his head. Combined with the curly red hair, he looked like a miniature Napoleon Dynamite.

"How did you get word about this? Cell coverage at the Crystal is non-existent."

"Good old-fashioned amateur radio. One of the Canyon Rafters drivers relayed the message through ARES."

Danny instantly knew who Steve was talking about. ARES - The Amateur Radio Emergency Service, had many adherents, but one stood out from the crowd.

"Tell Smitty we're on our way."

"Thanks again for the assist. Call me when you get them out of the ditch. Morris out."

Danny glanced back at the coroner. Joey's eyes were now focused on the scene unfolding ahead.

The view of the Grand Canyon at altitude never lost its majesty, even for Danny. As a boy, he explored a good deal of the trails and tributaries at its base. He learned his constellations lying on top of a sleeping bag, enthralled with the night sky.

The afternoon sun was already working its way toward the western horizon, casting golden shadows into the canyon's depths.

"You all right, Joey?" Danny asked. He knew that the medical examiner had never been in a helicopter before. In fact, Joey Price didn't want the gig in Flagstaff at all. The pay was not very good and he was a little too far from his family in Albuquerque. But Dr. Price couldn't be picky. He was described as "difficult" by his last two employers. In the incestuous world of forensic medicine, word gets around. Joey had been "between opportunities" for over a year. When the M.E. position opened up for a second time in twelve months, both sides decided that Dr. Joseph Price was the least objectionable candidate for the least objectionable situation.

"This extrication assignment seems a little below your pay grade, Sheriff," Joey finally said.

"You're right, Joey. We have other people on the team who typically handle these things. But there's something unusual about this one. It's a sight I wanted to see for myself. Ever done an autopsy on a jumper?"

"One or two."

Danny thought about the damage a fall from the canyon's rim could do to a human body.

"I'll bet they were nothing like this one."

Danny was the first one out of the chopper as it set down within sight of the river.

Marty Laurent was waiting on a stretcher. A homemade splint held the fracture in place. The dead body was covered with a tarp, about ten yards away.

Danny knew that Dr. Price preferred the dead to the living. The sheriff was pleased that his M.E. concentrated first on the patient who was still breathing.

Marty Laurent grinned at the flight nurse.

"Mabel! Come take a look at what a really cool compound fracture looks like in a home-made splint!"

Danny could see Dr. Price's almost imperceptible nod. He clearly had noted the "Pitkin Paramedics" patch on Marty's blue fleece. Not quite a doctor, but a member of the family.

"Nice job with the splint," Joey said. "I expected you to be more shocky."

"Not my first rodeo," Marty answered. "And Smitty and his team took great care of me."

The Sheriff knew Kevin Smith well. He was the best driver Canyon Rafters had. "He's not the most cooperative patient," Smitty said. "I hate customers who think they know more than I do."

Joey Price turned to the nurse.

"OK, Mabel. You can take over with your boyfriend. OK to give him some narco to get him ahead of the pain. If it's not hurting now, it's going to hurt like hell soon."

"Drugs are for pussies." Marty smiled at the nurse. "Sorry, Mabel. Drugs are for wimps."

"Shut up, Marty," she said. "Tell me where it hurts."

The nurse gently slapped the side of his head.

"Up here? Oh wait. That's empty."

Danny joined Joey as the coroner pulled back the tarp. The M.E. gave the body a cursory scan.

"What a mess. This guy sure loved the body ink. More tats than I can count. Cervical fracture at C3. The left radius and ulna are shattered. So is the left humerus. The clavicle is toast, too. Deep contusions everywhere." He opened an eyelid with one hand squeezing a finger nail with the other. "I'd say he's been dead about forty-eight hours. We'll confirm all that when I open him up."

Danny translated Joey's clinical assessment, making his own notes. Broken neck, fractured arm, shoulder and collar bone. Bruises consistent with a fall.

He noticed that Joey was focusing on an outline in the layer of damp fabric. The doc snaked two fingers into the pants pocket and pulled out its contents, a nicotine vaporizer.

"Be careful with that thing," Danny said. "I want the prints."

Joey pointed to the tattoo under the victim's eye. "Well, there's one thing we likely know about him. Guys with permanent teardrops don't end up dead without some help."

"OK, gang," the Sheriff said. "Help us load these two into the chopper. I'll need names and phone numbers from all of you. Smitty, can you handle a little cop work and pull that together for me?"

"You got it, Chief."

"Do me another favor and take a quick look to see if anything else is out of place. My guys won't be down here till tomorrow to poke around. Don't touch anything. Just report."

"Will do," Smitty said. "When do I get my badge?"

Danny looked at the tarp-covered body, comparing its silence to the exuberance of the man on the stretcher. He crouched and put his hand on Marty Laurent's shoulder.

"Let's get this kid to a hospital before he tries to get up and walk there."

SEVEN

Police Headquarters - Phoenix

Ned Gerrard liked hiding out in the Phoenix Police Department Server Room. The AC was especially effective and he rarely had company. The IT specialist assigned to the City's Information Security and Privacy Office, "ISPO" to everyone who worked there, made his daily inspection after his late lunch hour. It didn't take long to run down the checklist. Ned usually stretched it a bit to let his meal settle and catch up on social media.

His ears were finely tuned to perceive the normal hum of the server cooling fans and the comforting clicks of the few hard drives that had not yet been upgraded to solid state storage.

When the rhythm of the machinery shifted, Ned's senses caught it.

Looking up from his smartphone, he watched in growing alarm as each box began to shut down. Ned jumped to his feet and ran along the rack space.

A hardware failure in a single machine happened from time to time. But all the boxes at once? Ned grabbed for the wide area network cable that connected the master router to the outside world and pulled it free of the device.

Too little, too late, he thought, as every server in the room ground to a halt.

Ned tapped the speed dial entry for the City's Chief Information Security Officer.

"Boss," he said when the ISPO chief came on the line. "We've got a problem."

EIGHT

Coconino County Morgue - Flagstaff

Dr. Joey Price thought about the five legally acceptable manners of death; natural, accident, suicide, homicide, and undetermined. An autopsy was the only way to reveal the true cause.

Visitors compare the morgue at the Coconino County Medical Examiner's office to a big industrial kitchen.

To Dr. Joey Price, it was a playground.

He entered the immense walk-in refrigerator containing the inventory of what once were human beings. Most were unclaimed bodies, corpses with phosphorescent green skin the consistency of leather. Each chest was marked with the Y-shaped incisions that revealed the treasures of the Medical Examiner's trade. The one he wanted had yet to be sliced.

The autopsy room had the capacity for two simultaneous examinations. North-facing windows, rows of ceiling-installed LEDs and fine-detail spotlights illuminated the theater of operations. The instruments used to probe the body for clues were similar to those in an operating room, with several grisly exceptions. Scalloped bread bakers' knives were unique to Joey's profession, as was the mallet and hook that encourage recalcitrant body parts to break free. An electric stryker saw used to remove the skull and reveal the brain hung from a spring next to a light fixture that illuminated the table. A plastic box held a large needle and thread used to close up the body when the docs retrieved what they needed to determine the cause of death. There was a consumer-grade dishwasher nearby. Sterility was not nearly as important when the patient was already dead.

"Good afternoon, Dr. Price."

Dr. Robert Knutson entered the room. "Dr. Bob" was a legend in Flagstaff. He was in his late 70s, still practicing, still learning, and an unpaid coroner's assistant who was fascinated with the tales a dead body might tell.

"Hey, Bob. Suit up. Let's see what this 'Illustrated Man' has to tell us."

Joey watched as Dr. Bob scanned the plethora of tattoos on the body's torso as he dressed. "That's artwork that would have inspired Ray Bradbury. OK if I take a picture?"

There was no gunpowder residue, paint flakes or other exterior clues. Aside from the clear indications of trauma, the body looked relatively normal. Joey had already taken X-rays, hair and blood samples and gathered the other minutia that might lead to an iden-tification.

Joey grunted. Bob started snapping.

"Looks like he might be from Texas," Joey said. A rendering of the Longhorn State stood out among the other iconography on the dead man's chest. "You have obviously noted the teardrop under his left eye?"

"Prison language for death. The inmates often mark a killer without permission. It wouldn't surprise me if that's what happened here."

Joey picked up a scalpel, a reminder of how his worked compared to his father's butcher shop. To the uninitiated, the two physicians looked like meat cutters. Joey allowed that it was an apt analogy. Their wardrobe included a blue surgical gown and cap, a plastic apron, coverings for shoes and sleeves, latex gloves and a clear plastic splash shield to protect faces from any retribution the body might throw at them.

"You've got six months under your belt now, Joey. How are you settling in with the team?" Dr. Bob asked.

The doctors rolled the body from the steel gurney onto the examining table.

"It's a change."

"You've got a long resume for a young guy. Lots of change."

"I'm on the spectrum. An acquired taste."

"Has that been hard?"

"Not for me. I like who I am."

Dr. Bob smiled. "I do, too. You don't say much, but when you do it's worth listening to. I wish more people were like that."

Joey made rare eye contact. "Thanks. I really appreciate it."

Dr. Bob centered the torso on a rubber block, extending the body's arch, providing better access to the chest and abdomen. He pointed to a scalpel.

"May I?" he asked.

"Slice away. We found this one under a rock at the Crystal Rapid. Perhaps forty-eight hours dead."

Bob Knutson gently opened a broad Y-shaped incision in the body's chest.

Peeling back the skin revealed the corpse's internal organs.

"This guy is a mess," Dr. Bob said. "Looks like he took a swan dive into the canyon."

The parade of bruises and contusions made the internal organs almost unrecognizable. For Joey, it triggered the same morbid fascination that first attracted him to the profession. "My first," he said. "The admin is pulling up the records of 2 others like him."

Dr. Bob tilted his head toward the plastic bag that contained the dead man's blood. "I'll be interested to see what toxicology tells us."

Joey reckoned that Dr. Bob had seen a lot of death since moving to Flagstaff, enough to form intuitive opinions that often turned out to be fact.

"His type doesn't end up like this unassisted."

The wall phone next to the freezer rang. Joey frowned. He didn't like interruptions when he was playing in the sandbox.

Joey pressed the speaker phone button with an index finger.

"Dr. Price."

"Dr. Price, it's Jennifer."

"It must be important if the Sheriff's administrative assistant is interrupting an autopsy."

"It is. Can you come over to the sheriff's office? Something is wrong with the computers."

NINE

Paloma PD HQ

"We are here today for a preliminary review of the Maryland Meth Lab matter. Ben, give us the executive summary of your findings."

Jess studied Chief James J. O'Brien's bearing in the conference room at Paloma Police Headquarters. His military background was evident in the angular way he sat in the chair at the head of the long conference table. The perfectly manicured hair, the starched uniform with four gleaming silver stars on each epaulet and the well-polished Glock, holstered at a perfect 90-degree angle attested to both his position and his attitude. His deep voice reverberated off of the worn conference room wallpaper, off of the array of photographs of cops receiving community kudos, off of the shooting trophies he loved to display on shelves where inspiring books on leadership would be, if he had ever read any. His tone gave Jess the uncomfortable impression that judgment had already been passed. All that was left was determining the severity of the punishment.

Kojak and Butler got into the room early enough to take the seats farthest from the chief, as if distance might mitigate the pain.

Mowery sat next to them. Jess, as usual, was in the hot seat, right next to O'Brien. Captain Batavia sat on the other side of the table, a thick folder arranged with OCD attention to detail in front him. Ali, always the last one to show up for a meeting, sat to his left.

Jess wasn't going down without a fight. "Wait a minute, Chief. How can you have the person who ordered us to bust the joint alone investigating his own screw-up?"

The chief glared at her. "You'll have your chance to respond in time, JRam."

Batavia was expressionless. Jess could feel visceral hatred on the knife edge of his voice.

"Thank you, Chief. On the tenth of the month, Detectives Harrison and Ramirez, accompanied by Officer Butler attempted service of a warrant at 595 Maryland Street. Harrison and Butler made contact with an armed subject and retreated. Detective Ramirez entered the house and did not retreat when she heard the other officers had done so. The investigation has determined that her actions resulted in the death of one suspect and a serious injury to the other. In the course of service of the warrant a fire was started in the dwelling that caused an explosion that destroyed the house, significantly damaging two adjoining houses and breaking windows as far as a block away. Detective Ramirez's failure to follow department policy has been found to be the primary cause of the damage, which has resulted in the filing of five different law suits from relatives of the dead man and citizens who suffered dwelling damage as a result of the explosion. Our investigation will likely conclude that Detective Ramirez should have retreated from the dwelling until appropriate backup arrived. Had she done so, the loss of life and property would not have happened."

Batavia put the document neatly back in his folder. He averted his eyes from Jess's piercing stare. That was the Readers' Digest version, she thought. Pure fiction.

O'Brien turned his attention toward Harrison. "Detective Harrison, tapes of radio traffic indicate that you reported shots fired and withdrew for backup." Kojak nodded, rubbing the bruise on his chest. Forty-eight hours later, it was still sore. Jess could feel the pain throbbing in her arm, too. She guessed from the dilated pupils that Kojak had accepted the doc's offer of narcotics.

"Detective Ramirez, you have stated that your radio was in operation but you did not withdraw."

Jess gave her union rep time to intervene. He did not. She realized she was fighting this battle alone.

"The moment I knew that my backup bailed the perp whacked me. How was I supposed to 'withdraw'?"

"You've testified to all that. The timeline shows that you were in the house alone for a full two minutes. When you heard 'shots fired,' you should have never entered the premises."

Jess flipped through the printed copy of her testimony to find the right page.

"All of this is noted on page fifty-seven, paragraph three."

Jess looked at her union rep. He was shaking his head, telegraphing to her to "shut up." Kojak focused on the ceiling. The rookie's eyes were downcast.

Ali shifted in her chair. Jess knew that her partner had a short fuse and was trying hard to keep the powder keg in her head from exploding.

O'Brien looked at the IAD officer. "Ben, what does your department recommend as corrective action?"

"Two weeks suspension with pay for Detective Harrison and Officer Butler. Thirty days unpaid leave for Detective Ramirez with corrective action upon her return."

Jess knew that "Corrective Action" was a code word for whatever punishment the chief felt like doling out. He could be uncomfortably creative.

"Officer Mowery, any comments on behalf of the union?"

Mowery addressed Batavia. "Isn't 30 days without pay a little harsh, Captain?"

"We haven't discussed the 'Reckless Endangerment' issue yet,

Officer Mowery. I'll be doing that with the chief shortly. It's a contributor to the remediation recommendation for Detective Ramirez."

Jess gritted her teeth, replaying the car chase she and Ali were part of several weeks earlier. When they maneuvered the suspect's vehicle into a spin, it had flipped and exploded, killing the armed robbers who had just killed two employees for 1200 dollars in cash at a liquor store. The gasoline mushroom cloud that incinerated the bad guys was caught on someone's phone camera, leading most of local evening newscasts. Jess had probably saved the state several million dollars in prison expenses in the process. This was the freeway thing Ali was needling her about. It was going to be an issue after all.

Detective Mowery parroted words Jess knew he had said at dozens of hearings just like this one. "The Union feels that the punishment is overly severe. Unless it is mitigated, we intend to file a grievance."

The chief was dismissive. "File away, counselor. Harrison, Butler, Clark you are dismissed. You can leave, too, Officer Mowery. Ben, thank you for your usual thorough work. JRam. Stay here."

The men headed for the door, stopping in their tracks when Ali grabbed Batavia's sleeve and pulled him back into his chair.

TEN

Coconino County Sheriff's Office - Flagstaff

"What do you mean they are gone?"

Danny Lopez knew little about technology. He still had his administrative assistant, Jennifer Lee, print out his emails. He dictated the responses.

"The entire database," Jennifer said. "All the autopsy and investigative data, traffic tickets, court records, everything. Gone."

Danny was incredulous. He knew little about technology, but assumed that, like every other tool in his arsenal, it was supposed to be reliable. "Just here in Flagstaff?"

"No. The statewide system. I called Phoenix to see about restoring from a backup. They've been hacked, too."

"Don't we keep hard copies of that stuff?"

Jennifer shook her head. "Not for the last three years. The State went paperless in 2015."

The magnitude of the problem was becoming clear to Danny. "How did it happen?"

"Nobody knows yet. ISPO searched the system logs. It appears that they were wiped, too. Whoever did this, knew what they were doing and covered their tracks."

Joey Price was drawing circles on the desktop with his finger. He didn't look up as he spoke. "This is a pro job. Someone doesn't want us to put any puzzle pieces together."

The sheriff was not in the mood for Joey's unfiltered feedback. He tried to ignore it. "What do we do now, Jennifer?"

"IT says Dr. Price should disconnect his laptop from the network and save his work directly to the local hard drive until they get to the bottom of the issue. The hacker deleted all the backups, even those off-site are gone. When they connected to the physical hard drive they keep in the safe deposit box at the bank, it got wiped. The FBI's computer forensics team has been contacted."

The FBI. Danny was well aware that when the Feds engaged, local law became an inconvenient obstacle. "Well, that takes us out of the game. They like to play things close to the vest until they have it solved. Any other agencies reporting something similar?"

"None so far."

"So we have one dead guy on Joey's examining table and no data to draw any conclusions."

Joey shook his head, still focused on the circles. "That's not quite true. We still have Dr. Bob."

ELEVEN

Paloma PD HQ

Jessica could tell that Ben Batavia didn't appreciate being dragged back to his seat by a woman. But when Ali went on a tear, there was no stopping her. Jess saw the chief grab the arms of his chair, bracing for the barrage.

"This is crap, Chief. Why do the boys get two weeks paid and you're screwing Jess with a month of nothing?"

"Nobody asked your opinion, Gates."

Every cop gets a nickname along the way. Ali quickly picked up "Gates", an homage to Microsoft's Bill Gates. It wasn't meant to be complimentary.

"Well, let me ask a few questions then. So Ben, what's your rationale for throwing Jessica under the bus?"

Batavia looked to the chief for help. O'Brien looked back, an expression Jess translated as, "Answer the question."

"Detective Ramirez did not follow proper procedure."

"And these other two guys." Ali nodded at Harrison and Butler, who stood frozen in the doorway. "Their bailing on a partner who was in harm's way doesn't constitute any malfeasance?"

Batavia was silent.

Ali continued. "Chief, isn't proper procedure for SWAT to handle takedowns like this?"

Jess tossed the policies and procedures manual she held in her hand to her partner. Ali put a finger on the paragraph Jess had highlighted. "The Narcotics Response Team will execute all interdictions. When unavailable, Special Weapons and Tactics will respond. And what about HAZMAT? If it was suspected that the subjects were cooking meth in there, why would we deploy three officers into a potentially deadly crime scene without personal protection gear?"

She didn't wait for O'Brien's answer.

"So Ben, who made the call to send these Three Musketeers to Maryland Street? Oh wait. It was you, wasn't it? And why send Jess at the last minute? Could it be that you're still holding a grudge because she rebuffed your sexual advances?"

"Officer Clark!" The chief held up a hand to silence her. "That's enough."

But Ali was on a roll, coiled like a barely controlled jungle cat preparing to strike.

"I'm just trying to make sure I'm understanding things, Chief. And Ben, what about that bit at the strip club where you made Jess play the role of your girlfriend. How well did that work out for you?"

The bust was a fiasco that ended up with the entire undercover team in handcuffs. It was an early, defining moment in Jess's career that elevated her to heroine status with every female in the organization. It transformed her into Batavia's sworn enemy.

"Gates!" The chief's voice was louder. And in this instance, his use of Ali's nickname was not a compliment.

"Here's what I think is going on, Ben. I think you want to do whatever you can to discredit a good cop because she wouldn't buy into your plan to get into her pants."

Batavia's face crumpled into a sneer. "You're out of line, Gates."

The chief was on his feet. "Not another word, Officer Clark."

"I'm almost done, Chief. Here's what I'm gonna do, just to make sure I'm not misunderstanding this." She shot a withering glance at the union rep who stood next to Harrison and Butler in the office doorway, mesmerized by her performance. "You know that no cop in her right mind would tell HR that you've created a hostile in our tight little family. That's career suicide. And since our union rep, Officer Mowery here, is a total incompetent, I'm gonna whisper this story to Alejandro Gonzalez. You remember who he is, Ben? The lawyer who took the City for five million dollars the last time your boys made a little error with an arrest in the barrio? Yeah, that's the one. I might do that. But Chief, I'm a team player and I'm willing to shut up and be a nice girl if you encourage Captain Batavia to modify his recommendation to 30 days paid leave so our girl can heal from that little scratch the stick man with the Bowie knife gave her. Maybe a citation for bravery? Nah, that's a little over the top. Do what you will with the boys here, but mess with my sister and I'll give her some recommendations of my own that none of us will like very much."

She burned her stare into Batavia's eyes. Jess thought it was a thing of beauty. "Sound like something you can live with, Ben?"

"Mowery!" The chief barked at the union representative. "Get Officer Clark and the rest of this crowd the hell out of my office, now. I want to talk with JRam, alone, then with you Mowery. Wait outside until I call for you. Captain Batavia." It wasn't Ben now. "Thank you for your recommendations. If you want to change anything before you submit the final to me in writing, you may. You're all dismissed. JRam. Stay where you are."

Ali made for the door. Jess thought she looked like a little girl who was skipping down her driveway to play with friends.

The men were all standing, stunned, at the doorway, watching the proceedings. The tale would quickly circulate throughout the House. Jess could imagine how they would tell it.

Replicating Ali's skillset for what the chief paid her was nearly impossible. But everyone had a breaking point and Jess could sense that he was nearing his.

O'Brien waved an arm as if he was clearing trash off of a table top.

The cops didn't need another invitation. Everyone was out the door as if the fire alarm had gone off. The chief walked from the conference table and returned to the big leather chair behind his oak desk. He pointed a finger to the spot in front of it where he wanted Jess to stand.

She recognized the power play and wasn't having any. She picked one of the two leather chairs where friendlies were offered a seat and sat.

"Jessica." It was the first time he had uttered her first name. It did not mean she was being welcomed into his inner circle. "We have training and policy to prevent situations like this. You are lucky to be alive."

"Ali was walking a little on the wild side."

"Ya think?"

"But she's got a point and you know it."

"You're high maintenance, JRam. Everyone else here can get along. Why are you always rocking my boat?"

"If that's your perception, sir, then you don't know your own house."

To Jessica, the conversation felt like two adversaries, circling one another on a Karate mat. Every word had a deeper, unspoken meaning. And you kept your intentions veiled so as not to give an opponent any opening.

The Chief tried throwing a punch.

"This isn't a job you have to do, JRam. If you're not happy here, nobody is forcing you to stay. I hear that they are hiring over at the University."

"No thank you, sir. This is my house in my city. No amount of chauvinistic *mierda* will get me to quit. I have every right to be here and to be treated as an equal to the men without harassment."

Jess could see the hair on the back of the chief's neck rising. When a woman brought up the "harassment" word, it triggered him.

"Thirty days will help the wound heal and give you some time to think. We'll call it medical leave so you can keep cashing your paychecks. But I don't want to see your face in the station or on the street until your suspension period is over. Thirty days from now you will return to this office and we will discuss your future." He was done with her. "Any more questions?"

"How do you sleep at night?"

She shouldn't have said it. It added nothing productive to the conversation and it was disrespectful. But Jessica Ramirez had endured much worse over a decade in O'Brien's house. She instantly forgave herself for breaking protocol.

And Jess enjoyed watching the chief's face turn purple. Both adversaries knew she had better bail before they said things they could not take back.

TWELVE

Flagstaff

"Killers always sign their work," Joey Price said. "They want us to know who they are. The map to their undoing is hidden in the graffiti."

Danny Lopez studied the diverse group that sat on either side of the long rectangular table in the morgue's conference room. Joey Price, Bob Knutson, and Jennifer Lee were in deep conversation. The smell of freshly installed carpet and wood paneling gave the place the feel of brand-new construction. An Apple TV was connected to a projector. A grim slide show of dead bodies danced across the screen at the front of the room.

Joey nodded in Dr. Bob's direction. The floor was now his.

"Here's the John Doe from today. We'll name him Subject A. Six-foot-one, about 275, we place him in his late fifties. His injuries are consistent with death due to massive trauma - a fall from great height. There is no liquid in the lungs, so he was likely deceased when he hit the water. No telling how far up stream he was but, as the Sheriff has said, he was found submerged at mile 98.9. His only clothing was a pair of blue jeans. Not even skivvies."

Jennifer rolled her eyes.

Dr. Bob chuckled.

"When you're 78, you get to call 'em as you see 'em. Now let's look at Subject B. Similar injuries, but was found at mile 122. A little better dressed. Add a T-shirt to his ensemble. He landed head first, so whatever picture we might circulate won't do much good. He's also unique because the nature of his fall scraped most of the skin off of his hands and arms. No fingerprints."

A series of gruesome photographs of a shattered corpse flashed on the screen. Jennifer covered her eyes. Even Danny, who was well inoculated to what the police photographers called "spaghetti shots" had to stifle a shudder.

"Now here's Subject C. We know who this guy was. Harold Raymond Lattimer. Last known address, Federal Correctional Institution, Phoenix. Released three months ago, awaiting a new trial for allegedly killing his girlfriend. Had a really good lawyer who got him free on bond. He jumped bail and was never heard from again until you found him at mile 111.6 two months ago."

More pictures.

Dr. Bob folded his arms. "Notice anything in common?"

"Looks like they all had at least one tattoo," Danny said.

"There's something else."

Dr. Bob flashed a shot of a toxicology report on the screen.

"All three men died from a fall, not from drowning. And we know that two of the three had Bergulon in their systems when we found them. I'm betting our Illustrated Man's blood comes back positive for that, too."

"What's Bergulon?" Jennifer asked.

"It's one of the brand names for Pancuronium Bromide, a nerve agent," Joey said. "In Belgium and the Netherlands, it's used in euthanasia. It's also part of the lethal injection cocktail that kills death row prisoners. Administer it alone and you lose the use of your muscles but continue to have full sensory feeling. Ideal for a sadist who likes to torture his victims before dispatching them."

Danny was focused on the commonality of the drug. It was the modus operandi that linked three probable murders together, confirming that they were dealing with a serial killer.

Joey continued. "On death row, they first give the prisoner sodium thiopental to induce coma, Bergulon is then introduced to stop respiration. Give it to a conscious patient and they still feel the pain but can't do anything about it. Without a ventilator, they stop breathing in about ten minutes."

"So what do you guys think we have here?"

"You have someone who administers the drug to his victims," Joey said. "He tosses them into the canyon when their muscles are spaghetti. And it's virtually impossible for us to know where because the Colorado can carry them well downriver before anyone notices."

Like the best administrative assistants, Jennifer Lee had become Danny Lopez's second brain. Her years of service had given her the equivalent of an advanced degree in criminology. He also appreciated that she understood his penchant for thinking rather than writing. She held up the yellow legal pad she used to augment his memory and read from it. "The more troubling questions are: Who would do this? How do they get the drugs and how do they get them into the victim? How was someone able to hack into a federal-grade network and cover their digital tracks? And why?"

"The timing of the murders and the hacking incident don't make them connected," Danny said. "At least not now."

Joey held up a zip lock bag with the vaporizer in it. It was covered with the black residue of fingerprint dust. "No data yet, I bet this little guy introduced the drug into our victim's system."

Danny looked to Dr. Bob for corroboration.

"The drug is typically injected intravenously. There is no known instance of it being ingested through the membranes of the lungs."

"No *known* instance is the key phrase, here," Joey added. "That doesn't mean it's impossible."

The method of death was clear to Danny now. He was ready for more puzzle pieces. "What other commonalities did you see?"

"These dead men can tell a few tales," Dr. Bob said. "Joey and I spent a little time admiring the needlework on our Illustrated Man. Tattoos can talk if you show them to the right people. Ten will get you one he's a felon, like Subject C. If we circulate his photograph, my guess is that he'll come back dirty, too."

Danny was trying to put the puzzle pieces together.

"So we have a serial killer who targets bad guys."

"Not just any bad guys," Jennifer said. She held up a print out of a newspaper story from the *Arizona Republic*. "Bad guys who beat the system."

She read the article aloud.

Phoenix, Arizona - Harold Raymond Lattimer, who is accused of killing his long-time female companion, is free on bond after a mistrial was declared last week in Phoenix.

Lattimer is alleged to have bludgeoned Denise Wallace to death with a baseball bat after an argument last September. Police found the victim and what they believe was the murder weapon side by side in the Lattimer home in suburban Phoenix on September 23. Fingerprints on the bat were inconclusive, but neighbors reported a violent shouting match earlier in the evening and witnessed Mr. Lattimer leaving the house in a hurry, an hour before police were called.

Lattimer, who served five years for bank robbery in the 90s, does not dispute the argument, but proclaimed his innocence, stating that his girlfriend was alive when he left the house. The Maricopa County Medical Examiner fixed the time of death within a window when Mr. Lattimer could have killed the woman, but lawyers successfully argued that the evidence was circumstantial.

The director of Phoenix's Sojourner Center, an advocate for victims of domestic violence, complained that the situation will only further embolden other abusive spouses. Police expressed frustration that they couldn't prosecute the case. Lattimer remains free.

"Not anymore," Danny said.

THIRTEEN

Paloma PD HQ

Jess felt suffocated. Leaving the chief's office only slightly relieved that.

Ali was leaning against the wall next to the locker room, arms folded, her facial features morphed into an expression of disgust. Jess felt the blood returning to her head and with it the competitive combativeness that she loved about their relationship.

Her partner grinned. "So how was my performance?"

Jess started for the door, wanting some fresh air. She fired back at Ali over her shoulder. "I was doing fine in there with the chief, Alexandra."

The game was on. Ali trotted after Jess. "What? I beat the shit out of Batavia for you."

"I could have handled it... What are you doing? Bucking for Mowery's gig?"

Ali was by Jess's side now, punctuating her sentences like a boxer delivering a right hook.

"If I were you, I would have told the chief to fuck off."

"You were pretty close to doing just that yourself, girlfriend."

"I'm sick of this macho bullshit. Why do you keep coming back for more?"

Every time, Jess thought. Every time the shit hits the fan, Ali asked the same question. "You already know the answer, Ali. For me it's about the community. If I can keep kids like Ricardo from ending up in the penal system, there's hope for the future."

Jess said these things. But for the first time in her career, she was questioning them. She knew Ali could sense this.

"Yeah, yeah, yeah. You spew that all the time. But we know we're hooked. This is an addiction. You look at a van and scan it for where the drugs might be hidden. You watch faces at the grocery store because you have a sixth sense for an armed robbery that's about to go down or that little girl who might be in the hands of a human trafficker. You run toward the gunfire when everybody else is running away. And when a killer like that skinny-ass meth addict puts your own gun in your mouth, you're already planning how you are gonna take him down, even if it means blowing a hole in his chest that's so big you can watch the sunset through it. We're cops, Jessica. Assholes in charge, macho meatheads with a badge, bad guys with guns; there isn't anybody or anything that is going to change that."

"That was Shakespeare on a shingle. I haven't been this turned on since I kissed that FBI guy."

"Don't play kissy face in a sandbox you might have to shit in, Jess. Anyway, let's both take the next thirty days and see what life is like away from this frat house."

This caught Jess off guard. "What do you mean 'both'?"

Jess stepped outside, squinting her eyes in the cloudless sunshine and inhaled the fresh air. Ali looked jubilant.

"Mowery just told me. I went a bit too far in there. The chief tossed me out for a month, too."

Jessica needed to think. She stopped by the local sporting goods store and purchased the upper half of a scuba wet suit and pointed her Tahoe toward the one place where she knew her contemplations would be undisturbed.

She was among the first to jump into the indoor pool when the Paloma Family YMCA opened. As she walked toward the racing platforms, she thought about how it still had the same look and the same chlorine smell she knew so well during her years as a competitive swimmer.

Jess cut a length of neoprene from a scuba wetsuit to protect the freshly stitched incision on her arm from the elements, securing it on both ends with waterproof tape. "Doctors be damned," she thought. "Nothing will keep me away from the water."

Jessica mounted the platform. She jackknifed into the lap lane, strong strokes and powerful kicks creating a wake as her graceful freestyle cut fresh eddies in the undulating currents.

FOURTEEN

Paloma PD HQ

In the summer of 2002, Jessica Ramirez was seventeen. As a junior at Paloma Central High, she'd held six statewide swimming records, capping her career by tying the 50-Meter freestyle time set by her idol, Dara Torres, a Latina with a background that mirrored her own. The papers called Dara the "Torres Tornado." A dozen universities had offered her a full ride. Torres had used swimming as a way out. It was a path Jess fully intended to follow.

When she answered the phone that July evening, Jessica thought it was a joke.

"Hey, Jessica. It's Dara Torres."

Jess recognized the voice. The hint of Mexico in Dara's confident greeting was exactly like the one Jess knew well from the dozens of television interviews she had recorded and memorized.

"THE Dara Torres?"

"The real deal. I've been watching you and so has Coach Quick. We thought you might be interested in trying out for the 2004 team. Brooke Bennett wants to meet you, too. Of course, there's no guarantee that you'd qualify. But something tells me you've got the skills and the attitude to blow past us all."

The rush of emotions Jess felt was overwhelming: To learn from the best of the best, new friends, world travel and validation that hard work doing something you care about pays off. She struggled to compress them all into a sentence.

"That would be fabulous."

"Think about it and let me know in a week or so."

"Thank you very much for calling, Dara. I hoped I would meet you since I first saw you swim."

"I've seen your videos," Dara said. "And believe me, I'm looking forward to meeting you."

Jess's heart was pounding as she reported the conversation to her family at the dinner table. Her younger sister, Maria, didn't follow swimming, so the names meant nothing to her. But Athens did. The games were to be played at the Olympiad's birthplace. Jess's mother may have been just as excited as her oldest daughter. But Mexican wives deferred to their husbands.

All eyes were on Papa Luis.

"I think not. It will be a distraction. We make a better living with our brains than with our bodies."

"But Papa." Jess knew that Luis was unaccustomed to an argument, but she persisted. "This is history. Think of what having the Ramirez name associated with the team could mean to la familia. Our legacy. It's every swimmer's dream. And I know I can make it come true."

"You may not understand it now, Jessi, but you will later. In time, you'll lose physical strength. Mental strength lasts a lifetime. My answer is 'No.'"

"I'll be eighteen in a year, Papa. And then I can make my own decisions."

Her father's expression darkened.

"La familia es más importante mi'ja. As long as you eat my bread, you will sing my song."

In the coming weeks a contingent from the Olympic Swimming Program would sit at the family dinner table to try unsuccessfully to change Luis Ramirez's mind.

Jessica's Olympic dreams were dashed.

FIFTEEN

Flagstaff

Danny Lopez scratched his chin, a sign that his mind was working in high gear. To his left, Joey had his thumb on Dr. Bob's iPhone and was flipping back through the ghastly gallery of autopsy photos, comparing each in rapid succession. He could tell that Bob Knutson wanted to go home. Danny knew that it was about time for the doc's Manhattan cocktail and perhaps nine holes of golf before dinnertime.

Jennifer tried to bring everyone's focus back to center.

"What are our next steps?"

Danny walked to a dry erase board and began to write.

"One - Document Dr. Bob's recollections in a formal statement, printing out the photos on his phone. Two - Get the photos of the two identifiable victims in circulation, especially Subject A. Focus on the Texas Mounties with that one. The map on his belly is too good a clue to pass up. His tats may still shed some more light on things. Three - create a profile of our perp. We know he has access to some high-level chemistry and perhaps a team of hackers who are keeping us from connecting the dots. If he does have a thing for killing bad guys, there has to be a way he makes contact with them. We could assume that he's from Flagstaff because he does his dirty work near here, but my guess is he's not local and just brings his victims here to dispose of them."

Jennifer tapped her yellow legal pad. "What about our other problem? Do we wait for the FBI to deal with the hacker?"

The sheriff knew little about computers, but was aware that every hour could make a recovery much harder to achieve.

"I'd love to get a forensic computer criminologist to look at our network to tell us how we were hacked. Waiting for the FBI to come play in my sandbox grinds my gears."

"Where will you find one of those geniuses around here?" Joey asked.

The sheriff sighed. "I wish I knew."

SIXTEEN

April's Boutique - Phoenix

"Good men are like orgasms," April said, wiping a fingerprint off the glass display case. "There aren't nearly enough of them and you end up doing the real work yourself."

Ann began the tedious process of removing stock from each display case, carrying trays of merchandise to the safe. She could feel April's enjoyment in quoting one of her favorite aphorisms as her boss pressed on.

"So today will be a first."

"What do you mean?"

"This will be the first time I've seen one of your beaus."

"He's not my beau."

April typed a password into the cash register to collate a report of the day's receipts. "You always talk about these men you date. The story always ends the same way: They leave you. But you never let us meet any of them."

"I'm a private person."

"I've never known a woman who was embarrassed to show off her man. Unless she has a sixth sense for picking losers."

Ann deposited an armful of jewelry into the safe.

"What are you implying?"

"Nothing." April was definitely implying. "I'm just interested to put a face and a name together for the first time ever."

"You should talk, Ms. 'I'm divorced for 20 years.' Your history with the opposite sex hasn't been stellar. Shall I list them?"

April frowned at the cash register display. The online take was down one-point-five percent, year over year. She made a note to find out why.

"That we have in common. The only difference is that you've met mine and I have no proof that yours ever even existed."

"Let's just say that I'm attracted to magicians. They are always disappearing."

"It's a pattern, Ann. You must be doing something to make them disappear."

"Men are pigs. Perhaps we should try dating women."

April shuddered. "Two needy, self-centered drama queens at the same table? I'd rather eat alone."

"Not me. Not tonight. Mr. Wonderful is taking me to the Century Club. Even if he turns out to be a douche bag, at least I'll get top shelf liquor, a fillet and a creme brûlée out of it."

"And at most?"

Ann smiled. "A moment he'll never forget."

"What's that supposed to mean."

Ann closed the safe and spun the dial. Her work for April was nearly complete, but the night was just beginning.

"That was his parting shot. 'I have a feeling this is a moment I'll never forget.'"

The ringtone for Ann's *Amore* dating application spit out the opening bars from "It's Raining Men." She glanced at the screen and smiled.

April looked shocked. "Don't tell me you are stringing along two prospects at the same time?"

Ann tapped a message into the app's chat box. "From the look of his profile, this one will be a brief encounter. First things first. I'm getting hungry for some red meat at the Century Club."

April sniffed. "I hope you carry protection. This guy sounds like he could be a walking STD factory."

"Oh I carry protection."

Ann could sense her boss's disgust as April continued to review the day's receipts with a jeweler's attention to detail.

"Protection goes beyond condoms and mace," she said. "I've never met another girl with such a tragic taste for losers."

The store was empty. The movie that repeated perpetually in Ann Blakely's brain appeared again at the front of her conscious-ness. The one man she really wanted to kill was already long dead, stolen from her by a heart attack. She could see her psychiatrist's face, warning her about transference, the danger that you might transfer your hatred to an innocent. For Ann, it was a revelation, a perverted pathway to healing that became an addiction. She would transfer her hate all right, but not to the innocent.

Ann inventoried the "protection" in her purse. There was the unlicensed, untraceable Walther pistol, a small dispenser of mace and a tactical pen that could be used to puncture a carotid artery. She patted the zippered pocket where she kept the two nicotine vaporizers that were her weapons of individual destruction. It was missing the reassuring bulk that told her the items were there.

Ann Blakely unzipped the pocket and realized that there was only one device in it. Her own. Where was the other one?

She carefully retraced the events of the night at the canyon. She could recall giving Mahoney his. But she had no memory of taking it back.

That was a problem.

SEVENTEEN

The Ramirez Household - Isbell Street, Paloma

The old neighborhood had declined. Jessica was painfully aware that the Ramirez household was one of the few that had not fallen into disrepair. What had once been a thriving community of blue-collar middle class evaporated when the auto plant closed and the jobs vanished.

Drugs and the gangs that sold them moved in. Those who could afford it moved out.

At the same time, the place still felt like home. The aroma of Mexican spices, the family pictures, the music of Leo Dan, Rocío Dúrcal and other Latin artists from the 1960s playing softly in the background. For Jess, it remained a haven of comfort in the midst of a tumultuous world.

Throughout Jess's life, dinner at Luis and Rosa Ramirez's home was always an extended family affair. She and Ali sat on an overstuffed couch in the small living room that had been her grandfather's before cancer took him at age 82. Jess's grandmother, "Abuelita" Elana, was in her usual spot, a recliner that faced a fifty-inch flat screen television. Jorge Ramos's review of the day's *Noti-*

cias on Univision purred out of the speakers at low volume. All were nursing glasses of Sangria.

This was not standard practice in the typical Mexican household. Jess and her sister, Maria, had long since broken with a number of traditions. And the concoction was Adelita's personal recipe: Rioja wine, Grand Marnier, Gran Duque De Alba Brandy, fresh squeezed orange juice, pineapple chunks, thin-skinned Mexican limes and club soda.

Ali sighed. "A girl could get used to this little slice of heaven. I need to come here more often."

"What you need is to learn how to cook so you can attract a husband." It was Maria, shouting from the kitchen.

"I'd rather eat takeout with a beautiful woman."

Jess laughed. Ali's sexual preference was ignored in this Catholic household. "Good cooking hasn't done much for you, Maria. You're almost thirty and still single."

"Speak for yourself, sister. I like being single. Most of the boys around here are *pendejos* anyway."

"Pendejos?" Ali knew little Spanish.

"Idiots," Jess answered. "Maria has gone out with most every eligible fish in this small pond. They have all thrown her back."

"I heard that, *mi'ja*. Shut up before I punch you in the face."

The two cops' cell phones beeped at the same instant. The text message read, "Shooting within two blocks of your current location. Latino male suspect, five feet four inches tall, 125 pounds, wearing a black hoodie and blue jeans."

"Jesus. Another one," Ali said. "Do you guys have a security system in the house?"

Jess laughed. "Just Maria. She's better than a watchdog. And just as ugly."

The voice from the kitchen barked. "I said shut up, Jessi."

"See?" Jess said. "The best watchdog in the neighborhood."

"You ought to at least let me install a few items. Looks like your smoke detectors don't even have batteries in them. I have some stuff in my vehicle."

"You would have to sneak it in," Jess said. "Papa doesn't even like locking the door."

Ali cupped her hand next to her mouth and whispered, "Distract him after dinner."

EIGHTEEN

Phoenix

The Century Club attracts the city's most prosperous and powerful. It sits atop Chase Tower in Phoenix. A 180-degree panorama, exquisite cuisine and five-star service command an expensive menu and a dining experience to match.

Perhaps, Michael thought, that's why the outfit Ann still wore from earlier in the day, and the way she purposefully added more sway to her walk to accentuate it, turned heads. Ann was as out of place as a dirt clod in a punch bowl. The fact that she was his guest bought some dispensation from the Maître D'. Not so with the older members who still believed the place deserved jackets, ties and dresses cut below the knee.

Michael knew that Ann sensed it and could not have cared less. She saw a septuagenarian watching her and pretended to brush some dust off her blazer to call attention to her chest. Michael could tell that it made the old man's day.

"You're getting attention," he said.

The acid was still in her voice. "I thought they were looking at you. These people are rich, accomplished and principled. They can smell frauds a mile away."

"Everyone here has a little larceny in 'em. You don't get wealthy without sidestepping a few rules."

"Look at that monument over there," Ann said, as they passed a bejeweled, blue-haired woman. "That's a world class judgmental sneer and she's shooting it our way."

"I know! Isn't it wonderful?"

"How can we make the most of it?"

The maître d was pointing to a table by the window. Michael slid his hand in the pocket of Ann's blue jeans and squeezed. She slapped it away.

"No touching!"

"Just checking to see if you have a wallet. Not sure I can afford this place."

"Liar."

"Look," Michael whispered, "I think she just choked on her caprese salad when she saw that."

"What do you think she'll do if I knee you in the jingle bells?"

"Save that for after dessert."

The sun was well beneath the horizon and the dim lights of the city twinkled below. Michael held Ann's chair, admiring the contours of her back. He glanced at the blue hair. She was still watching them. He opened his mouth and wiggled his tongue at her. The old woman covered her face with a jeweled hand and jabbed a finger into her husband's arm, directing his attention their way.

Michael waved and smiled. The old man smiled back and nodded.

A waiter materialized in a tuxedo that would have been perfect for prom night.

"What would the lady care to drink?"

"A Porn Star Martini please. Shaken, not stirred, as Mr. Bond might say."

Michael nodded, adding, "The usual," which was a Double Old Fashioned on the rocks.

The waiter bowed, presented the menus and departed for the bar.

"We'll have to see if they have passion fruit," Michael said. "This may be a first."

Ann raised an eyebrow. "If they bring me one, it -will- be a first. Nobody outside of the Covent Garden Cocktail Club in London seems to know how to make one."

"2 ounces vodka, preferably Aylesbury Duck, one ounce passion fruit purée, one ounce vanilla syrup, one half ounce lime juice, shaken on ice and served with a shot of Prosecco on the side."

"You seem to be well versed in mixology. Sophisticates substitute vanilla vodka for the syrup. So why is your pick-up routine so lousy?"

"Was it really that bad?"

"The worst. How much of it was true?"

"Very little." Michael was feeling good about his progress. Everything was going as he had hoped. And yet, the whole mating dance fatigued him. *He* felt like a porn star, going through the motions in front of a camera crew for the thousandth time with another well-worn partner he barely knew. He thought about the one lover he really wanted, wishing she was sitting across from him now.

I'll think about her later, he said to himself. This was a game he intended to play, and win.

NINETEEN

The Ramirez Household

"La cena está servida," Rosa said. Dinner is served.

The entrée was Carne Asada, Adelita's family recipe. Thinly sliced ribeye was grilled and seared, spiced with cumin, garlic, jalapeño chile pepper and cilantro, intermingled with chopped avocado, lime wedges, radishes and lettuce and wrapped in a home-made corn tortilla.

"Eat up," Rosa commanded. "But remember... Natallas for dessert."

As the plates of food were passed, Jess turned to her father. The events of the past few days steeled her for another attempt at convincing him to get out of the decaying neighborhood while he still could.

She took a long dose of Sangria. Liquid courage was necessary for any conversation with Luis.

"Papa, why do you and Mamá still stay here?"

The query caught everyone's attention. Nobody ever questioned the patriarch.

Luis Ramirez always thought before he spoke. As he studied Jess, she felt as if his eyes could see inside of her soul.

"This is our home. I was born here. You and Maria were born here. I remember Abuelito telling us what it was like to move in after the War. There were uncertainties then, too. Not every day was a good day. Abuelito contributed to the creation of a safe neighborhood. We can still contribute now."

Jess could relate. One of the reasons she became a cop was to try to make the barrio a safer place. But where her family's safety was concerned, things were different.

"Times are different, Papa. Abuelito left Mexico to build a better life. There is no shame doing the same thing now. Our barrio is not what it once was. We can't change it."

She quoted one of the Spanish proverbs he used to tell her at bedtime when she was a girl.

"*Lavar puercos con jabón es perder tiempo y jabón.*"

Ali shoveled another spoonful of Mexican rice into her mouth.

"You're gonna have to put that into English for this gringo."

Jess translated.

"'Washing a pig with soap is to lose time and soap.' It's the same as George Bernard Shaw's advice: 'Never wrestle with pigs. You both get dirty and the pig likes it.'"

Her father answered in the same cryptic way he always did.

"*Donde hay gana, hay maña.*"

Where there is a will, there is a way.

That was the adage that had been Jess's north star. It kept her focused on her dreams when they seemed out of reach. It was on her mind as she was sparring with the chief. It centered her when O'Brien's male-only culture threatened to suffocate her.

"Yo entiendo... I understand, Papa. But now, I'm not sure I believe."

Her left forearm still ached. The wound was granulating nicely but still had a long way to go to heal. The memories of her encounters with internal affairs, the chief, were fresh and raw. She sought affirmation to stay the course. Today was the first time she had ever considered leaving the department.

Jess's mother passed her the carne asada. "When will the doctors let you swim again?"

Even with twelve years intervening, the swimming questions still cut her to the core.

"I swam today, Mama."

Maria shot her a questioning glance. "I saw the doctor's follow-up notes. You are supposed to avoid getting that thing wet for two weeks."

"They have their timetable. I have mine."

"Maria tells me that you have thirty days of extra vacation, Jessi."

"Tell Mamá the truth, Maria. I was suspended today. Internal Affairs says I did not do the right thing at the Maryland house. All of us who were there got suspensions."

"Now, who's not telling the truth?" Ali said. "The Captain changed his recommendation to 'medical leave.' Still not a blemish on your girl's spotless record."

"Ali is the one who got herself suspended," Jess said. "Opened that big mouth one too many times defending my honor."

Luis lapsed back into Spanish. *"A las mujeres bonitas y a los buenos caballos los echan a perder los pendejos."*

Jess made the translation in her head. "Beautiful women and good horses are corrupted by idiots."

Ali raised a fork. "I have no idea what your father said but I totally agree with him."

"Papa is right," her mother said. "Don't let anyone or anything smother the fire that burns in your heart. Use the time to remember the reasons you chose this road."

I didn't originally choose this road, Jess said to herself. She looked at the frame that hung over the fireplace. All her swimming medals were there. Olympic scouts sat at this very table. She had potential, they said. She could be a medalist. All she needed was the training Olympic Coach Rich Quick could provide.

Papa was adamant then. Brains over body. Her response was a career in law enforcement. She wondered now if that decision had been more rebellion than reality.

TWENTY

Phoenix

Michael considered his dinner date. The dancing glow of the candlelight accentuated her allure.

"Let's agree that tonight it's the whole truth and nothing but the truth."

Ann chuckled. "I bet that would be another first. You're up."

"I'm thirty-five. I'm a money manager. I hate the job but I'm good at it and like the income. I've slept with more women than I can count and none of the relationships have lasted more than a few months. There, that's a start. Your turn."

"29. Grew up in San Francisco. Majored in hospitality business at USC. Landed a gig overseas after graduation. Two sisters. Parents are dead. I live alone and stumbled into April's place after I moved here. The boobs are 500cc's of silicone but everything else is as nature provided."

Michael had no reason to believe that anything Ann said was true. The goal tonight was to gain her trust.

"Hospitality? Why is a smart girl like you working in a boutique?"

"Oh, I still like being on the receiving end. Just soured on the work."

"You impress me as a well-traveled woman with the status to get free upgrades."

"The only upgrade you're getting is the pleasure of my dinner company. Stop being a moron."

"Relationships?"

"I've had my share. They don't last, so we have that in common."

"What's missing? I mean where your partners are concerned."

"I'll answer that one after you do."

Michael had to think about it, realizing he never really considered it before.

"I think I get bored. I've known some extraordinary women, along with more than a few un-extraordinary women. Once I figure them out, I lose interest."

"Love them and leave them?"

She had pinpointed Michael's truth. He wasn't proud of it.

"That sounds horrible. But it's about the size of it."

"So you are incapable of sustaining relationships, period?"

"Not true. I have half a dozen men I would consider friends and many acquaintances of both sexes. I can be reliable and present. Where women are concerned, I seem to have a short attention span."

"A psychotherapist would say that you're an emotionally unavailable male, driven by a stereotypical upbringing to favor autonomy over intimacy. You screw 'em and leave 'em because that's how your brain is wired. The more interested a woman becomes, the more you want to run away."

She had him nailed.

"You seem to know the subject well."

"My father was a shrink. Old school Freudian, brought up probably much like you were. He was very good at what he did for a living but cold as ice where hearth and home were concerned."

"Was a shrink?"

"Dead. Heart attack at fifty-nine."

Michael put down his drink. The loss of a parent at such a young age was a big deal.

"I'm so sorry, Ann."

"Don't be. I'm glad he's dead. I wanted to cut out that heart with my bare hands. Some days I'm angry that I didn't get the chance."

"I guess what I meant to say was, I'm so sorry for the pain you've had to endure for much of your life. Experiences we have as kids can have a profound impact on the adults we become."

"It has. I'm tired of talking about it. What was your family life like? I'm guessing it was damn near idyllic."

"My dad was definitely the opposite. He loved my mother and wasn't afraid to show it. He was a good provider. Spent lots of time with my brother and me. Never missed a little league game, school assembly, was at every parent teacher conference. He remembered the right things about her, too. Things I could never remember like their first date, first kiss, the moment he knew she was the one. He got her flowers for the right occasions and would sometimes just show up with a dozen roses. She would give him a look and he would say, 'I was just thinking about you, babe.'"

"Sounds like the perfect husband."

"There must have been something missing for her. He found out she was having an affair. The plot was right out of a soap opera. He came home early from a business trip to surprise her with jewelry and found her in bed with someone else. Turns out she had been playing that game for years."

"Not exactly the impression you gave me on the street when you were trying to seduce me, Michael."

"We all have images we sell in public. Nobody is attracted to dysfunction."

Ann swirled the red liquid in her cocktail glass. Michael felt the first hit of a real connection between them.

"One of life's ironies. Victims of dysfunction can find it disgusting and arousing at the same time," she said. "Did they divorce?"

"He was ready to forgive her for everything. She dropped the papers on him. Wanted her freedom. She's had three other husbands since."

"Now I get you," Ann said. "You have the same trust issues with women that I have with men."

"A marriage made in heaven."

"Don't get your hopes up. It will never work."

Ann waved at the waiter and pointed to their water glasses. "He must have sent to China for the alcohol."

Michael was impressed. Her candor, whether true or not, was disarming and he was beginning to be attracted to the rest of her.

"You've analyzed me," he said. "What makes you tick?"

"My mom overcompensated on the caregiving side. The more my dad stepped back, the more she poured it on. Her sense of self was totally tied to his affirmation. When it wasn't there, she turned up the neediness. It drove us all crazy. It was finally too much. She closed herself up in the garage with the Lexus running. That was my senior year. Quite the graduation present."

Michael wasn't sure how to respond to this revelation. Was it true, or just another puzzle piece designed to throw him off the scent? The best he could do was, "So as a result you distrust men?"

"Let's just say it's very hard for me to like men. But I enjoy intimacy and it's more fun with someone who knows how."

Their drinks came. Michael took a sip of her Porn Star Martini. It might not have been exactly like Covent Garden, but it was in the neighborhood. Ann ordered a second one without waiting for permission.

"What's your food preference? Surf? Turf? Twigs and sticks?"

"I eat red meat."

Michael felt that the words and the way she said them were layered with meaning. This was not like any mating dance he had ever experienced. Something about this whole encounter felt very wrong.

Tuxedo appeared.

"The Fillet Oscar, rare please. Baked potato with butter. No sour cream. Sautéed spinach and the wedge salad with ranch, hold the blue cheese. No bread."

Michael noted that she had barely looked at the menu. He shrugged in the direction of the waiter and said simply, "For two."

The tuxedo nodded and departed.

Michael wanted to know more. "What worst thing would you say about yourself?"

Ann turned on the sarcasm. "Wow. Why not ask me an 'uncomfortable' question?"

"I'll tell you, if you tell me. It's still Truth Night."

"I have a temper. You wouldn't like me when I'm mad."

"I'll try to avoid provoking you."

"You've already come close. Now you answer the question."

He took a deep breath. It was time to sell the story. "I'm technically a convicted felon."

TWENTY-ONE

The Ramirez Household - Paloma

"When was the last time you took any real vacation?" Maria asked. "Like never!"

Jess saw her grandmother fidget. She always had the hint of a smile at the edges of her mouth as if she knew some special secret. It looked like she had just heard an off-color joke.

Elena Ramirez lifted a hand, a signal that Jess knew was a sign that it was her grandmother's turn to speak and everyone else's turn to listen.

"You should visit Daniél and Christina."

Maria lit up like a roman candle. "That's a great idea, Jessi. Tio Danny runs the police out there in Arizona, doesn't he? It's beautiful country. Their kids are grown and gone. I'm sure they would love to see you!"

Ali added her own postscript. "And to meet your gringo associate."

Jess was doubtful. Her head was full of inner conflict and uncertainty, two things that she had never allowed to come to the surface. The events of the last forty-eight hours had knocked her off her center. She was now questioning every pillar on which she had based her life's purpose. What she wanted most was time to think. "I don't know. It's a long way and an expensive trip. Who will watch after you all while I'm gone?"

Maria nearly choked on the salsa corn cakes. "You're never around, Jessi! A meal here and there perhaps but you are always either working or sleeping. It's no wonder you haven't found a husband. No men know you exist unless you stop them for speeding."

"I agree with Mamacita," Rosa said. "Go visit Tio Danny in Arizona. Compared to your life here, it will feel like a vacation."

Ali concurred. "Let's blow this pop stand."

Everyone had voiced an opinion except Luis. Silence fell as the women waited for his pronouncement. He answered in a single word, in English so even Ali would understand.

"Go."

TWENTY-TWO

Phoenix

Michael Allen watched as Ann Blakely took a long drink of her martini. "I could tell the moment I saw you. Your face looks like the felonious type."

He feigned incredulity. "Really? I bent some SEC rules and lost my license for a while. Got a good lawyer who found the right judge to get me a new trial. I can work until it's decided. He thinks I'll 'beat the rap' as the saying goes."

"Did you do it?"

"Do what?"

"Commit a felony?"

It was time for Michael to sell the backstory.

"Technically, yes. But the law is a real gray area in that space. It made the firm a ton of money. They are supporting me one hundred percent. Lots of people do it. I just got caught."

"So because your mom broke the rules, you can't commit to a woman and feel you need to break them, too? Pathetic."

"That's probably a pretty good analysis. I've never done therapy, but as I listen to myself now, it makes sense."

"How many years would you get if convicted?"

"A lot more than I'd like. I prefer freedom."

"And you'll do whatever it takes to keep your freedom."

"Wouldn't you?"

Ann shook her head. "You're testing my temper."

Michael asked the question that had been on his mind since she had acquiesced to his street corner act. "So why did you agree to have dinner with me tonight?"

"I like the Century Club?"

She said it as a question. He wasn't buying.

"We're still in truth mode."

"I'm coming off of a breakup and needed a fresh victim. That thing you said about 'a moment to remember'? You were just in the right place at the right time."

Michael replayed their earlier conversation. There was one thing that still needed clearing up.

"Are you really a lesbian?"

"It depends on who's looking at me across the table. I'm all about equal opportunity."

Michael didn't like what the alcohol was doing to his mind. His eyes were focused on Ann's mouth. The way it scrunched and twisted, revealing her mood made it delectable. He wanted to taste it.

"Focus, Michael. Focus," Michael said to himself, as he conjured up a retort.

The salads appeared.

"Maybe we are a perfect match. We are both royally screwed up and we mutually distrust one another. That puts us in league with 90% of the couples on the planet."

"If it's still 'Truth Night,'" she answered, "I'll tell you this. I've known some really bad men, but in your own way, you are one of the worst."

"Naw. Think about it! There had to be some animal magnetism or we wouldn't even be playing the game. And besides..." He pointed toward the napkin on his lap. It discretely covered his ever-expanding interest in her. "We both have the equipment and perhaps a night of meaningless intimacy might be what the doctor ordered."

Michael could tell that Ann's blood alcohol content was increasing. He felt himself becoming more attractive with each swallow.

"You really are a classless idiot," she said. "If I wasn't so hot for the fillet, I would be walking out on you right now."

"Wait until you see what I can offer for dessert."

The second martini arrived. When it was gone, she ordered a third.

Michael Allen wrestled with conflicting emotions. His assignment was to do whatever it took to confirm what his superiors already thought they knew about Ann Blakely. It felt like that would require some bending of the rules where intimacy on the job was concerned. And that triggered a completely deeper level of unease. The woman he really wanted felt inaccessible. His heart beat for her anyway. And yet, the combination of candlelight and alcohol made him wonder what Ann looked like naked.

Duty and desire were overpowering. Michael Allen decided he would find out.

TWENTY-THREE

The Ramirez Household - Paloma

It was the kind of evening when you knew that winter was finally over. There were buds on the trees, the April showers conspired with the sunshine to green up the grass and the aroma of hot dogs and roasted peanuts floated gently across the porch, a sign that the minor league baseball season was again underway nearby.

Jessica sat next to her father on the wooden porch swing that overlooked the Ramirez front yard. It was another tradition, where a young girl's questions were asked and the wisdom of generations was dispensed.

The process always began in silence. Even now, it took Jess time to get up the courage to query the patriarch. She studied his features. The years had marked him. The smooth golden skin was now wrinkled and pocked with age spots. The deep circles under the eyes spoke of too many late shifts on the assembly line. The thick shock of hair remained. But it was now mostly gray, no longer jet black like her own. The muscles that were once thick sinew, pressing the edges of his short-sleeve shirt, had softened.

The eyes still twinkled as they studied the details of the

evening. She wondered what thoughts were swirling inside her father's mind. Memories of broken dreams? Fears for his daughters' futures?

Whatever they might be, he never shared them.

Jess thought about her inability to communicate with this complicated man. In uniform, she was capable of confronting nearly every permutation of humanity. Fear disappeared in the heat of conflict. But her father could reduce her to a stuttering mess.

She took a deep breath.

"I need your advice, Papa."

His eyes didn't deviate from their inspection of the yard. His head dipped almost imperceptibly into a nod.

"The university approached me last week. There is a coaching job opening up in the aquatics program. It would mean less stress, more regular hours and a lot less danger. The money is about the same. If I prove myself, there would be more."

Another nod.

"As someone who was asked to try out for the Olympic team, I would be good for recruiting."

She had rehearsed that one sentence a hundred times. How to say it so it would be respectful but also let him know what she had lost the day he shattered her dreams.

Her father blinked but said nothing. She knew the words had hit home.

"What do you think I should do?"

With that, Luis Ramirez sighed. He leaned forward, resting his arms on his knees, his head cradled in two calloused hands.

"Children don't come to us with an operating manual," he said. "All we can do as parents is remember what our parents taught us and trust our intuition."

Jess watched her father's eyes as he focused on the golden badge that seemed to glow in the dark on her belt. Even on suspension, she couldn't take it off.

"I wasn't happy about your decision to become a police officer, either. But I knew another broken dream was too much for you to bear."

His hands came together, fingers intertwined as he gave Jess his full attention.

"What do you really want, querida?"

Jess wanted many things. She wanted to know what it would have been like to stand on the platform with a gold medal around her neck and the whole world watching as the national anthem played. She wanted respect and acceptance in her profession, to retain her womanhood while being treated as "one of the guys." She wondered what it might be like to have a soul mate she could confide in, a warm body on the other side of the bed who would hold her when the nightmares came and love her for who she was, completely, passionately, unconditionally.

How could she say all of these things to this stoic man whose mono-focus was on providing for his family, expecting unquestioned respect and acquiescence to his point of view. To Jess, he was an anachronism. But she still desperately wanted his approval.

She hung her head, ashamed at her inability to say what was really on her mind.

"I guess I don't really know."

"Come to me when you do."

Jess realized her father had won another round. He focused again on the buds that were sprouting from the limbs of the oak trees they had planted together in the front yard over thirty years ago. There would soon be a canopy of leaves, shading the house from the afternoon sun. Jess thought it an apropos metaphor. Her father was only trying to protect her from the heat. But in the process, he blocked out every ray of sunshine.

Ali appeared on the porch. She gave Jess a conspiratorial OK sign with her fingers.

"If you only knew what that filthy hand sign you just gave us means to a Hispanic," Jess said.

"It means either 'kiss my ass' or 'blow me,'" Ali answered.

Her partner had no filters. It was a trait Jess shared everywhere but here. Ali walked up to the porch swing and kissed Luis Ramirez on the cheek.

"What do you say, Papa? Is it all right to take your daughter out for ice cream?"

Luis closed his eyes and waved a hand. The hint of a smile appeared at the corners of his mouth.

"Take her away. She tires me."

Jess punched her father in the shoulder.

"Papa!"

Ali grabbed Jess's hand and pulled her down the front stairs.

"Wait! I have to say goodbye to the family," Jess said.

"I already did. Let's get going before I go into hypoglycemic shock!"

TWENTY-FOUR

Paloma

When owners of The Tasty Twist lost the lease on their stand-alone location near the Paloma University Campus, their fanbase followed them the three blocks to cramped quarters in a strip mall. The fact that the place was located next to a marijuana dispensary turned out to be a stroke of strategic genius. The newly medicated were magnetically drawn to the smell of frozen dairy products. The ice cream parlor was almost always crowded.

Jess and Ali parked their sundaes at a rare open table outside. They savored each mouthful as if it was fine wine, punctuated with erotic moans that made mothers of young children quietly steer clear.

Jess turned her spoon upside down. The cool sweetness of the ice cream tickled her taste buds.

"Why did you become a cop, Ali? You're a digit head who could make ten times the bank in the private sector."

"Why did you become a cop?"

"Do you always have to answer my questions with a question?"

"Let me guess. You tell everyone that you want to serve your community and be a role model for other girls. But the real reason is so you can show those boys you can do anything they can do."

"Guilty as charged. And you?"

"I'm a big fish in a small pond. I spend my free time with college nerds who get paid to ethically hack into the most secure networks. I don't have a wife or kids, so the crappy pay we get gives me some play money. And I get to carry a gun and take out my sexual angst by arresting really bad people who probably would hate me anyway. How could life be any better?"

Jess thought life could be a lot better. The men could treat the women as equals. Judges could plug the loopholes that kept putting perps back out on the street. Society could open its eyes to the root causes of poverty, hopelessness and the crime it engendered. She knew none of these things when she became a cop. Now they were the reasons she wanted to stay in the game.

"And you keep risking it by shooting your mouth off to higher ups who would love nothing better than to get you fired."

"Parallels again. We're not much different, girlfriend."

"Nobody is going to stand in the way of my dreams. I know what it feels like to lose. I intend to keep fighting until I win."

Ali looked at the eight inches of white gauze bandage that covered the wound on Jess's right arm.

"How's the arm?"

Jess raised it upward, making a fist. The move hurt, but she didn't show it.

"It will be one sexy scar. None of the goons we work with could handle something like this without opioids."

"So are we going to visit Uncle Danny or what?"

"I'm on the fence. It's boring out there compared to here."

Ali rolled her eyes. "They have lots of drug issues and crime, just like we do. Not enough cops and more than enough trouble. Sounds a lot like home to me."

"Yeah. I guess I'm not real excited about being there and having to sit on the sidelines."

"I know you, Jessica. You're wallowing in self-pity. Stop bull-shitting me and make the call."

7:30 p.m. PST - Flagstaff

"SHERIFF DANNY LOPEZ PLEASE. This is Jessica Ramirez calling."

After a moment she heard the familiar voice on the other end of the line.

"Jessi?"

Just hearing her uncle's voice made Jess feel better. Waves of comfort and excitement flowed over her.

"¡Tío Danny! ¿Cómo estás?"

"Sobrina Jessica! I haven't heard from you in ages. What's up?"

Jessica, the niece, felt embarrassed to have to confess to her uncle. Jess, the cop, always told the truth, selling it with confidence, even if she didn't always feel it.

"I got bounced for thirty days for blowing up a meth house. Thinking of visiting relatives in Arizona. Could you use some company?"

"I have a bit of a storm brewing right now. Not sure I'll have time to be a gracious host but you are more than welcome to come. Christina will be delighted to see you."

"Is it OK if I bring a friend? Ali got herself banished, too."

"Gates? The computer guru?"

"Yes. We can leave tomorrow. Planning to drive the scenic route and be there in two, maybe three days."

"You can leave tomorrow and be here tomorrow night. I need Gates bad, sobrina. I'll send you airline tickets in the morning."

It took Jess a minute to process her uncle's words.

"What's happening?" she finally said.

"I've been hacked. And I think I may have a serial killer on my hands."

TWENTY-FIVE

Police Headquarters - Phoenix

"Status report."

The head of the Phoenix Information Security and Privacy Office wanted answers. How, the ISPO wondered, could a virus break through the multi-layered electronic wall he had personally helped construct around the City's information technology infrastructure. The CISCO people personally implemented his award-winning design. A small army of staff inspected each device once a week to make sure nothing had changed, documenting their work in old-fashioned handwritten journals that were compared with electronically generated log files. What went wrong?

His number two couldn't hide his own discomfort. His shirt was drenched in a flop sweat and his face told the story of a long, sleepless night.

"We just completed another audit. It looks like the intruder was actually on premises right after our last security pass and manually opened a port in the chief's office at the Police Department. It was port 8250, an oddball. Usually it's port 80 so they can hide behind web traffic or port 21 so the attack can simulate email."

"What do the ID swipes say?"

"The cleaning people come through about 10 p.m. every week-night. We contacted the service and they report sending a temporary employee out on Monday evening. The regular janitor didn't show and nobody has heard from him since."

"Who was the temp?"

"A new hire. The agency was tapped for extra help that night, so this person got the call."

"Have the police chased him down?"

"Chased her down. The record says her name is Jiang Qing. She only worked that one night and quit the next morning."

"Why do I know that name? It's familiar."

The number two already had the Wikipedia page pulled up on his smartphone. He flipped it in the ISPO's direction.

"Jiang Qing was the name of Mao Ze Dong's wife."

"An alias?"

"Complete with full documentation and paperwork. Green card, driver's license, even a passport."

"Do we have her in custody?"

"No, sir. When our officers went to the address on her ID, it was a fast food restaurant."

"So we've been hacked by professionals. I assume the port is locked down."

"Yes, sir. We're doing daily audits now with hourly reporting that sets off an alarm if anything is out of the ordinary."

The ISPO's number two held his breath. The boss could tell that there was more and his colleague was uncomfortable saying it.

"And..."

"We have not been able to find a way to restore the database. Even the files in the cloud backups are gone. And when we install a fresh drive, the firmware in the machine wipes it clean."

The ISPO was never a good poker player. His face conveyed a combination of pain and resignation.

"OK. It sounds like you followed procedure to the letter. Any idea where the outside data was coming from?"

"None at all, sir. I'm afraid I'm out of my depth."

For the first time since learning of the breach, the ISPO gave the hint of a chuckle.

"That makes two of us. Let me know if we get any alarms overnight. I'll have some federal help here in the morning. Any other folks on the statewide network impacted?"

"Every law enforcement agency in Arizona was compromised. That's the commonality."

"Have their IT guys unplug, too. If Jiang Qing infected us, the virus could already be spreading beyond our borders."

The number two nodded.

"That's another problem, sir."

The ISPO looked up from the notes he was writing on a legal pad. It felt to him like old-fashioned technology was the safest way to document things now. What else could go wrong?

"If the firmware on the servers are compromised, we can't be sure that the same thing hasn't happened to the routers. We could be wide open to outsiders and not even know it."

The ISPO scribbled a note on a fresh sheet of paper and signed his name to it.

"Call our vendors. Get them out of bed if you have to. I want everything replaced, top to bottom within forty-eight hours. Until then, disconnect every link to the outside world. Let's try to keep this virus inside the House."

TWENTY-SIX

Crystal Point - Phoenix

"How much did this place cost?"

Michael liked the feeling of Ann's head on his chest. The thin sheet that was her only covering accentuated her contours. She inspected them in the mirror that hung over the mahogany dresser against the only wall that wasn't framed by floor to ceiling windows. Ann liked what she saw. She was a brunette again. Not quite as dark as her natural color. The blue contact lenses were also gone. Brown eyes. Brown hair. It suited her. The implants were working well, too. Perhaps a bit more saline before her next project. The type of man she wanted to attract liked them large.

Michael pressed a button on the night stand. Curtains opened, revealing one of Phoenix Arizona's most breathtaking views.

"The 20th floor of one of the city's most exclusive residences? Not inexpensive."

"Are we talking six or seven figures?"

"Low sevens."

"So this is how felons live in Phoenix?"

"You're not going down that rabbit hole again are you? We've had such a wonderful evening."

"OK. I'll leave it. For now. What cocktail can I make you?"

"A Vesper Martini, if you please, ma'am. 'Shaken, not stirred.'"

"Stirred is actually better. Ian Fleming got that one wrong."

"I prefer shaken. The ice is more effective that way. I like mine at 27 degrees Fahrenheit. If I could make it even colder, I would."

"Liquid Nitrogen would do the trick. There are ice cream stores that use the stuff now. A guy like you could probably afford the equipment."

He slipped a hand beneath the sheets.

"I'll explore it."

She batted the wandering fingers away.

"Another thing I don't understand. The insatiable male. Don't men ever grow out of it?"

He nibbled on her ear.

"If I ever do, I don't want to live anymore."

"Sheesh. I sure know how to pick 'em."

She slid out from beneath the sheets. She sensed his hungry eye following her curvaceous silhouette, floating in the direction of the bar that was next to the dresser.

She measured the ingredients, put crushed ice into a glass to prepare it, pouring the remains of the ice bucket into a quartz crystal shaker. Securing the top, she slid it into a custom chamois coverlet so her hands wouldn't freeze. She shook.

She made sure Michael could only see her back. His imagination would have to paint the rest of the picture.

Ann returned with a martini glass in one hand and a Blue Moon Belgian White beer bottle in the other.

Michael was astonished by her choice. "The best booze in Phoenix within reach and you drink a beer?"

"I'm full of surprises. Here, handsome."

She handed him the glass. It was the perfect temperature. The familiar aroma of the alcohol mixed with her perfume in an appealing way.

"To crime," she said, tapping the bottom of her beer bottle against his glass.

They drank.

TWENTY-SEVEN

Crystal Point - Phoenix

Thirty minutes later, Michael Allen was sound asleep. The level of Benzodiazepine Ann added to his martini would keep him comfortable for a long time. She took her clothes into the bathroom, showered, dressed and reemerged, fairly well put together in relatively short order.

Ann opened her laptop and checked her watch. It was nearly 3 a.m., almost 6 on the east coast. There were things to do. She cursed silently, realizing she had forgotten to ask Michael for his WiFi password. That would add another ten minutes to the task.

She clicked an encrypted folder on her screen's desktop and entered a twenty-five-character passphrase with the speed of a stenographer. A toolkit menu appeared under the logo she knew well.

The Maitland Corporation.

She selected the password recovery utility and started the application.

Ann Blakely leaned back in the comfortable depths of the Corinthian leather chair she had placed by the window as a work space. She sipped the Blue Moon and tried to decide if Michael was worth taking to her special place, 78 miles north of Flagstaff. There were others who were much darker, more dangerous and in greater need of her attention.

She liked this one. He challenged her intellect and had the money to spoil her. Perhaps he still had some value to offer. At least for a while.

She returned to the chair. A green icon blinked on the desktop. The familiar four bar WiFi symbol popped up in the upper right corner of the screen.

Time to go to work.

THE SECURE CRYPTIX chat application flashed on the screen. Ann logged in. In a moment, a soft beep confirmed her connection.

Капитан
Status?
Vega
On Schedule.
Капитан
I know about your distractions.
Vega
That's on my time
Капитан
I own your time until our project is complete.
Vega
Are you dissatisfied with my progress?
Капитан
It has been satisfactory... so far.
Vega
Until it isn't, leave me alone.
Капитан

You cannot afford to fail

Vega

I won't.

Капитан

Status of the test?

Vega

Proof of concept worked flawlessly

Капитан

I believe you made an error

Vega

?

Капитан

These distractions. They may draw attention to our more important work.

Vega

That's my problem. I can handle it. Trust me.

Капитан

I can't afford to trust anyone. You must deliver.

Vega

And so must you. The bank transfer. Make it.

Капитан

It shall be done today.

Vega

Today is almost over where you are.

Капитан

It shall be done. You must focus on our objective.

Vega

It shall be done. We are on schedule.

Капитан

Next update?

Vega

When I feel you need one. Must sign off. Work to do.

Капитан

There is no room for failure.

Vega
Have I ever failed?
Капитан
There is always a first time. It can't be now.
Vega
It won't. Signing off.

ANN DISCONNECTED and turned her attention to the East Coast.

TWENTY-EIGHT

The Third Day - The Beltway Outside Washington DC

The black Lincoln Town Car inched its way through the typical mid-week morass of the morning DC rush hour traffic. Terry Taylor sat in the back seat, the white collared shirt and red power tie already constricting his neck. The Head of the Federal Bureau of Investigation's Cyber Action Team was more comfortable flying below the radar in a polo shirt and cargo pants.

Today he had an audience with the director.

Taylor recognized the number blinking back at him from the secure cell phone in his hand.

Taylor ran his friend's details through the mental contact database that served him so well. He and Phoenix FBI Station Chief Bill Roberts graduated in the same class at Quantico. Though vastly different in temperament and core competencies, they maintained a close friendship over a quarter-century career with the Bureau.

African Americans still had a much tougher time advancing in many law enforcement cultures. Bill Roberts' bottom line was delivering results and going wherever the Bureau sent him. When the Phoenix job became available, Arizona's 4% black population statistic didn't matter. It was leadership and Terry Taylor knew that Bill Roberts intended to be a leader.

Taylor reflected that his path couldn't be more different. Harvard educated with family connections on both sides of the party spectrum, he had the interpersonal skills and the relationships to earn the director's trust. He was proud of the reputation he had created, "Directors come and go, but Terry is the guy who gets the jobs done."

"Brother Bill! How goes the inferno in Phoenix?"

This morning, Bill's voice was particularly sober. "You know me, Terry. I only call on birthdays and bad days. I'm afraid this is the latter."

"What's the story on this meltdown at the cop shop?"

"Someone got into Phoenix PD HQ and opened a port on a desktop computer. They set up a secondary WiFi access point and our perp used it to infect the statewide police information network. It looks like their intent was to see how far they could get in wiping out records."

"I hear they did a good job. The folks at Amazon Web Services and Akamai have already been on the phone screaming at me this morning. Their backups and the backups of the backups are toast and they are worried that this thing might infect other clients."

"Sorry to ruin your day, partner. Do you have any sense for who did this and why?"

"It could be any number of scenarios. The Chinese are always knocking on every door to see if they can elbow their way into everything from the power grid to airline scheduling systems. Organized crime has the sophistication and the budget to try to cover their tracks by cratering our data warehouses. It could be another Edward Snowden, or perhaps just a lucky adolescent sitting in his mother's basement."

"Why Arizona?" Roberts wondered. "Does this have anything to do with the person we have under surveillance?"

"That's what I'm hoping you can help me find out."

"I'll need some horsepower. Our tech guys barely know how to reset passwords."

Taylor smiled. There was a reason Bill Roberts kept getting promoted. He got results.

"You always under promise and over deliver, my friend. It sounds like your team is being pretty creative where your assigned subject is concerned."

"Perhaps. But this breach is beyond our capacity by a mile."

"We'll get you some resources before the end of the day. Incredibly, your little slice of heaven isn't the biggest thing on my radar, so it won't be the first team initially. I can spare one guy for the rest of the week and the cavalry will descend soon thereafter, assuming I can get a couple of other things under control."

"Anything you can share without having to kill me?"

"Just whispers, really. But if they are true, and if by some random chance there happens to be a connection to your current assignment, you'll be at the top of the list before you can blink."

"I guess one guy is better than nothing. How are you keeping ahead of the shit storm with the budget cuts Congress keeps tossing at you?"

"You know how it goes. We fire good people on the inside and hire them back as contractors on the outside. Maitland picks many of them up. Your guy will actually be one of theirs."

"Maitland?" Bill Roberts didn't often express emotion, but Taylor could tell that this development tripped his trigger. "Aren't they the people you all investigated for inappropriate contact with the Russians last year?"

"Those are the guys. We ultimately couldn't get enough proof and their CEO is a big contributor to the President's campaign. You know how that goes."

"Can I trust them?"

The Town Car was pulling up to 935 Pennsylvania Avenue, NW. Taylor looked at his watch. It was time to go. "Bill, old friend, I'm counting on you to answer that question for me."

TWENTY-NINE

Crystal Point - Phoenix

When Michael Allen woke at nearly 11 a.m. the next morning, Ann was gone. The midday sun burned his eyes.

He reached for the remote to close the curtains and found a small business card next to it. The card said "April's Boutique" on the front. On the back was a handwritten note:

"I work weekdays, 11 a.m. until 6 p.m."

He put his palms against his temples.

"No phone number."

He fingered the speed dial on his cell phone. There was an answer on the first ring.

"Good morning, sir."

"Did you log the router session?"

"Yes, sir."

"Good. Messages?"

"You need to go to Flagstaff. The locals are free-styling."

"I am making progress. Why me? Why now?"

"You are requested to come by the office when convenient. It will be explained."

Michael stifled a yawn and looked at his watch. He was expecting a dressing down from the Station Chief for sleeping with a suspect. That wasn't in the FBI operations manual. In typical situations, that would be enough to get a case thrown out of court and end a career.

Everyone up the line agreed that this situation was anything but typical.

"I can be there in an hour."

"I will pass on the message, sir."

Michael disconnected the call and tossed the cell phone across the room. It landed on the leather chair by the window.

The distraction from his primary mission annoyed him. He had a terrific headache. It was either the booze, the rich Century Club cuisine or the girl. Whatever it was, it was worth the discomfort. Where Ann Blakely was concerned, he felt he was right on track.

THIRTY

Phoenix Sky Harbor Airport

The Sky Harbor airport public address system announced that passengers deplaning from Delta flight 2666 could be met at baggage claim.

Bill Roberts stood at the edge of the security zone with his second in command.

"You look like you haven't had any sleep, young man," he said. "There is such a thing as taking an assignment too seriously."

"I live to serve," was the best reply his colleague could muster.

Roberts' closed mouth twitched. It was the closest he came to a smile. The chief knew exactly what this definition of "service" meant and he didn't like it.

From the midst of the swarm of arriving passengers, a young man matching the description Terry Taylor had forwarded appeared. He fit the paradigm of a computer geek, five-foot-five, about thirty pounds under weight, and dressed in an unbranded solid-black T-shirt and well-worn jeans, a backpack slung over his left shoulder. He looked way too young to be carrying the responsibility Taylor had put on his shoulders.

The youth pulled his Maitland Corporation ID card out of his pocket passing it to Roberts with one hand, extending the other to accept the chief's handshake.

"Mario McCallister," he said. "Looks like I'm your man for the next few days until the really smart people arrive."

Roberts smiled. "You wouldn't be here, unless you were one of them, Mario. This is my second in command. He's undercover on a case that might end up being interesting to you. Meet the man most likely to win the best actor award for posing as a convicted felon: Special Agent Michael Wright."

THIRTY-ONE

72 miles North of Flagstaff

The woman lay on her back. Out here sky wasn't dimmed by the city lights. She could make out the tiny communications satellites moving among the star field, traversing the heavens in their elliptical orbits.

"Did you do what they said you did?"

That was the key question.

His face darkened.

"Is that what this whole thing is all about?"

There was a menace in his voice, perhaps the same voice that was the last thing two dead women heard. It would have frightened his normal prey. But she wasn't normal.

He leaned closer, his foul breath stinging her olfactory glands.

"What do you care?"

"I don't!"

She sprung to her feet and stood at the edge of the blanket, silhouetted in the glory of the dark spectacle that framed her perfect body. The unbuttoned cotton shirt fluttered to the ground.

She turned to run, laughing, bareback in the direction of the stars, her exquisite flaxen hair dancing behind her.

"Catch me if you can!"

He followed her.

The thin screen of woods that framed their coital stage opened like a movie curtain to reveal the majesty of the Grand Canyon. She insisted that they hike to this spot, a favorite of hers she said.

The girl made love with an intensity and urgency that felt more like punishment than pleasure. But it was a chastening she knew he was more than willing to endure again.

She ran for about 200 yards, slowing to a trot as she approached the canyon's rim. The rangers told tales of how easy it was to die here. Nearly 800 had lost their lives across its vast expanse since the counting began in the 1880s. Words like "accidental," "suicide" and "murder" were often hard to distinguish. Dozens of unsolved cases remained. They all shared one thing in common: the inevitable ending, a broken, lifeless body, buried and soon forgotten.

She was pleased with how things had progressed.

She could tell that her toughness both aroused and concerned him. He didn't trust females. Two were dead because they broke that trust.

The woman was at the edge of the precipice now. She turned to him. Her smile was broad, inviting.

"Come sit next to me. Let's look into infinity!"

She perched on the edge of the canyon wall, dangling a pair of exquisite legs into the gentle breeze that mixed the heat of the rocks with the cool of the evening. Below, far away, the boiling voice of the Colorado River sang its eternal song.

She counted on his taste for danger. Beauty and death inches apart. The combination was intoxicating.

He sat.

From a small bag, she produced a pair of handheld vaporizers, a favorite of a generation of smokeless smokers who were being hooked on nicotine like never before.

She handed him one of the devices. Without the flannel shirt, she knew her moonlit figure was distracting, almost irresistible. She put the other vape pen into her mouth, wrapping her lips around the end in a way intended to make him want to relive the highlights of the evening. She took a long pull, exhaling the characteristic aroma of menthol out of her nostrils.

As he inhaled his own mixture, she put a hand on the back of his neck and pulled him close, kissing him deeply. She sensed his wariness starting to dim as she gave him a taste of the rich hint of vodka that first primed the path toward their earlier coupling.

She let go of his lips, looking intently into his eyes.

"Is that the river in the distance?" he asked.

"Yes."

"How far down?"

"Five hundred fifty-three feet."

"That's pretty specific."

"I've been here before."

"You mean I'm not the first?"

"Nor will you be the last."

She kissed him again. It was a test to see if his mouth was becoming numb. Its unresponsiveness to her caress told her it was.

"What is it like?" she said.

Her face was just inches from his. It had transformed into a cold countenance, nothing like the smiling seductress who lured him here.

His speech slurred. "What do you mean 'what is it like'?"

"What is it like to kill a woman?"

She saw that the man was starting to lose his balance. It was her own hand that kept him from falling before she was ready for it.

"What the hell is this?" he slurred.

She checked her watch, calculating his body weight and the strength of the mixture. He should be incapacitated by now.

"Kind of a truth serum," she answered. "A preparation for your final earthly judgment."

The blow seemed to come from nowhere.

The man was on top of her. Her feet pressed against his chest. His thick hand encircled her throat.

"Not so fast," he growled.

She could see him squinting to keep his vision clear. There wasn't time to think about where she had made the error.

The hand started to close around her throat. She gagged in as much air as she could, directing her energy to her legs, pressing the man's 300 pounds backward toward the cliff.

He lost his grip on her neck, but was able to snag the thick belt around her waist. The pair tumbled over the edge.

Failure and dying were never things that she had even considered. Their sudden nearness generated an unaccustomed emotion that terrified her: Fear.

Somehow, she found something to grab. The small outcropping wouldn't be enough to restrain both of their bodies. In a few more seconds it would break loose from its moorings and they would both be dead.

The only emotion she felt now was rage. To be denied her addiction to retribution was inconceivable. Dying in this place at this time was not an option. She channeled her anger into every sinew of the five fingers that held fast to the ledge. Even with the added focus, she knew there were only seconds left until the tiny muscles failed.

The Bergulon finally started to do its job. His grip start to relax.

Her target could still scream. It was a sound she knew would populate her nightmares for the rest of her life. Its animalistic hysteria was at once chilling and pleasing. As with every victim's shriek, she cataloged it, associating the sound with the one person she really wanted to kill. The one person who was already dead and beyond her reach.

With her own strength starting to ebb, Ann Blakely managed to find a foothold. Then another. In a few moments, she lay, exhausted and hyperventilating on the soft grass as she heard the splash, five hundred fifty-three feet below.

THIRTY-TWO

Flagstaff Pulliam Airport

The American Airlines Canadair RJ 700 touched down on Runway 210 ten minutes late. Pulliam Airport was a compact facility where passengers still deplaned onto the tarmac. Jessica Ramirez and Alexandra Clark stepped out of the aircraft and into the cool of the Arizona evening.

Jess was delighted to see Danny Lopez's broad smile as she deplaned. Beside him was an unfamiliar presence, north of six feet and dressed in a National Park Service Ranger's uniform.

"Welcome to Grand Canyon state, ladies."

The three embraced in a group hug.

"Meet Stephen Morris, Chief Ranger for the National Park Service Grand Canyon District."

Morris bowed and extended a hand.

"My pleasure," he said. "Danny has told me a lot about you."

"I hear you've had some interesting developments in your jurisdiction," Jess said.

"Concurrent jurisdiction. We've staffed up the unit these past few years, but we still let the local constabulary take an occasional case. Sheriff Lopez has one of the best homicide teams in the West. We're glad to let him take the lead on this one."

Ali raised an eyebrow. "What jurisdiction let's somebody else handle a nice juicy murder?"

"This one will ultimately involve all of us. Danny has had a little more experience cooperating with multiple agencies than I've had."

Danny grinned. "A politically correct way of saying you don't want to herd the egos?"

Steve Morris covered his ears.

"I can't confirm or deny that."

Jess watched her uncle inspect the dressings that still covered the laceration on her right arm.

"That's quite a prize you got there," he said. "What happened to the other guy?"

"In the Paloma City Morgue. 'Ego Girl,' here put him to sleep."

"She's actually getting a little soft," Ali added. "I had to roll backup when she couldn't raise her gun to take out a guy with a pissant AR15. You'd think a girl who lost only 80% of her blood could be a better shot."

"I had it under control until you butted in," Jess shot back.

The sheriff raised a hand.

"From what O'Brien tells me, you two were both damn near perfect in how you handled the incident."

This bit of information took Jess by surprise. O'Brien kept the assessments of his officers close to his bulletproof vest.

"You talked with O'Brien?"

"Of course. I always do a background check before I share my secrets."

Jess's natural distrust for the system was evident. "That's not how IAD positioned it. We're both in some pretty hot water when we get back."

"Oh he told me all about that, too. You haven't had a career unless you've run afoul of Internal Affairs at least three times. This too shall pass."

Danny locked eyes with his niece. Jess couldn't tell if he was serious or bluffing. "The chief also said you were both insubordinate and royal pains in his ass. I think he's hoping you like it here and decide not to go back."

She didn't know if it was the desert air or the company, but Jess was already feeling her mojo returning. "He'll never get rid of me," she said. "As long as la familia is around, I'll be around, too."

Jess and Ali swung their backpacks over their shoulders.

"You certainly pack light," Danny said. "Looks like Christina will be doing some laundry."

Ali laughed. "We figured you'd at least give us some polo shirts. If the chief sees us come back with official Mounty gear, perhaps he'll treat us with a little more respect."

"I've done better than that," Danny said.

Jess watched as he produced a pair of five-pointed stars, pinned to black leather wallets.

"For the next thirty days, you are hereby special deputies of the Coconino County Sheriff's Department. And I've got some priority work for you both."

THIRTY-THREE

The Fourth Day - Flagstaff

Tia Christina's hot breakfast made Jess feel right at home.

She watched Tio Danny dip a forkful of French toast into the spool of syrup that encroached on the scrambled eggs, sausage and fresh fruit piled high on his plate. Christina was definitely a better cook than wife number one.

The sheriff was already in the zone, wrestling with a puzzle he knew little about. "How in the hell can someone break through government-level network security and crater an entire system, including all the backups?"

"I won't know until I take a look," Ali said. "But nothing is impregnable anymore. If there's just one connection to the Internet, you're vulnerable."

"That will be your first task when we get to the office. I'm glad you brought Gates along, Jess."

"She can't cook worth a damn, but she has a few useful skills. Why isn't the FBI all over this?"

"They are. The phone lines and email still aren't working very well. Gates here has maybe a day until the Feds take her toys away."

Ali devoured another load of fruit and yogurt. "Let 'em have it, Tio Danny. My brain is already full."

"You'll give me a better briefing than I'll get from our DC brothers and sisters, Gates."

Jess knew how Ali loved having her ego stroked.

"I'll agree with that," she said. "Nothing beats having a gifted artist in residence."

Reticence was the Hispanic way. So, Jess wasn't surprised when Tia Christina weighed in. "Are all your friends this crazy, Jessi?"

"I have compassion for lost souls," Jess answered.

Ali spoke through a mouthful of food.

"Lost souls that pull your bongos out of the fire, girlfriend."

"Give her something to do, stat, Tio. She's already driving me crazy and it's not even 9 a.m."

"Perhaps I'd better split you two children up today," Danny said. "Jessi, I'll be putting you in a 4X4 to take some evidence to a lab in Phoenix. Our latest guest at the morgue brought us a little present and I want to make absolutely sure it gets there."

Jess produced a small notebook and pen. "What can you tell us about all this?"

"Drownings in the Colorado are up year over year. That's not necessarily a big deal. These things ebb and flow depending on the volume of tourists, the weather and sometimes just plain bad luck. But three of the bodies we've found don't seem to fit the pattern. We can usually trace the victims back to a camping group, a raft expedition or hikers who checked in with the rangers. These guys weren't on anybody's radar. They all popped up in the same ten-mile stretch of river. They all exhibited injuries consistent with a fall from the canyon's rim. And I'm almost certain they all share another thing in common: a criminal background."

"And you think these incidents are connected to your data breach?" Gates asked.

"I can't say for sure. But you know how our instincts work. It wouldn't surprise me if the breach was cover. We went to on-line data storage three years ago. I've got a new coroner who doesn't have the institutional knowledge yet to put the pieces together. And now, without data, we're at square one."

"What's my cargo?" Jess asked.

"The latest victim had a nicotine vaporizer in his pocket when we found him. The docs think he was poisoned before he took his swim. The drug is consistent with what toxicology said was in the blood stream of one of the others. We have some prints that are on their way to be analyzed and we are hoping to ID our victim before the end of the day. I want confirmation of what's actually inside that vape thing. I think the killer may have used it to poison our victims before dispatching them. I have a ton of deputies who could run this errand. But you're the one I trust to get it there safely."

"It sounds like a pattern we can work with," Jess said. She was already feeling like she and Ali were part of the team. "Do you think there is any connections between your data breach and these murders?"

"It still feels too coincidental to me. The Feds and the NPS guys will be all over this when they digest what we've sent them. Until Gates figures out how we were hacked, I've been sharing information the old-fashioned way. FedEx and phone calls. We've bought some time to explore but in twenty-four hours, my guess is we'll have a lot of interested company."

Danny Lopez's cell phone vibrated. He recognized the number.

"Good morning, Jennifer. Our houseguests made it here safely."

Jennifer's voice was tense. "You had better get over here, Sheriff. We've had a break-in at the morgue."

THIRTY-FOUR

Coconino County Morgue - Flagstaff

Joey Price sat on a desk in the foyer of 4402 East Huntington Drive. His short legs swung back and forth like a 6-year-old sitting on the edge of a fishing dock. It helped him to think.

He was fascinated by parabola painted by the prismatic safety glass crystals on the carpet.

The sheriff's bark didn't faze him.

"Report."

Joey's mind parsed the facts. Danny and his out-of-town visitors stood in the outer lobby. The lower pane of the glass front door was smashed. Shards of safety glass littered the floor. The likely weapon, a single red brick lay in the middle of the mess.

"I've told you that the security here is too rudimentary," he said. "Whoever broke in knew what they were doing. They cut power to the entire building, fried the recorder and camera system and disabled the alarm. Then it was as simple as tossing the brick and they were inside."

"What's missing?"

"I left the autopsy notes along with a vape pen on the counter next to the deep freeze. That's all that's missing."

"Please tell me you took your laptop home with you and have a backup."

"Absolutely."

"But we've lost a crucial piece of evidence, the one item that might help us identify and convict whoever is doing this."

Joey was totally unconcerned.

"I wouldn't say that."

Joey already knew that the sheriff had a long fuse. When it burned up, his temper could be a hurricane.

"I have the FBI on my case, Dr. Price. And I have neither the time nor the patience to deal with what looks to me like a rookie mistake."

From behind his back, Joey produced a sealed evidence bag. Inside, still covered with black fingerprint dust was the vaporizer. He swung it in the air in time with his rocking legs.

Joey felt a rare emotional sensation. He loved having the upper hand.

"What the hell?" was all Danny could manage.

"I went down to the Greenhouse Marijuana Dispensary. They happened to have an identical device there and I bought it. I figured that our Federales would confiscate the evidence and I wanted to understand how the thing worked. I left it out last night along with a print out of the autopsy notes. I was planning to bring both to you first thing this morning."

"This," he said, waving the bag with a flourish, "was in my personal safe at home last night. No sense in tempting the fates, don't you agree?"

Danny put a hand to his forehead. Joey recognized the opening stanzas of a world class migraine.

"Joey, I..."

"Don't mention it, boss. I take security a little more seriously than the taxpayers who manage our budgets do."

Danny waved a hand at Jess, pointed to the bag and motioned for her to take it.

She examined the item through the clear plastic that protected it.

"I guess this is my traveling partner today."

She shook Joey Price's hand.

"Nice work, Doc."

"I think that's what the sheriff is trying to say."

"Get this cleaned up," Danny finally yelled over his shoulder. "And call the power company before the bodies in our freezer start to smell like yesterday's fish."

Joey looked at Jess and Ali. The corner of his mouth bent upward into what constituted a smile.

"Already done."

THIRTY-FIVE

Raft Put-In Point - Colorado River - Grand Canyon National Park

Kevin Smith went through the inspection of his S-Rig white-water raft with the attention to detail of a jet pilot. He took a closer look at "Rosie" this morning after her tumble at Mile 98. She seemed to have weathered the adventure well.

Smitty thought about Marty Laurent, about how dangerous these rides among the churning foam could truly be, about the dead man with the teardrop tattoo.

He paused, marking the point on the checklist that was clamped to a clipboard in his left hand, and looked around him.

The canyon was almost 1,000 feet deep here. He could see the horizontal lines painted at intervals from the ground to the precipice, road signs that depicted watermark moments across thousands of years of history.

Kevin marveled at how something so soft and pliable as the most fundamental liquid on the planet could overcome solid rock. With time and persistence, it was possible for the weakest to overcome the strong.

The squelch circuit on the Yaesu FT2D amateur radio hand-held he carried on his belt popped.

"N4FMQ from N5ZGT."

Kevin recognized the voice before his friend identified with his call sign.

"N4FMQ. Go ahead Brian."

"There's another about a mile north of the take-out point."

"Another what?"

"Another body."

THIRTY-SIX

Phoenix

As usual, Jess had done her homework. Smart people come to Phoenix for the climate when the mileage on abused bodies starts to impact quality of life. Richard Walker was one of them. The former FBI chemist and forensic pathologist relocated on the very day he was eligible for retirement. He formed High Desert Diagnostics to ply his trade to a rarified clientele that included both governmental and private customers. A lifetime of contacts brought him more business than he could ever want. He could afford to be picky.

"Dr. Walker?"

Jess poked her head into the laboratory, unsure if anyone was home.

"Over here. Look for the *September Torch* poster on the wall and turn left."

September Torch was one of my all time favorite bands. The man had taste.

"Ahh. You must be Danny's niece, the one who blows up houses."

Jess wasn't sure she appreciated how her uncle had character-
ized her.

Walker peeled off a pair of rubber gloves and proffered a
hand.

"Nice to meet you, kid. I hear you have something for me."

Jess produced the clear plastic bag from a butt pack where she
kept her undercover work essentials: handcuffs, firearm, a taser and
several extra clips of ammunition.

Walker was impressed. "You must have been a girl scout. 'Be
prepared.'"

"Nope. Couldn't afford the uniform. It must have damaged my
self-esteem. I've been wearing one for the last ten years."

"I like the polo," Walker said. "The color suits you."

"Tio Danny must have brought you in on the sales pitch, too. It
seems like everyone from my family to my chief is hoping I won't
ever come home."

"I like it here." Walker seemed to be in the mood to pontificate.
Jess noticed that talking at length was a habit older people often
acquired.

"It's often too hot and the monsoon season isn't very fun. But
the pace is a little slower and I haven't seen 32 degrees since I
left DC."

Jess swept the well-appointed room with her eyes. She knew
little about the profession, but everything here looked to be state of
the art.

"How does just one guy afford all of these toys?"

"I have a rarefied clientele who are less concerned with my fees
than they are with my results."

"And you do this alone?"

"I have a kid who helps me in the afternoons. Interns are great
indentured servants."

"Danny says you find things that others don't."

"I found the Bergulon after the other lab guys missed it. I'm
told you have a possible modus operandi for its ingestion."

Jess handed him the bag. Walker held it in front of a large, lighted magnifier and began his inspection.

"Guessing the fingerprint guys won't find much. If our suspect is smart enough to use this to kill, he's smart enough to keep his prints off it."

"Our coroner is more interested in understanding how you can concentrate enough juice in a small weapon like this to incapacitate a victim."

She took another vial from her butt pack.

"And then, there's this."

"Let me guess. A blood sample from the deceased."

"That's it. Hoping you can tell us if any of that drug was still in his system."

"You've given me an interesting project," Walker said. "Let's see what stories this little toy can tell us."

He gently sliced open the bag with a scalpel. "Let's take a look."

The pathologist put on plastic gloves, a mask and eye protection, handing the same to Jess.

"If that stuff could kill a big guy like your friend in the freezer, we had better take extra precautions."

She backed away.

"I'll stay well clear. Not interested in coming anywhere near what's in those things."

Walker studied the liquid inside the vaporizer, carefully transferring what remained to a small Sevidence vial that sat on the counter. He capped it with a rubber cork and carried it to an array of machines that lined the far wall. Using what he called an "air displacement pipette", Walker carefully placed samples into a half dozen different receptacles, each designed for the unique intake of the machines that would analyze it.

"When I started, we still used microscopes and litmus paper," Walker said. "It's all computerized now. These few devices measure atomic absorption and emission, gas and liquid chromatography, refractometry, rheometry, viscometry, thermal analyzers, and the like. Every chemical has a unique signature. This should tell us what we have and help us calculate what happened to the victim's metabolism when he inhaled it."

Jess knew that the clock was ticking until the Feds would engage.

"How long does it take for results?"

"Normally weeks, sometimes months. Fifty-five days is the current backlog at the state lab."

"But..." Jess said, anticipating an addition.

"Since it's Danny, I can give you rough estimates in about an hour for everything. It won't be ready for a Judge and a court until we go through the normal channels. But I can have a conclusive confirmation of the drug in sixty minutes. You can stay here with me and be bored, or do some exploring in town and come back after lunch. It sounds like we think we know what we've got. Leave me your cell number. I'll call you sooner if I find anything unusual."

Jess turned for the exit.

"Hey," Walker said. "The person who did this? He's very smart. Probably a Bio-chem major if not a full-fledged M.D."

"Watch yourself," Jess said. "If he realizes we have her stuff, he'll come looking for it." *his*

THIRTY-SEVEN

Flagstaff

"That makes at least four."

Dr. Joey Price got the news about the body at the end of his mid-morning staff meeting. He knew his penchant for staying up late and sleeping even later was welcomed by his seven-person team. It gave them time to prepare. Joey could be relentless in his questioning, a trait that might demoralize anyone who didn't understand the abrupt frankness that was a feature of his particular brand of autism.

The Medical Examiner appreciated how the Coconino family had come to understand his "love language." They knew it wasn't personal and his queries had made them a better, more cohesive machine.

He thought often about the more than 300 autopsies performed each year and the increasing burden of paperwork .

"The families deserve a full accounting," Joey would intone without emotion. "How their loved ones died becomes as important as how they lived."

When Danny Lopez's deputies pulled the latest fish out of the

Colorado, it quickly became clear that the departed fit their serial killer's MO.

"What does it mean when the time frame between the murders gets shorter?" one of the assistants had asked when Jennifer phoned in the news.

Joey didn't make eye contact. He passed a small SD data storage card between his hands with the dexterity of a magician.

"There's a countdown clock ticking somewhere," he said. "Our perp is getting short on time."

The assistant queried the entire team, but Joey knew that she expected him to provide an answer.

"I wonder what's coming?"

Joey popped the SD card into his pocket.

"Relocation. This bad person is about to disappear."

THIRTY-EIGHT

Flagstaff

In the data room at the Coconino County Sheriff's Office, Ali Clark was ensconced in her own analysis. Her computer was running diagnostics on the local network. That was the extent of what Danny had approved. But Ali was Ali. The woman they called "Gates" had designs on a deeper dive.

When Bob Knutson heard a computer genius was in town, he decided not to sit in on Joey's Thursday morning gathering. He wanted to look over her shoulder.

"What's that thing doing?" he asked. "In plain English please."

Ali always appreciated an attentive audience.

"It's searching for network vulnerabilities, unlocked back doors and such. I'm also examining a bunch of hard drives to see if it can find out how they were wiped and if any data can be recovered. That beat-up old PC over there is what we call a 'honey pot.' It should trap any further intrusion attempts. The geeks who do these things often set up bots to check their work. If our bad guy phones home again, we'll have some IP addresses to analyze."

"We had a kid that used to steal our mail," Dr. Bob said. "Not all of it. He was just a Field & Stream enthusiast. He figured out when they would arrive and intercepted them before Bonnie or I had a chance to check the mailbox. I guess it wasn't really stealing. When he was done reading them, he put them back in the box. He might have gotten away with it if he had not cut out so many coupons."

Ali laughed. "Criminals are definitely not the sharpest tacks in the drawer. How did you catch him?"

"Once I knew they were going missing, I sat in the hayloft out in our barn with my Pentax and a telephoto lens. That was what we called 'surveillance cameras' back then. I got some good photos of the boy doing his thing when he thought nobody was watching. I cornered him the next afternoon after he got off of the school bus and we negotiated a plea deal. I wouldn't tell his parents if he stopped 'borrowing.' For good behavior, I promised to give him the magazines after I was done with them. A win-win."

"What ever happened to him?"

"He's now the Coconino County Sheriff."

"Tio Danny?"

"We all have our sordid pasts."

THIRTY-NINE

Phoenix

Jess found a serviceable Mexican restaurant. It was popular with the Phoenix locals, jam packed with customers, many speaking Arizona "Spanglish."

Jess felt right at home. She savored an enchilada that her mother might have made and was watching the cash flow into the till. She figured the take during the last hour was over 2,000 dollars.

She was making a mental note to speak with the manager about emptying the register at more frequent intervals when she saw him.

"Perps stand out like sore thumbs," her FTO once told her. "The guy with the hood over his head on a hot day. Untucked shirts that obscure a weapon. The nervous kid who tries to look innocent, but tries too hard. Some have drivers. Watch for cars that are positioned for a quick getaway, backed into parking spaces with motors running and another guy with his face obscured in the driver's seat."

The thermometer on the bank across the street read 90 degrees. The air conditioning inside the restaurant was having trouble keeping up. This kid wore a thick sweatshirt with the hood pulled tight around the edges of his face, dark sunglasses obscuring his eyes. Jess noticed a beat-up Honda backed into the handicapped parking space out front. The kid's twin was behind the wheel, equally anonymous.

Something was about to go down.

Jess's penchant for always choosing a restaurant seat with a full view of the proceedings bothered her dates. It was an early sign of relationship control that made old-school males uneasy.

Today, that long-practiced habit paid off.

Jess eased the Glock out of her butt pack.

The adrenaline coursed through her. It focused her. She silently dared the kid to misbehave.

FORTY

The Phoenix Pubic Library

The Phoenix Library System has seventeen locations. The WiFi was free and fast and people left you alone. Ann Blakely's contract gig was on track. Now she was working on her own projects. Another guilty monster lay dead and broken in the Coconino County Morgue. Now that she had processed her near-death experience, even that added to the perverse pleasure she felt in the aftermath of a killing. But the thrill of dispensing her own definition of justice was brief.

Ann was hooked on retribution. And she needed another fix.

On her screen were the names of a dozen likely marks. She would research their cases to qualify them for her special attention. Then it would be time to create a new identity and bait the hook.

But first she wanted to check her countermeasures on the police IT network. From a quiet corner behind a row of romance novels, Ann clicked another application. It would take a few minutes for the packets to traverse through a dozen different virtual private network connections around the globe, but they would end up just down the street and report back. She covered the application screen with another window that summarized her research into "the ones that got away." Phoenix seemed to be a target-rich environment. "Geeze, these men are ugly," she said to herself. Why, she wondered, couldn't more bad guys look like Michael Allen?

She scanned the list for a likely candidate. Her eyes landed on a series of news items about a man under investigation for the mysterious deaths of three wives. He had enough of an alibi in each instance to walk. The cops were frustrated. The man was defiant. There were four children involved. Protective services wanted to take them away, but "Brent Foster" had the money and the lawyers to fend them off.

What was this duality of hate and eroticism that spun her top whenever she went after her prey? Whatever it was, it was beyond her control. She popped over to "Amore," the on-line dating website that seemed to be a common hangout for these people. Ann refused to believe she could get lucky there four times in a row.

She typed "Brent Foster" into the search box. A picture of a handsome thirty-something appeared.

"Independently wealthy widow seeks soulmate."

Perfect, Ann thought. Now to create my new identity.

"BINGO!"

Ali pointed to a corner of her laptop where an icon blinked bright red.

"I've found the leak and someone is exploiting it."

"Have you caught our magazine thief?" Dr. Bob asked.

"Not yet. But if they hang around long enough, I will."

FORTY-ONE

Phoenix

The perp in the hoodie made his move. He wrapped a skinny arm around the neck of a little kid and pulled a 9mm Springfield out from under his sweatshirt. "Nobody moves and nobody gets hurt," he yelled. "I'll only be a minute if my man behind the counter puts the cash drawer inside a to-go bag."

Of all the ways he could have done it, this was the one Jess liked least. Fast food employees are usually trained on how to respond in a robbery situation. But he had to involve a child. Jess could feel her blood boil.

The boy had a mother and she wasn't about to let her son get hurt.

"Let my son go! Let him go! If you want a hostage, take me."

"Move one step closer and someone is gonna get capped," the perp said.

The mother ignored the warning. She came a step closer. "I said take me. Please let my boy go."

The perp pointed his gun at her head, holding it sideways, gangbanger style.

"I warned you."

He lowered the weapon at the last second and fired a round into the woman's shoulder. She went down. There were screams. The child fell into hysterics.

Above the screams and crying, Jess's strong, commanding voice sang out. "Police. Move an inch and you're dead. Drop the weapon. You are under arrest."

She covered the thirty feet from her table to the perp in the five seconds he was focused on his payday. She was still about ten feet away, her Glock pointed at his head.

The perp froze when he saw the muzzle of the semi-automatic pistol trained on his skull.

"Right now, you have a chance of getting out of the joint before you're too old to remember who you are," Jess said. She repeated her command. "Drop the weapon."

Down it went.

"Let the boy go. Turn around. Bend over the counter. Hands behind your back."

He complied as Jess kicked the handgun into a corner. Cuffing him, she forced the perp to the floor. The boy ran to his mother, covering her body with his own.

"Gracias a Dios," the woman whispered.

"Estarás bien," Jess said softly. You will be all right.

She held her Coconino County star up for the customers and employees to see. "Call 911," she shouted. "Any medics in the crowd? I could use some help stopping this woman's bleeding."

She heard tires squeal as the getaway car peeled away. "Arizona plate. David Mike Lincoln - Five One Seven," she said aloud. "Somebody write that down."

FORTY-TWO

Flagstaff

"This bot is taking a world tour to get to us," Ali said as a string of IP addresses flowed into her laptop's log file.

"Can you trace a location with that information?" Dr. Bob asked.

"Perhaps. Whoever did this this is good. Very good."

NOW ANN'S computer was talking to her and she didn't like what she was hearing. Distracted by Brent Foster, she had missed the warning icon that was flashing behind her browser. Someone was reverse engineering her IP pathway. Ann quickly closed the laptop, cutting the power from its processors.

"Whoever is chasing me is good," she said to herself. "Very good."

The text alert on her phone blinked to life. There were only three words on the screen:

"High Desert Diagnostics."

ACROSS TOWN, the young contractor from the Maitland
Corporation was watching a stream of ones and zeros dance across
his computer screen.

"Translate for me."

Mario McCallister had been so transfixed that he didn't notice
the tall African American who seemed to be suddenly standing
behind him.

"Chief Roberts. You frightened me."

Roberts' voice was sardonic. "I don't believe that. What is your
screen telling you?"

"We have an intruder in the system from an IP address
assigned to the Library System."

"Do you have a MAC address."

"Yes, but it's probably spoofed. It's different than the one that
infected the system."

"You can do better than that, Mario. You're Maitland's golden
boy. Mine me some gold."

"It's a ViaTech 880 Laptop. An oddball browser I've never seen
before. It's interrogating the kernel of one of the servers at the
Phoenix Police Department. Whatever this person did has infected
the very core of the operating system."

"Have you or your buddies ever seen this before?"

"I haven't but I'll phone it in and ask."

Roberts thought about countermanding that idea. A small voice
was whispering a warning.

"Have you been reporting to your Maitland bosses since you
started on this?"

"Yes, sir. It's standard procedure."

"Well, stop doing it until I tell you otherwise. This is between
you and me and Associate Director Taylor in DC."

"Understood." Mario made eye contact with the director.
"There's something else here."

Roberts raised an eyebrow.

"I told the duty officer this morning and he's notified Agent Wright. Someone else is poking around in the system."

"Someone in Phoenix?"

"No. Someone in Flagstaff."

FORTY-THREE

Phoenix

"O'Brien was right." Jess sensed frustration in the raised voice she could hear all too clearly on her phone. "Trouble follows you around."

"It was a hold-up, Tio. What was I supposed to do, just eat my enchilada quietly and let it happen?"

"You are a temp employee, Jessi. You're not even sworn in this state. I took a big risk even giving you a badge."

"Did I stop the holdup?"

"Yes, you did."

"Beside the mom with a hole in her shoulder, was anyone else hurt?"

"No. But it took you out of action for almost two hours."

"Did anyone from the Phoenix House complain to you about any aspect of my conduct?"

"No. In fact, they said your handling of the situation was excellent."

"Then why are you giving me crap about this, Tio?"

"Because I am your Tio, Jessi. Your mother would kill me if anything happened to you while you were here. Do me a favor."

"What?"

"Next time, get take-out."

"I promise, Tio."

"So where is my analysis?"

"Heading back to Dr. Walker's lab right now. I'll be there in five."

IN THE LAB at High Desert Diagnostics, Richard Walker took the last pages of his report off the printer. There were two copies. One for Danny Lopez and one for the inevitable moment when Director Roberts would appear on the scene. He slid the Flagstaff printout into a manilla envelope. There was no telling when the FBI might show up and he didn't want to put the sheriff into any hotter water than he might already be navigating. Walker decided to play it safe, turning to the one place he kept the things the rest of the world didn't need to see.

The chime connected to motion sensor in the lobby softly sang as the package Jessica would take home to Flagstaff disappeared from view.

ALI CLARK SCROLLED through the list of IP addresses her laptop harvested from the hacker's return visit to the Arizona's flavor of "LEIN", the Law Enforcement Information Network. There were a dozen, from six different nations.

"Virtual private networks provide an almost unbreakable anonymity," she told Dr. Bob, "unless you are able to tunnel through to the subject's home network. While this is typically an impossible task, recent advances in the state of the art give us a tool to peek inside the machine at the other end."

Dr. Bob shook his head. "I don't understand a thing you just said."

"There's a way you can sit in the barn with your camera and take a picture of the person who is stealing your Field & Stream magazines," Ali answered. "If we get enough of these files, we can extrapolate the personality of the hacker. Each have their own unique signature. With a little luck, we can even get a handle on what type of computer they are using."

"What else do you need to do that?"

"Another log would be helpful," Ali said. "But getting that may be problematic."

FORTY-FOUR

Phoenix

When Jess entered the front door at High Desert Diagnostics., her cop sixth sense immediately told her something was wrong.

"Dr. Walker?"

There was no answer.

She drew her weapon and began to work her way around the maze of counter tops. When she rounded a corner, she saw what had once been Richard Walker, lying face up on the linoleum floor. There was no evidence of a gunshot wound. No breath. His eyes were open, pupils set in what paramedics called the "infinite gaze of death." On the ground next to his right hand was the vial which had the Bergulon in it.

It was empty.

Jess cleared the rest of the lab. Nobody else was there. She dialed 911, identified herself and requested an ambulance and the police.

Something else was missing, too.

The vaporizer.

Jess moved quickly. In three minutes, the place would be crawling with medics and cops. Was anything else out of place?

"Talk to me, Dr. Walker," she said to herself as she tried to remember the details of her visit earlier in the day. "Did you see this coming? Did you try to send me a message?"

She checked the email and text screen on her phone. Nothing.

There were sirens in the distance. Jess leaned against the wall, contemplating the *September Torch* poster, thinking about the retiree who paid the ultimate price for helping her try to figure out this puzzle ahead of the Feds.

"*Take It Home.*"

Jess whispered the opening lyrics of Torch's first hit as she thought about their common affection for the band.

> *Your gentle face has stories to tell.*
> *From heaven's clouds to the gates of hell.*
> *Let love's poetry begin.*
> *I know the answers lie within.*

It was then that the poster spoke to her.

She saw a slight bulge in the paper that wasn't there before. It pushed the Torch logo outward and up against the clear plastic cover that protected it.

Jess popped open the aluminum edges of the frame and gently pulled the poster away from its frame. Behind it was a manila envelope with her name on it.

She sprinted to her vehicle and slid the envelope under the front seat. She closed the door as a half dozen Phoenix police cruisers skidded into the parking lot.

FORTY-FIVE

Flagstaff

"You've turned this investigation into an unmitigated disaster."

The voice on the other side of the wall was familiar. Jess was trying to place it.

"Your agency's assignment was simply to bring back the body and perform an autopsy. Now we have another dead man in Phoenix and a crucial piece evidence is missing. Without approval, you let your own computer nerd do her own thing on a compromised system that was under FBI jurisdiction. You are doing the NPS's job investigating a crime scene. And you used a raft company employee to question potential witnesses."

"Let me walk you through the sequence of events," Danny said. "We got the call from Steve Morris at NPS to do a priority extrication. We did that. It's concurrent jurisdiction out here, so we're within protocol to investigate on NPS property. Even though the IT systems were hacked, we were able to reconstruct reports and draw some preliminary conclusions about a possible killer, including motive and method. Not knowing whether or not email or data systems were still being monitored, I sent everything to the

NPS via FedEx. It arrived yesterday. They got it to you and you're here today. The lab I used is the same one your Phoenix office uses, so I was expediting the work for you. And our network analyst was able to capture information about a second intrusion attempt in real time."

"We have that information, too," the agent interrupted. "Including an alert that a user in this office was messing with the system without permission."

"The bottom line," Danny said, "is that we did everything we could to help NPS and the FBI accelerate this investigation. What went down in Phoenix could have happened to anyone."

"Not true. When you realized someone had broken into your morgue, you should have locked everything up and sat on your hands until we arrived."

Jess could hear her uncle's voice rising.

"There's a killer out there. He's murdered four people in the last six weeks and there's no telling when he might do it again. Our goal is to serve and protect and that's what we were doing."

Jess realized that Jennifer Lee was standing next to her in the hallway. Her fist hovered a couple of inches from the door. Jess nodded to the admin. She knocked. "Excuse me, Sheriff. The detective and the doctor are here."

"Have them come in."

"This better be good," the agent said. "Your future is riding on it."

"Michael Wright. What in the world are you doing in Flagstaff?"

"Jessica?"

A rush of memory flooded Jess's brain. Her inclination was to jump into Michael Wright's arms. She came close but stopped herself.

"Sheriff," Jess said, "this is agent Michael Wright, white collar crime specialist for the Federal Bureau of Investigation and one hell of a good man."

"What in the world are you doing here?" Michael asked her. Danny was surprised at how abruptly his demeanor had changed. "This is about as far from home as you can get without seeing an ocean."

"I blew up a meth house and got suspended." She showed him the bandaged forearm. "Got this little present in the process. Ali and I decided to get away and visit Tio Danny."

"Tio Danny? This guy is your uncle?"

"I told you I would never leave La Familia."

"Jess, this is a huge mess your uncle has us in. I got pulled off of another case to come up here and find out how badly we are screwed." He paused a moment, looking at the bandages on her arm. "I'm so sorry about the arm. I hear that idiot Batavia is heading up IAD."

"We can talk politics later, Michael. Right now, Dr. Price and I have a few things to show you."

Ali's head popped around the side of the office door.

"Mike Wright. You better not be here trying to get my girl to come to DC with you."

The agent's concerned expression softened. "It sounds like your girl would be safer in DC, Gates. Two near-death experiences in the space of two weeks isn't part of our drill in Washington. Are you the nerd who has been poking around inside my digital crime scene?"

"Guys," Jess said. "May we please have your undivided attention?"

She produced the manila envelope.

"Dr. Walker left me this little love note before he was killed," she said. "It has the analysis you wanted to see, Sheriff. Bergulon is confirmed, both in the vape device and in our bad boy's blood. Same concentration as was found in another victim, a Harold Lattimer. Walker also corroborates Joey's hypothesis that the vape pen was how the drug was administered. Traces of Subject A's saliva were found on it."

"Let's hope so," Michael Wright said. "I need something really good to change the perceptions my folks in Phoenix have about this agency's conduct."

Ali pushed a packet of papers across the table to the agent.

"Maybe this will get the job done," she said. "Here's my analysis of the hack. The back door is actually in room 500, 620 W Washington St. The computer ID is PHX-CHF."

Michael closed his eyes and rubbed his forehead. "Their chief's computer," he said. "That's not gonna be good news."

"Have his IT guys close port 8250. That's what our hacker uses. Normally they keep the unused ports pretty tightly locked up. I don't know how that one got opened. But I can tell you a little about our perp. I think he's in Phoenix."

"Local?"

"Yup. It would be nice to have another IP log to confirm it, but I got a whisper with machine's MAC address and computer name."

Danny watched Ali pause for effect.

"Vega."

Mike Wright's eyebrows went up. Jess noticed the move. This was an important piece of information.

"All that and more is here in hard copy and on a thumb drive. And yes, I made sure I scanned it for malware before I put the docs on it."

"So you're that Gates. My computer forensics colleagues have been trying to get your attention for the last two years."

"Guilty as charged. And I don't answer emails from strangers."

———

JOEY PRICE LISTENED to everything without comment. He sat on his chair in a meditator's lotus pose, the fingers on his hands touching one another like a Hindu in prayer. If they would just shut up, he might be able to further enlighten them.

"This changes the picture," Michael said. "I'll need to get this information to Phoenix ASAP." He stood. "The cell coverage in this building is horrible."

Joey raised his hand.

"What have you got for me, Dr. Price?" the sheriff said.

Joey turned an empty, upturned palm back and forth several times. The last time, an SD data storage card miraculously appeared in it.

"I have pictures of the person who broke into my morgue," he said. "Anybody want to take a look?"

"How in the world..." Danny started to say.

Joey held up a small square cube.

"My camera. I wasn't sure if the battery on this thing lasted the whole night and you guys were so hot when you came over that I didn't have the chance to check it out. Like I keep telling you, our security is an abomination. If something's really important, I roll my own."

"Did you get a face?"

"Nope. But I got enough to give us an important data point."

Danny hated it when Joey paused for effect. The rest of the people around the table leaned toward the Medical Examiner.

"My thief is a woman."

FORTY-SIX

Flagstaff

Michael Wright left the conference room, adding the information Ali and Joey had provided to the manila folder with Richard Pearce's chemical analysis in it. Jess followed him.

Ali watched as Joey gave the sheriff another, What do you think about me now? look. Danny pointed to the door and motioned to him to get out.

Ali and the sheriff were alone.

"What's the story between those two?" Danny asked.

"Jess and Michael?"

"They act like they are old friends."

"They kinda are," Ali said.

"What's the backstory?"

Ali weighed the ups and downs of sharing the information with Jess's uncle, finally concluding that he would probably dig it up anyway. She took a deep breath and grabbed a bottle of water from the sheriff's stash in the fridge next to his credenza.

"We had better sit down, Sheriff. This one will take a while."

. . .

JESS WAS ABOUT three years into the job when the undercover guys needed a Latina female for a sting operation. She was a natural and began busting drug pushers left and right. They gave her the gig permanently and the detective badge that came with it, unheard of for someone only three years into the game.

The head of the team was a lieutenant named Ben Batavia. If you think Jess is hot now, imagine her seven years ago. Mid-twenties, great body, great physical shape, super smart. Everyone who was single and a few cops who weren't wanted to get into her pants. Batavia decided that it was his territory, especially after going to bat to get her the badge.

Naturally, Jess shut him down. "I don't play in a sandbox I might have to shit in," she said.

Danny interrupted the narrative. "Where did she learn that kind of language? Her Mamacita would slap her face and make her say a dozen Hail Marys."

"She works in a cop shop, Danny. What did you expect? We all swear like Teamsters and say 'please' and 'thank you' like ladies. We're complicated. Now stop interrupting my story."

Anyway, Ben didn't like being rejected and decided he would make her regret it.

We had this strip club in town. It was successful and the guy who built it cloned it into an empire of seventy-five others across the country. Jeff St. James was his name. He played by the rules, paid his girls well, gave them health benefits, a 401K and helped cover college costs.

As you can imagine, he attracted some really attractive women who saw the work as a stepping stone, not a dead end. And his place was classy for a strip joint. Good food, top shelf liquor and excellent service. Even in this "Me Too" environment, he did a great business, attracting a market share well beyond the usual pervert crowd.

Well, Batavia and his boys loved harassing this place. It's called "Sweet Dreams." You've probably seen their billboards on the interstates.

St. James was tiring of it, especially since he was following the letter of the law. He came into the station one night before roll call and confronted Batavia. There would have been blows exchanged, but for this visiting FBI guy who was in town working on a white collar crime thing. He happened to be around when all this was going down and got between them as the temperatures were rising.

Batavia didn't like it and cornered him later to tell him to mind his own Federal business, only he didn't use the word Federal.

The same night, Batavia tells Jess that they will be working Sweet Dreams the following week and that her role will be that of his girlfriend. She pushed back, but the lieutenant pulled rank.

Jess was really down after that and went to her favorite Mexican place to drown her sorrows in an enchilada. Wouldn't you know that the FBI guy was eating there, too.

"Can I join you?" he says.

"Thanks for the offer, but I really prefer to eat alone tonight," Jess answers.

"I heard about what went down at the station," he says.

"What are you talking about?" Jess says.

"Your lieutenant. I had a chance to see his customer service skills in action. I hear he wants you to play his soul mate next week."

"Who the hell are you?" Jess demands.

"Michael Wright," he says. "I'm FBI. I'm officially here on another project, but we've heard about you and I'd like to ask you to consider joining our team."

"You get right to the point," Jess says.

"I know talent when I see it," he says. "Ever thought about your next career steps?"

Jess tells him about La Familia Ramirez and how this is her town and how she won't leave as long as they are still around. Michael Wright admires her character and starts to get the same feelings for Jess that most of the other guys in the force have. But he keeps that part on a low burn.

"What if I could help you with your little problem?"

"What problem?"

"You don't have to play games with me. I'm a friend. Your Batavia problem."

"How could you possibly help?" she says. "There are enough blue suits here who would love to see me wash out. Now Lieutenant Batavia is one of them."

"I have some helpful friends and a creative mind," Michael says.

He goes on to tell her his idea. She kinda likes it but is still suspicious.

"You're not doing this just to get me into bed are you?"

He looks genuinely hurt. Men are good actors when they are truly horny.

"Not at all," he says. "I just want you to get a feel for what it looks like when real friends have your back."

"I hardly know you."

"But I think I know you. Even if I never get you into Washington, if I can help you exact a little revenge against these self-aggrandized cowboys, I'll feel like my life has been complete."

He finally convinces her that his plan is doable. He'll handle all the details. All she has to do is her normal job and nobody will know she had any part in it.

So the night comes when Batavia and his eleven undercover guys are gonna hit Sweet Dreams. Each gets two hundred bucks for lap dances and the goal is to see if the girls are violating the law on proximity. They can't get too close or too "touchy feely," that kind of stuff.

Jess comes in on Batavia's arm, feeling humiliated and has to stand by as one of the dancers gyrates in his face.

"Come on, baby," he says to Jess. "Let's see how they like you?"

She's sickened by the whole thing and walks away from him. The other guys are laughing at her. She retreats to the bar and orders a Coke. The bartender gives her a rum and Coke and she spits it out after one taste, cussing a blue streak.

You never blow your cover so she can't do anything about what *happens next. These two dancers come up and start shaking their racks within inches of her face.*

"What the hell are you doing?" she says.

"We're entertaining you," they say.

Jess pulls her wallet out of her purse and gives them her two hundred bucks. "Take this and leave me alone," she says.

"We can't do that," they say.

"Why not?"

"Because those guys over there paid us 2,000 dollars to do this for you and we're gonna give you their money's worth."

The boys pooled all their city money to pay for the dance.

They are literally rolling on the floor in stitches when all hell breaks loose.

Guys in FBI gear burst in and say, "This is a raid."

Naturally the cops give up their cover and everyone is showing badges. But it doesn't make any difference. The agents start cuffing them and reading them their rights, the whole Miranda thing.

Batavia gets the worst of it. He starts being belligerent and the agents pin him to the ground.

"Shut up," they say. "And you can forget about that pension. You're going to jail."

Jess walks up to one of the agents and says, so everyone can hear, "These men are police officers and are my partners. They are executing lawful surveillance on the premises."

"Don't interfere with a Federal Officer," the agent says.

They start heading the whole crew outside but leave her alone. What do you know, there's a god damned news crew from Channel 7 out there. Lights, camera, action.

The girl reporter is shouting questions at the undercover guys. Why they are spending taxpayer money at a strip joint? Do their wives know about this? Really embarrassing stuff.

The strippers are cussing them out. The regular patrons are cheering. The whole crowd starts singing that song, "Na na, hey hey, goodbye."

Off goes the paddy wagon to the station, lights and siren. Jess rides in the TV van with the reporter.

"How did you hear about this?" she asks.

The reporter is laughing so hard that her nose is running. Tears are rolling down her face. Her makeup is a mess but she doesn't care.

"Michael Wright told me about the whole thing," she says. "This is the most fun I've had in a year."

"What will you do with the video?" Jess asks.

"The only people who will see it are the courageous souls who show up at your Christmas party."

Off they go to the station, lights and siren.

Well, the paddy wagon pulls up to the back door and everyone is marched into the squad room. The whole night shift is there to see it. So is the chief. So is St. James. Everybody is laughing their asses off, slapping each other on the back, pointing and calling the boys names. There's lots of bad blood between undercover and the street cops thanks to Batavia's "holier than thou attitude."

The morale of the whole house is sky high, except for the poor undercover pukes who feel like the shit heads they are.

Finally, the chief says to un-cuff 'em and the rest of the shift goes back onto the streets.

It turns out that St. James has connections in the mayor's office and has a great reputation for how he takes care of his girls and follows the law. The chief makes Batavia apologize. St. James returns the two grand the boys spent on Jess's lap dance and agrees that the regular Blues can come and inspect the operation at any time. The embarrassed undercover boys get the rest of the night off to think about things.

As Batavia is leaving, Michael Wright pulls him aside and gently recommends that he should be nicer to the women on his team. "Next time," Michael says, "there will be more than just hand-cuffs and laughter."

That really melted Jess' butter. He winks at her from across the room and she beckons him to get a little closer. They slide into an *office and she plants one on his mouth, an Academy Award performance.*

"Wow," is all he can say once he gets his tongue back.

"Don't get any ideas," Jess says, rolling her index finger on the tip of his nose.

She can tell he has ideas. She has ideas, too. But they never have taken it any further.

Wouldn't you know? The lieutenant has his own friends at City Hall and eventually gets transferred to Internal Affairs Division. Word on the street is that he set up the meth house thing in the hope that Jess would screw up. Even when she didn't, he found a way to make it hurt.

"SO I HAVE this Ben Batavia guy to thank for you and Jess being here?" Danny said as Ali finished her story.

"You got it, Sheriff. If it were me, I would be following Michael Wright to DC in a heartbeat."

Danny put his chin on his hands. "Great question, Gates. Why haven't you gone to DC? Even though you have a profanity problem, your skills are on par with the best NSA people and you could make four times what you get in O'Brien's House."

"You can't tell a good story without a few well-chosen cuss words. Let's just say I like being a big fish in a small pond. Having options is empowering. And hey, I'm out here helping you catch a pretty smart hacker. Could life get much better?"

"What about my Jessi and this FBI guy? Is there some heat there?"

"If there is, they have done a great job keeping it in the oven."

"I just know the look," the sheriff said. "It's the same way I looked at Lola across the room at the elementary school dance where I knew she was the one."

"Lola?"

"My first wife. She turned out not to be the one. But I'll always honor her. If it wasn't for our split, I would have never found Christina."

"What did Christina say when you told her you got busted for stealing US mail from your neighbor?"

Danny Lopez registered surprise. Ali loved seeing what this revelation did to his poker face.

"Dr. Bob has a big mouth," he said.

Ali put a hand in front of hers. She could tell that Danny wasn't sure if she was signaling solidarity or stifling a laugh.

"Your secrets," she said, "are safe with me."

FORTY-SEVEN

The Northern Pines restaurant - Flagstaff

Trip Advisor rates The Northern Pines as one of Flagstaff's finest dining establishments. Jess ordered a Carnitas Green Chili Omelet. Michael got the brisket sandwich. He made fun of the fact that she was having breakfast for dinner.

"It's the jet lag," Jess said. "My body still doesn't know what time it is."

She ordered a margarita, "as a palette cleanser."

Michael got a beer.

"How did you end up out this way?" she asked. "Or would you have to kill me if you told me?"

"Just playing a role," Michael said. "If you worked with us, the undercover adventures would be much more interesting."

"Four dead guys, probably all perps, a hacker that takes down the entire network, a chick who breaks into the morgue for a vape pen, another murder, probably connected, and an armed robbery? It's been a pretty interesting twenty-four hours in paradise."

"Your uncle should have let us do our thing. Walker might still be alive."

"I'm sorry about that," Jess said. "Sheriff Lopez got the sense that the NPS guys were in over their head. After seeing a few of the puzzle pieces he was worried that our killer might strike again before you Federales had a chance to engage."

"I can't fault the work he's done. That's quite a collection of help he has over there."

"It's Flagstaff. He does pretty well with the shoestrings they give him."

"That coroner is a piece of work. One minute you want to praise him. The next you want to punch him in the mouth."

"You just have to learn his love language, Michael. He thinks he's the smartest one in the room, because he probably is. Where God gives the gift of brilliance, he also taketh away. Joey's got the brains. He's a bit unique in the personality department."

"That's not exactly the word I'd use," Michael said. He drained the last of his beer and signaled for another. "Who is this Dr. Bob guy?"

"A lifesaver. Seventy-eight and still seeing patients. He's got an interest in Joey's work. Been hanging around the morgue for something like fifteen years. And he keeps his own notes. He's the one who put Humpty Dumpty back together again when the database got wiped."

"What's Gates' assessment of the hack?"

"That's what you're up to, isn't it, Michael? I saw you tuning in when she reported. And there was that thing you do with your eyebrows when Joey said our vape thief might be a woman."

"Just getting a download. I have to report this all to my team and hopefully get Danny's butt out of the doghouse."

"You're lying to me, pendejo. But that's OK. All I know is what we heard. I've been spending most of the day debriefing Phoenix about the robbery and Walker's killing."

"What's their preliminary on that one?"

"They say the killer poured the rest of the Bergulon down his throat and watched him die before trashing the place. He must have seen it coming because he left me a love note... All the stuff I gave you was hidden in a picture frame."

"Phoenix didn't say anything about that."

"Because I didn't tell 'em. Somebody's way ahead of us on this, Michael. They seem to know our every move right after we make it. My gut told me to be a little circumspect."

"Circumspect. Is that one of those words you learned in college?"

"Kiss my ass, Agent Wright. You would have done the same thing and you know it."

Jess could tell that the fire in her eyes lit Michael Wright's candle. She could feel his eyes undressing her.

"You look so sexy when you get your dander up," he said.

"You're not gonna tell me what you're doing in Arizona, are you, Michael?"

"Will it get me past first base?"

Men, Jess thought. Still programed with crass instincts to procreate the species. Or was he just distracting her?

"Here's what I think. I think that our killer and the hacker are on the same team. And I'll give you one other thing to chew on. I think the person who is tossing all of these bad boys into the river is a woman."

"What makes you say that?"

"Only a chick could convince a felon to get close enough to a long fall, gas him with poison to soften him up and then kick him over the edge."

"Organized crime does that all the time."

Michael was trying to throw Jess off the scent and she knew it. Her temper started to rise.

"Don't bullshit me, Michael. I'm betting that the only thing these dead guys have in common is that they all got away with something. Women like nothing better than making men pay for their mistakes."

"You sound like your boss after we busted him at that strip joint."

He wasn't going to give her even a morsel. Jess sighed and gave it up.

"Where are you staying, Michael?"

"Here for the night. I thought I'd take in some scenery. Want to join me?"

There it was. She had been preparing herself for it. Now that it was happening, she felt like it was junior high again, the day Aldo Rodriguez first kissed her after the dance at the Y. Fear, excitement, desire and wariness all wrapped up into a pulsating ball of conflicting emotions.

One side of her brain was saying, "Don't show emotions or they own you." The other side was saying, "Screw his brains out and leave him panting on the hotel room rug."

Jessica smiled. "I can do both," she said to herself as she chugged the last of her margarita.

FORTY-EIGHT

Coconino County Sheriff's Office - Flagstaff

"Gates" was impressing the hell out of her FBI counterpart. Reinforcements had arrived and she was in the sheriff's office with a twenty-four-year-old geek that barely looked old enough to shave.

Ali was still skeptical. "So your name is Mario McCallister and you've been with the Feds for two years? That means they hired you right out of college. A pretty big assignment for someone still wet behind the ears."

"I'm just a contractor. With the Maitland Corporation." Mario said it as if it were a sexually transmitted disease. "I graduated from MIT at nineteen. Masters in computer science and network security." Ali could sense that this kid didn't like having to wave his credentials around, but was used to it. "Been working these little problems for my country ever since."

"Not so fast, kiddo. Your colleagues tell me you've had a few bumps along the way."

"What true hacker hasn't been in trouble? Look, they hire me to sniff out people like me. My sins were forgiven when I left the dark side."

Ali had more questions. What exactly did he do to run afoul of the law? He wasn't FBI. He worked for a contractor that didn't have the best reputation for honesty. And most importantly, how much did he know?

Before she could ask any of them, Mario spoke.

"Tell me what you think is going on with our hacker?"

"He got in through the chief's computer in Phoenix. Someone opened up a port and that was enough. The bot system this geek installed is a thing of beauty. Search and destroy stuff with code that wipes any piece of hardware that's added to the network. It bricked the off-site backups. Even the stuff in the cloud."

"Did he leave any traces?"

"Oh yeah. He modified the operating system kernels. Not enough to be detected. File sizes and functionality are unchanged. But you'll find something bad in there when you take it apart."

"If it's so sophisticated, how did you find it?"

"Are you saying that girls who work for pissant local police departments aren't smart enough to keep up with you savants?"

"You don't know me well enough yet, Gates. I love this stuff as much as you do. It's pretty darn cool that somebody local, with one-one-hundredth of the resources we have, cracked this thing."

"I work in a very boring shop," Ali said. "I have lots of time on my hands and spend most of it over at the University with their engineering nerds. We play a game where I set up a network and they try to compromise it. We have our reformed felons, too."

She smiled at Mario, hoping he wasn't offended. She decided he wasn't.

"One of them created something just like this. I make 'em build detector code at the same time they build the malware. His little sniffer smelled the stink and bingo."

"I'd like to see that in action," Mario said.

"I just happened to be online poking around when the bad guy phoned home. There are still bots all over the network listening for a command to report. He was logged in long enough for me to walk back across his VPN trail. I don't know why he didn't catch it. My app for that screams loud enough to wake the hearing impaired. I got nearly a dozen hops and was close to putting a pin in the map when he shut down."

"You said you got a MAC address?"

"Not just a MAC address. A signature."

"A signature?"

"These people have personalities like you and me. They can't help leaving at least a few cookie crumbs that give them away. I got the computer name. It's Vega."

Mario nodded.

Ali frowned. "I tell you all my secrets and throw you a huge steak in your lap and all you fucking do is nod?"

"What I don't say can keep you out of harm's way."

Mario said it without emotion. It was loaded with meaning. Ali's radar caught it.

"Vega means something, doesn't it?"

"I'm not authorized to say anything one way or the other."

"I can read you, digit-head Mario Brothers, like a comic book," Ali said. "Vega is the key. You don't have to tell me. But if you want me to help, at least point me in the right direction. We're on the same team."

"You don't even work here."

"Listen, Junior. I don't like it when assholes walk right in and take over our toys. And I'm beginning to think that there might be a connection between this Vega person and our murders. He's either been hired to cover someone's tracks, or he's our killer."

Mario was still evasive. "Show me how you detected the changes in the kernel. Our best and brightest couldn't find a thing. Even when the bots go to work, they don't show up on the sniffers."

"Not a chance," Ali said. "Unless.... "

She paused. She wanted Mario's full attention. She got it.

"Unless you start telling me what's going on here."

FORTY-NINE

The Grand Canyon Hotel - 72 miles north of Flagstaff

The Grand Canyon Hotel runs 300 dollars a night. It's a short drive from the South Rim. It has panoramic views that end up on every visitor's iPhone and enough amenities to be the only place within one hundred miles to earn three diamonds from the Triple A. Michael Wright's room had a sunrise view and a king-size bed.

Jess was stunned by the opulence.

"I thought you government guys stayed at Motel 6?"

"This was all that was available on short notice," Michael said. His eyes told her he was lying. His smile made it OK. He opened the mini bar and uncapped two bottles of Dos Equis, handing the first to his guest.

Jess decided to calibrate his expectations.

"I'm not staying the night. This is just some sightseeing and maybe dinner."

Michael's face darkened. "You're ninety minutes from your uncle, Jess and 2,000 miles from home. And you're a grown up. Cut yourself some slack."

She was done with the chess game.

"Listen, shithead. I've told you everything I know and you haven't given me squat. And now you're trying to lure me into that king-size bed. I'm in deep shit with the chief back home. My uncle has a serial killer on the loose in his neighborhood. My arm hurts like a son of a bitch. And I'll tell you something else I discovered was missing when I found Walker dead. My business card. Whoever this dirt bag is, now knows who I am. And as it stands, if he or she comes after me, I won't have a clue until it's too late. So do something useful besides trying to seduce me."

"Welcome to the game," he said. "After all this time, after getting shot at, yelled at and undermined at every turn, you're finally realizing what it is we all do for a living. There are bad people out there Jessica. Sometimes we're the only thing between them and those we love. That's why we both keep a shield in our wallets and carry guns. Most of the time, we don't think about the downsides of that career decision. But sometimes enlightenment rears its ugly head and we see things as they really are. This is that moment for you. If you are the woman I think you are, you'll sleep it off and keep pointing that courageous spirit in the direction of the thin blue line. All I want you to understand is that you're not alone."

Jess thought it was a damned good soliloquy.

She took his measure. The definition of his muscles pressed against the open collared shirt. She liked the smell of his cologne, the way his hair curled into a comma over his forehead, and the square jaw that radiated strength and character.

She worried about the caring heart she could sense behind his shields. Cops who survived a career inoculated themselves against stress. They could compartmentalize the gruesome and the grieving, taking down evil with one hand while showing measured empathy for the victim with the other.

Did Michael have what it took to be a survivor?

Jess realized that this complicated boy scout was arousing her. Sex was the ultimate stress reliever for adrenaline junkies and it was easy to fall into bed with someone who understood the lifestyle.

Jess never accepted advances. At first it made her an outcast. Ten years later it earned her a grudging respect from some and bitter hatred from others.

She didn't care. She was in control. That frightened many of the men who tickled her coital fancy, but made her irresistible to others.

Michael Wright, she concluded, fell into that second category.

Jessica Ramirez put her hands on Michael's shoulders and shoved him backwards onto the bed.

"OK, big man," she said. "We'll argue about it again in the morning."

She flipped open the top two buttons on her shirt with a thumb and forefinger.

"Show me how I'm 'not alone.'"

FIFTY

Phoenix

Ann Blakely's apartment didn't come close to Michael Allen's opulence. The one-bedroom efficiency was within walking distance of April's Boutique and had a dozen different WiFi access points she could break into whenever she needed the bandwidth. She was logged into one named "GameOfThronze" now.

The vaporizer, her vaporizer, was on the kitchen table inside the plastic bag with the Coconino Sheriff's tape on the outside. So was a copy of Richard Walker's analysis, confirming the exact mixture that worked so well on Mahoney and proved to be the last liquid to cross the lips of the owner and sole proprietor of High Desert Diagnostics.

She fingered a blue and white business card with a name and cell phone written in ink on the back. Both data points were pulsing across the darkest corners of the Internet, reflecting a full portfolio of personal details back to her screen.

Brent Foster would have to wait. She needed to deal with the Latina now.

FIFTY-ONE

The Fifth Day - The Grand Canyon Hotel

Detective Jessica Ramirez stirred. A ray of sunlight penetrated a tiny break in the curtains in the sprawling suite at the Grand Canyon Hotel. Still fresh in her mind was a vivid nightmare. A woman in a black veil was leading Michael toward the edge of a cliff. No matter how loud Jess screamed, he didn't hear. When the pair approached the brink, the woman turned to Jess.

"I will destroy everything you love," she growled. "Beginning with him."

Michael seemed to be sleepwalking. He held up a pair of hand-cuffed wrists, put his fingers to his lips and blew Jess a kiss. Then he leaned backward, his body floating in the air into the vast expanse as if on a magic carpet. The veiled woman clapped her hands and Michael Wright plummeted out of sight.

Jess opened her eyes. Something heavy and constricting was wrapped around her waist. She was face down on her pillow, her head tilted just enough to the left to breathe. A mixture of sweat and stale cologne bombarded her nostrils.

She was naked, lying in the center of the king-size bed. Michael

Wright's left arm held her comfortably against his body as he continued to sleep. The half-smile on his face made her think he was replaying the events of the previous evening.

He was drawing closer to Jess and she wasn't sure she liked it.

Michael Wright stirred.

"You are amazing, Detective Ramirez."

Jess turned toward the dancing panorama of light and color that painted prismatic pictures on the walls of the hotel room. It occurred to her that it mirrored the uncertain vibrations of eroticism and terror that were at the center of her nightmares.

"I have no illusions about this," she said. "There is a different scent on the shirts in your closet. You've been up close and personal with someone else. And pretty recently, too."

Michael chuckled. "All in the line of duty. What I do is for God and country."

"Including what you did last night?"

The smile vanished. He looked deeply into her eyes.

"You are an extraordinary woman, Jessica. What happened last night was about us. Just like you, I'm tracking a woman, too. She's deadly dangerous and scares the hell out of me. The only way we can beat her is to get close enough to fully understand her intentions. I've done the research on her for the last two years, so I got the field assignment. She's attractive, smart and very good at everything she does..."

"Everything?" Jess interrupted.

"Everything. Including destroying innocent lives. Many will suffer unless we can stop her. I was fairly certain she could have killed me the other night. I'm still not sure why she didn't. But that's the job I signed up for. What I didn't expect was finding you, sulking in the corner of that little restaurant, harassed and unappreciated by small-time cowboys who could never hope to be worthy of your affection. I didn't expect that you would have stayed at the center of my mind every moment since. I didn't expect the surge of feelings that washed over my soul when you de-fanged me in the middle of my epic rant at your uncle's office. And I never expected that one night in your arms could be so fulfilling and so sad all at the same time."

Jess brushed a finger against Michael's earlobe.

"That's quite a speech. You're making me care about you, shit-head. In my world, that's a liability."

He touched her cheek. She saw his biceps ripple with the move. It was not an unpleasant sensation. The darkness in his expression vanished as his face morphed into a grin.

"You have to admit that we could share some pretty amazing adventures together if you would just let me into your heart."

Jess rolled Michael on his back and mounted him.

"So what you're saying is, 'ignore my instincts and just enjoy the ride'?"

"We can't replay our yesterdays and there is never a guarantee of a tomorrow. All we can do is make the most out of today."

Jess was determined not to let Michael "into her heart." But that didn't mean denying herself his pleasure. She grabbed his chin and gently shook it. Her feminine charms undulated in time, capturing Michael's full attention.

"Then just for today, let's see if you are as good in the sunshine as you are in the dark."

Michael Wright glanced at the wall clock out of the corner of his eye. Jess caught it.

"What? Are you running a stopwatch on this? I can either out-pace you or out-last you. The choice is yours."

"That's the sexiest invitation I've ever had," he said, rolling her over on her back and covering her mouth with his own.

FIFTY-TWO

Flagstaff

"Alexandra Clark."

Ali felt the disorientation of waking up too early in a strange place. Her voice was still clouded with sleep as she answered her cell phone. Who the hell was calling this early?

"Gates, it's Mario McCallister."

The pine paneling in the small guest room she shared with Jess at Danny and Christina's place came into focus. The other bed was empty. Still perfectly made up from the previous morning. Jess must have got laid last night, Ali thought. She rolled over on her elbow in the tiny twin bed, holding her cell close to her ear.

"Mario? Why are you waking my ass up at..." She looked at her watch. "Holy shit. 5:55 a.m.?"

"I got permission from Director Roberts to bring you in on this thing. How soon can you meet me in Phoenix?"

"You drove back to Phoenix last night when there are so many wonderful motels in Flagstaff?"

"I like to sleep in my own bed."

Ali twisted her neck until it cracked.

"Me, too. I'm only on day three of this temporary duty thing and I'm already missing mine."

"I'm at the office now. Get here as soon as you can. I want to show you some IP addresses that I think will interest you."

"Jesus, Mario. Do you know what time it is?"

"Do you want in on this thing or not, Gates?"

Ali swung her legs outward and sat up on the edge of the bed. "Can I shower first?"

"If you do, you'll smell better than most of the people on my team."

"You guys never grow up, do you. This is all just a fucking video game."

"Growing up is overrated. Get here as soon as you can. I'll have chocolate milk and Cocoa Puffs waiting for you."

Ali yawned. "I'd rather have a large Coke. I'll text you an ETA when I'm on the road. Where do I go and how do I get past security?"

"21711 N 7th St. Tell security that Mario sent you."

FIFTY-THREE

Phoenix

Капитан

Status?

Vega

On schedule.

Капитан

And the Detective?

Vega

How do you know about her?

Капитан

This project is important to the organization. You must expect that I have my own auditors.

Vega

I have it under control.

Капитан

We have no room for error.

Vega

This can be managed. I have an asset engaged.

Капитан

That will initiate an investigation. We do not need distractions.

Vega

It will happen in her home town. It is nothing more than misdirection and will disengage an adversary.

Капитан

It must not divert you from the timeline.

Vega

You said I could have free reign to complete the task. This is what I need now. I will handle it.

Капитан

As you wish. No more distractions. No more men until you accomplish your objective.

Vega

I will do my part, my way.

Капитан

Your way has created a problem. Focus.

Vega

We are on schedule. I will deliver.

Капитан

That is the only acceptable outcome. Neutralize the police woman.

Vega

Signing off. Will communicate when it's done.

FIFTY-FOUR

72 Miles North of Flagstaff

Jess was finally getting a chance to drink in the Grand Canyon's beauty. It was a place she had only seen in pictures and on television. Now she was walking beside a strong, handsome man, about to peer into the chasm, cut from sheer rock over millions of years by the inexorable flow of rushing water.

"Tell me more about this other woman you slept with." Despite Michael Wright's silver tongue and extraordinary skills in bed, she felt a stab of jealousy.

"It was my job, Jess. I learned more about her in the space of twenty-four hours than we had in twenty-four months."

"So casual sex is now part of the FBI's operational manual?"

"That's not fair. I was directed to do whatever it took to gain her confidence. Getting her to come to the condominium was essential. We hoped she would send a message through our WiFi router. She did. It's given us our first real clues to what she may be planning."

"Planning what?"

"You know I can't talk about that."

"If we are to be a thing, Michael, you have to be honest with me."

"Is that what I am to you? A thing?"

"You know exactly what I mean. Put yourself in my situation. Would you open your heart to a woman if you knew she couldn't level with you and was incapable of being faithful?"

"Slow down, Jessica. Last night you were telling me to calibrate my expectations. I'm grateful that we are beginning to learn a little more about one another. Let me finish this job and then we can talk about what happens next."

"So what can you tell me about Miss Wonderful?"

"She says she's from Frisco, a hospitality business major who didn't like being hospitable. She works in a boutique in Phoenix."

"But you don't believe the backstory?"

"Nope."

Jess was annoyed at Michael's continued evasiveness.

He jumped the small safety fence that kept the curious from getting too close to the canyon's rim. "Come see this," he said. "It's a view that will put all our problems into the right perspective."

Jess cleared the fence and walked ahead of Michael Wright. She couldn't make sense of what she was feeling. There was gratitude for his tenderness. The thrill of making love was still coursing through her. There was fear, fear of a commitment that might end in tragedy, fear of falling too quickly and deeply for a man she really didn't know very well. There was the guilt, hardwired into her Catholic DNA. And there was anger. Her upbringing was very clear about commitment. Sex was not something you used as a weapon. This woman she was chasing may be dangerous, she said to herself. A jealous Jessica Ramirez could be deadly.

Lost in thought, she found herself standing on the canyon's edge. As she finally focused on the scene in front of her, the realization that the prospect of instant death was just inches ahead of her made her head spin.

Jess's ears began to ring. Sweat drenched her body. She felt pulled toward the horrific depths and was consumed with nausea. A memory, long sublimated, returned like a rocket. She was seven years old. Her father invited her to sit with him on the roof of their house to watch the fireworks on July 4th. She made it three rungs up the ladder when this same sensation engulfed her. The next thing she knew, her father was trying to revive a quivering body, passed out on the sidewalk.

"Jessica? Jessica, are you all right?" Michael's voice felt a thousand miles away as Jessica Ramirez spiraled toward unconsciousness.

FIFTY-FIVE

Newark, New Jersey

The New York Financial district encompasses an area encircled by the Brooklyn Bridge expressway, West Street and FDR Drive. Battery Park lies to the west with Tribeca and the Lower East Side to the north. 61,000 people call it home and over 300,000 earn paychecks there on any given weekday. At its heart are the headquarters of every significant financial institution including the major stock exchanges, investment banks and the technological support organizations that serve them. The business of American Capitalism flows through it. The nation's economic security was dependent upon it.

Since the 9/11 attacks, security in the area has increased dramatically. The best and brightest focus their energies on keeping the assets; architectural, human and technological safe.

Across Newark Bay, The Asian Container Lines vessel, Spratley, named for the disputed island chain in the South China Sea sat anchored among a dozen other boats like her in the Port Newark Channel. Two men sat alone in the captain's dining room pouring

over a table covered with maps. It was after 8:30 and the morning
sun was well above the eastern horizon.

A small laptop was connected to an ultra-secure communications link. The person on the other end of the connection could
hear and see the proceedings. The only thing the duo could see was
a small black square where line after line of green characters
displayed the far end of the conversation.

Vega:
Do you have the fiber optic network maps?
"Yes, we do," said the taller man. Both were short by American
standards. The taller of the two spoke with an Eastern European
accent.
Vega:
Let me see where you have identified your points of presence.

THE SHORTER MAN held the map up so the camera could see
it. The taller man went over its features.

"These are the locations where the SONET rings are most
vulnerable. We will be deploying the devices at twenty-seven
points." He referenced areas on the three fiber optic rings encircled
the district. The other man switched maps. "And these are the
back-ups. They are not self-healing and can be easily compromised
at these ten points. The incident will also disable connection to all
area cell towers."

Vega:
And the control circuit?
"There will be a wireless solution in each of the seventeen key
buildings. 80% have already been prepared."
Vega:
How long do you estimate the network will be down?
"The architecture is designed to do the maximum amount of

damage. It would take a highly skilled team of fiber optic technicians at least a week to restore it.

Vega:

Are you on schedule?

"Yes."

The shorter man spoke up.

"What about the internal networks and the off-site telecommunications centers?"

Vega:

Leave them to me. Most are already prepared.

"How do we know we can count on your software to accomplish the objectives?"

There was a delay. The green cursor kept silently blinking for a long time. Had they made Vega angry with the question? They wondered if their fear was evident in the camera's eye.

Vega:

Field tests are complete. You do your part. We will do ours. When will you have the devices deployed?

"Work is already underway. Two more days at the most."

Vega:

Any chance of detection?

"It is highly unlikely. We have trusted assets, fully credentialed. Untraceable."

Vega:

They must disappear when the job is finished.

"They were carefully vetted. No immediate family members. They will vanish." He quoted a Chinese proverb. "A candle lights others and consumes itself."

Vega:

I will contact you in 48 hours. You will both be very rich in 72.

THE CONNECTION CLEARED. The two men were visibly sweating.

"Are the Cìkès in position?" the taller man asked.

"The man Vega directed us to hire has the dossiers and is prepared to execute on our command."

"And the other targets? The people in the Midwest."

"He is already there and will act soon."

"Do you not wonder if Vega intends to have us eliminated, too?"

"It is a strong possibility. We have no other connections to the organization, whatever it may be. And we share something else in common with the fiber optic technicians."

"What is that?"

"No immediate family."

FIFTY-SIX

Phoenix

"Mario sent me."

Ali smiled as she said this to the security guard at the Phoenix FBI office. Twenty-four hours and she was already inside Mario McCallister's head.

The guard studied her, comparing what he saw to the picture on his computer screen. He nodded, handed her a visitor badge and pressed a button that unlocked the door to the bureau's inner sanctum.

"Room 2 1 7," he said. "The elevator is on the right."

"So you decided to trust me?"

Ali inspected Mario's small cubicle. A Macintosh CPU hummed away beneath it. Two monitors were filled with applications, browser windows and notes. The desk was totally empty, except for a keyboard and mouse.

"I didn't," Mario said. He pointed behind her toward the door. "He did."

Michael Wright's smiling countenance stood in the doorway.

"You do promise to keep everything you see and hear confidential, don't you, Gates? We have some very uncomfortable accommodations for those who violate Federal laws and I could come up with a half dozen felonies with your name on them."

"You sure know how to seduce a girl, Michael," Ali said. "Speaking of which, do you care to comment on why my roommate's bed was un-slept in last night."

Michael held up his hands. "It's a matter of national security. A need to know basis."

"Will you get outta here and let me play with my new friend?"

"Help us find this perp, Gates. There are troubled waters ahead for all of us if we don't get on top of this."

Mario felt his phone vibrate. It was a familiar number but he couldn't quite place it.

"Mario McCallister speaking."

"Mr. McCallister? This is Travis, the IT technician at the Phoenix Police Department. I work for Ned Gerrard. I have a confession to make."

FIFTY-SEVEN

Flagstaff

The IT network at the Coconino County Sheriff's office was still a mess. Jess abandoned the place and was sitting in a booth at the Fire Creek Coffee Company, "Roasting, brewing, and sharing coffee in Arizona since 2008, on historic Route 66." The WiFi was relatively fast and she was able to access her cop resources back home on her laptop.

She entered the names "Alton James Mahoney" and "Harold Raymond Lattimer" into *All-Search*, one of Ali's many creations, which plumbed a dozen different databases, both inside and outside of the law enforcement firewall. The program was chugging away when Aunt Christina appeared with two cups of *Lucha Libre*.

"The only place in town with coffee from beans grown in Mexico," Christina said.

Jess stifled a yawn. "I can use the caffeine."

"So tell me about this big FBI man who likes rescuing lovely young Latinas."

"I wasn't rescued, I'm not lovely and I'm not young, Tia."

Christina put her hand on her spine, leaning backwards in her chair until it cracked. She winced.

"Compared to many, you are young, Jess. You are evading my question. What happened at the Canyon?"

"It turns out I have a fear of heights, Tia. Vertigo, they call it. I took one look over the edge of that thing and flipped a nut. Michael tried to clean me up, but I discovered what it's like to drive for an hour in a closed car covered in your own barf. The perfect ending to a romantic encounter."

"I thought that was a lesson most girls learned in college."

"It's no joke. I can fly airplanes. I can look out of skyscraper windows. But put me on a step ladder and I become an unconscious puddle of puke. Enough of this. I am working, Tia! Trying to help Tio Danny solve these murders."

"That can wait a few minutes. We haven't had time to talk since you arrived. How are Luis and Rosa?"

"Still living in Abuelito's house. I can't convince Papa to move. Your brother is so stubborn, Tia. He always says that he has *"una vida comoda,"* a comfortable life. I am afraid that the house won't be worth anything by the time he realizes he is no longer comfortable and needs to get out. The insurance value is already more than what he could get for it."

"He is a proud man, like your grandfather. *Sé la solución.* Be the solution. That has always been in the blood of every Ramirez since the family came over from Spain with the conquistadors."

Jess felt a growing frustration. "The solution is leaving. Abuelito left Texas to make life better for the family. Why can't Papa move a few miles away to a safer neighborhood. It's closer to his doctors, better shopping and our Church."

"Give him time, Jess. He is proud, but he is also smart. He will do what is best for the family."

Jess was studying her laptop screen. *All-Search* was still working. Christina leaned in to make eye contact.

"Just like you do, Jess. Danny told me about how they want you to go to Washington. But you won't leave your comfortable life, either."

"That's different, Tia."

"Is it? Now tell me about the FBI man."

Jess sighed. She pushed her laptop aside and lay back against the thick upholstery.

"He is a very good man, Tia. We both live dangerous lives. I'm not the 'falling in love' type."

"Isn't it a little late for that?"

"What do you mean, Tia?"

"I know the look, Jess. You are already a woman in love. How do you say it? The bird has left the station. The train has flown."

"I won't say it."

"You don't have to. Danny told me what happened when you two saw each other at the office. The FBI man calmed right down. Danny said it was like shooting a bear with a tranquilizer."

"He's a bear all right." Jess was remembering the coital highlights of the past eighteen hours.

"Don't fight it, querida," Christina said. "Listen to the universe. Pain is inevitable in this life. Suffering is optional."

"You speak in riddles, Tia."

"We all get hurt. There are those who descend into victimhood and doom themselves to a life of suffering. There are others who decide to transform their pain into the fire that forges the toughest steel. It is the storm that helps us appreciate the beauty of the sunshine. Danny was already in law enforcement when we met. We had both failed with marriage number one and came into the relationship with our eyes open. We knew that each morning when he left, he might not come back that night. At first it terrified me. But I learned to savor every moment we had together as if it might be our last. We have loved more deeply and appreciated the little things more greatly. We have lived a life, not an apology. You can do that too, querida."

Jess saw that her aunt's eyes were wet. The thought crossed her mind that she had never cried since the night her Olympic dreams were dashed.

"Tears, Tia?"

"Tears of gratitude, my beautiful Jessica. May God bless you in the same way."

The laptop beeped. Jess pointed to it.

"I must," she said.

Christina took a long swallow of her Lucha Libre. "Adelante," she said. *Go forth.*

FIFTY-EIGHT

Phoenix

Mario McCallister brought two rows of numbers up on his computer monitor. "Take a look at these two IP lists," he said. "The one on the right is yours. The one on the left is ours."

"You tracked the hacker, too?" Ali asked.

Mario nodded. "Notice a pattern?"

"Different IPs but a geographic triangulation. Our perp seems to love Bulgaria, China, Venezuela and England."

"Yup. What else?"

"The IPs are spoofs for sure. Fake as the false teeth on a politician."

Ali felt a lecture coming on. Perhaps she still had to prove to this kid that she knew her stuff.

"A spoofed IP address in a TCP connection requires the source of the traffic to either be able to monitor or predict the response from the target host in order to forge the proper answer. The device has to be able to understand the real address or the packet disappears in the noise."

Ali thought about her little monologue and had an idea.

"You've discovered the routers where the IP packets are coming from."

"And..."

"And you've used them to decode the true addresses and perhaps..."

Ali realized she was holding her breath.

"We know where it originated. The MAC address and computer name you predicted is a perfect match with what we've got. We know the machine and we know where it's initiating the connections."

"It's local, isn't it?" Ali said.

Mario smiled. "Several locations across the Phoenix Public Library system and a condominium we know about. The hacker initiated a connection there and we logged the whole session."

Ali whistled. "You're closer to this perp than I realized."

"You helped confirm it, Gates. And you gave us another important gift. We know what a compromised computer looks like and can make them stand out like a constellation on a clear summer night."

"We can do more than just know where they are," Ali said. "We can fix them without the intruder knowing we did."

"That," said Mario McCallister, "is exactly why you're here."

Ali's cell phone vibrated. She looked at the screen and frowned.

"Is something wrong?" Mario asked.

"Someone is in Papa Ramirez's basement."

FIFTY-NINE

Paloma

Maria recognized the ring tone.

"Ali! What are you doing calling? Is Jessi all right?"

"We're fine, Maria. What's going on at the house. My sensors show that someone is in your basement."

"It's the man from the gas company, Ali. He was in the neighborhood and said people have been smelling gas. He thought we might have a leak."

"Did he show you ID?"

"You cops are always so suspicious. Of course, he did. He came in a company van and a uniform. I think he's attractive."

"Listen to me, Maria. I want you to call the gas company right now and make sure that the man in your house is who he says he is. If he isn't, I want you to call me immediately. Will you do that for me?"

"You worry too much, girlfriend."

"I'm serious. Will you do it for me?"

Maria sighed. "Yes, ma'am. I will."

"OK. I'll be waiting."

The man in the gas company uniform came up the basement stairs as Maria disconnected the call. He looked handsome in uniform, she thought. Maria caught sight of a pair of ivory dice on a tiny chain that hung from his neck, drawing her eyes to the hair on his chest. The triangular form of his torso and the undulating biceps beneath his shirt sleeves bespoke a man who spent time in the weight room.

"My crazy friend," she said. "She wants me to ring up your office to make sure you are real."

The man laughed. "That happens all the time. I'm glad she's being safe. Here is my card with the office number on it. If you like, you can call it right now." He held up his ID badge. An index finger partially obscured the photograph. "Give them this information and they can confirm."

"I hate having to work my way through the stupid automated system," Maria said. "'¡Para español oprima el número dos!'"

"Yo entiendo," the man said. "This number takes you directly to my supervisor. No waiting."

He speaks Spanish, Maria thought. Another plus!

She entered the number on the card into her cell phone and hit the "send" button. In a moment a female voice answered.

"Field Services, Elaine speaking."

"Hi Elaine, this is Maria Ramirez calling from 314 Isbell Street. Ed Collins came to our home today, employee ID number 32677. I'm checking to make sure he is the real deal."

"Eddie?" the woman said. "Tell him to hurry it up. He has four more calls on his route and I have backlogs in two adjoining districts. Can you put him on the line?"

Maria put her hand over the mouthpiece. "The woman wants to talk with you."

The gas man held up his hands and whispered, "Tell her I'm already on my way to the next job. She'll let me have it if she thinks I'm flirting with a beautiful customer."

Maria blushed. "I'm sorry, Elaine. Ed just left. I just wanted to make sure he was in fact an employee."

"He sure is," the woman said. "And he better get moving or we'll all be working overtime tonight."

"Thanks very much for confirming."

The gas man wiped a hand across his brow. "That was a close one," he said. "Thanks for protecting me. Since I'm a single guy, they always load me up so the married employees can go home on time."

A single guy. Maria felt an exciting chill race down her back. This was getting better by the minute.

"You should be in good shape downstairs," he said. "I'll write my cell phone number on the back of the card and if you smell gas, call me directly. If I come by later today to make sure everything is OK, what time would I find you all here?"

"Mamá serves dinner precisely at 6pm," Maria said. "I hope that's not too late."

She was hoping to show him off to the family.

"I'll make sure to be here no later than 6:15."

"That's perfect. Mamá is making Steak Ranchero. I'll have her make enough for one more."

"That would be wonderful. I'm looking forward to meeting them."

The gas man handed Maria his card with a cell number on the back. His grin was melting Maria's heart.

"Tell me about the necklace," she said. "I love the dice."

The gas man blushed. "A gift from my mother. She says it brings me luck. I guess it has today."

Maria always wondered what "love at first sight" might feel like. Now she knew.

"Thank you for being a customer," he said.

Thank you for being so handsome, she said to herself.

SIXTY

Flagstaff

"Progress!"

Jessica Ramirez smiled as she spoke into her cell phone to her uncle.

"What have you got for me, Jessi?" The sheriff sounded impatient.

"The bodies we identified have accounts on the Amore dating site. Within the last month, they both connected with a woman."

"How in the world did you get that information so fast?"

"All-Search confirmed that Mahoney and Lattimer were offenders. Both had recent convictions overturned."

"And your department also searches dating databases?"

"Nope. I did that one the old-fashioned way. I joined a half dozen different ones until I got the hits I needed."

"You on a dating site?"

"My name, your money. Don't be too upset if you see some strange charges on Aunt Christina's credit card."

"What are your next steps?"

"You got a warrant to have Amore give us the IP addresses and customer information for the women."

"I did?"

"That's what I told their security team. They will email me the information before the end of the day. Told 'em it was 'life and death' and that I would overnight the warrant."

"You are going to get me in trouble again, young lady."

"Like I told Tia Christina, I am neither young, nor a lady. But I get shit done."

"With that mouth, you'll be spending a lot time in the confessional. I bet Father Diego would love hearing about the week you've had so far."

Jess figured the dig about her night with Michael would come up at some point.

"Heaven for climate. Hell for company," she said. "At least I'll have a lot of friends there."

The phone vibrated. Another incoming call. From Ali.

"Tio, I gotta go. Ali's on the other line."

"OK. Tell Christina this is coming out of her budget, not mine! Chow."

Jess switched lines.

"What's up, girlfriend?"

"Jess. Glad you picked up. Listen, it may be nothing but one of the sensors I installed in the basement of your parents' house fired about an hour ago. I called Maria and she said a gas man was down there. She promised me she would check his credentials and call me back if something wasn't right. I'm thinking it's a good idea for you to ping her, just to make sure the guy was on the level."

"When did you put sensors in Papa's basement?"

"Remember Carne Asada? While you all were washing dishes, I was downstairs keeping your world safe for Democracy. Nobody goes into those dirt basements unless they absolutely have to. Your dad wouldn't let me put a sensor on the doors or windows upstairs, so I had to do something."

"We've been cops too long," Jess said. "We both worry too much."

"I don't know, girlfriend. This little case we've stumbled into doesn't seem so little anymore. Whoever killed that Walker guy has your business card and it's pretty easy to track things back home. Right now, I'd err on the side of over cautious."

Jess looked across the table at her aunt. She didn't want to alarm anyone, yet.

"I'll call Maria right now and text you the highlights."

"They are on the basement windows with a motion detector in the rafters by the utility conduit. The motion thing is what triggered."

"Got it. Anything interesting to report in Phoenix?"

"Lots but not on the phone. I'll be back tonight and we can debrief over your aunt's awesome cooking."

"She can teach you a couple of things if you want to learn."

"Why do I need to learn, when I have you all? Let me know what you find out."

"One more thing, Ali. Do you think one of your student friends could do a little research for me?"

"What do you have in mind?"

"I'd like to know how many women from Detroit graduated from American universities with double majors in Organic Chemistry and Computer Science over a four-year period between eight and twelve years ago. It's a rare combination so the list shouldn't be so long."

"Where did you get that information?"

"Pillow talk."

"Do I want to hear details?"

"Not while my aunt is in the same room."

"So you're thinking our two perps may be one person?"

"One woman."

"What gave you that idea?"

"Just a hunch. And perfume on a man's shirt collar."

"Perfume?"

"White Shoulders. I used to wear it myself, back when I cared about those things."

"I'm on it," Ali said. She was gone without a further word.

Christina was on Jess's case the instant she hung up.

"What was so important that you had cut off my husband. I thought finding that common thread with the bad guys was big news?"

"Just Maria being stupid, Tia. Listen, I gotta head to the ladies' room. Can I give you money for all of those credit card charges?"

"Are you kidding? This is the most fun I've had in years. I can't wait for Danny to see the bill."

SIXTY-ONE

Paloma

The security guard hired by the real estate holding company to watch over the abandoned K-Mart facility in the south end of the city noticed the gas company van parked next to the back of the building. That seemed odd. The utilities had long since been turned off. The guard was a retired cop, making a few extra nickels on top of a pension that barely covered his living expenses. He didn't have the strength or the speed to chase down shoplifters anymore, but he still had a concealed carry permit and a police officer's sense for something that was out of place. He parked his vehicle parallel to the van and circled around it. Peering into the back window, he noticed the body. A single gunshot between the eyes. He dialed 911.

"MARIA?"

"Jessi? I hear from two of my favorite girls in the same day."

"What did the gas company say?"

"Did Ali tell you about that?"

"Yes, hermana. Did you call them?"

"Of course, I did. I spoke to Eddie's supervisor."

"Eddie?"

"Yes, Eddie. He's single. He's handsome. And he's coming to dinner tonight at 6 p.m."

"So they confirmed that he worked there?"

"Yes, ma'am. Edward Collins. Employee number 32677."

"He had picture ID?"

"Jessica! Stop being a nag. I did exactly like Ali told me. He's for real. He's coming back tonight to make sure everything is OK. I can't wait for the family to meet him!"

Jess looked at her watch. It was nearly noon in her time zone. That meant the gas man would be back at 314 Isbell in about three hours.

"OK, Herman. I'll check with you later. Tell the family *los amo*."

"JRam." Jess recognized Lou Harrison's voice. "What are you doing calling in while you're on suspension. Word here is that you and Gates are relaxing in the Arizona sunshine."

"Listen, Lou." It wasn't *Kojak* now. "It may be nothing but a gas company man came to my family's place earlier today. I need you to see if an Ed Collins, employee number 32677, works there and have his supervisor confirm his route."

"Got it. What's the concern?"

"The family never called. He just showed up."

"Is this JRam the worry wart?"

"It's JRam the cautious. You and I blew up a million-dollar meth lab a couple of weeks ago and there's a bad guy out here who got hold of my business card. There are at least a half dozen people somewhere who probably don't like us very much right now."

"You got it, partner. I'll do some digging and call you back. How urgent is this?"

"He's supposedly coming back to the house at 6 p.m. If something's gonna go down. That's when it's likely to happen."

"Do you want me to send a unit over there to check things out?"

"Not yet. I don't want to overreact and scare *la familia*. Just call me immediately if anything looks funky."

"Will do. How's the arm?"

"Sexy scar, big man. Where are my flowers, the roses I asked you for when you were lying on top of me in the street after that house blew?"

"You know I'm a married man, JRam. Don't even talk like that."

"If you help me out with this, Kojak, *I'll* send *your* wife the flowers."

SIXTY-TWO

Chicago O'Hare Airport - Gate A27

The man who called himself Edward Collins got to the airport just in time to make his flight. This had been an inconvenience. But he was well paid for his trouble.

He thought about the woman who had given him the assignment, one of the rare clients who he had seen face to face. For a moment a memory of that meeting flooded over him. They both had broken personal protocol with the liaison. Throughout a night where they had explored every corner of cupid's grove with ravenous, animal-like intensity.

The sex was anything but mechanical, but there was no emotion attached for either participant.

Living dangerously cultivated voracious appetites. While no words were spoken, both knew that the other was totally satisfied. Both knew that it would never happen again.

There was just one souvenir that remained. It was a silver necklace she presented him with as he was about to walk out the door. His hand reflexively felt for the pair of silver dice that danced on his collarbone as he walked up to the gate.

"Boarding all rows, all zones for LaGuardia," the agent said over the gate area public address system.

The man handed her his ticket.

"Just checking to make sure the WiFi is working on this aircraft."

"Yes, sir! And texting is now free on all of our flights."

"That's great. I have a message I need to send at 6 p.m."

"Is it someone's birthday?"

"A condolence call," he answered, tapping a text message and a long string of numbers into his cell phone.

4,917 miles away another cell phone on the table of a small bar near the Kremlin beeped. The Mongolian dipped his head, almost imperceptibly to scan the screen. The attention the wait staff paid to every detail marked this bar as a place once frequented only by the highest-ranking Party members. Today, the Mongolian owned the business. It was nearly 1:30 in the morning. A skeletal staff remained to serve his every need.

The man's bearing radiated military, although the open collared shirt and sport coat did not.

He lifted a glass filled with top shelf Russian vodka, draining it as he pressed a thumb on the phone's keyboard to reveal the full text of the message.

It came from an address at the Maitland Corporation. He picked up his phone, motioned to the nearby waiter to refill his glass, and sent a reply.

SIXTY-THREE

Flagstaff

"Jessica. It's Lou."

Real names, she thought. This can't be good.

"Ed Collins was in fact a gas company employee."

"What do you mean *was*?"

"A security guard found his van abandoned at the old K-Mart facility on the south side. The guy was in the back in his undies. Shot once in the head. A pro job."

Jess looked at her watch. It was 5:45 in Paloma.

"Get over to my parents' place stat and get 'em the hell out of that house. We've got less than fifteen minutes."]

"Already on the way with transportation and backup. We'll be there in five. I'll call you when everything is clear. No time for the bomb squad on this one."

"Watch yourself, Lou. This is some serious shit."

"To Protect and Serve is what we do."

"Call me."

"10-4."

"ALI, I think your hunch was right. They found the gas man shot dead at the old K-Mart. Harrison is headed to get the family out of the house now."

It was hard for Alexandra Clark to hear Jessica's cell connection over the drone of the cooling fans in the server room.

"Shit, girlfriend. He told Maria 6 p.m. That's in ten minutes!"

"I wish I was there."

"I think that's what our perp is hoping you'll do."

"What do you mean?"

"You're getting close to something, Jess. This bad dude wants you off the case."

Ali could hear unaccustomed emotion in Jessica's voice.

"Thank you for all you've done, girlfriend. It sounds trite saying it just like that."

"You can thank me in another nine minutes when I hear Mamacita's voice."

"DETECTIVE HARRISON!" Lou registered Maria Ramirez's surprise at seeing the phalanx of cop cars and four police vans on the street in front of the house. "We're about to have dinner."

"Not tonight, Maria. I need you to round everyone up right now and get out of the house."

"What's going on?"

"No time to talk. Does Mamacita need help?"

The detective pushed past Maria with two more blue uniforms in toe. The rest of the family was at the dinner table. Rosa Ramirez held a large plate of Steak Ranchero.

"We need you all to leave right now," Harrison commanded. "No questions. Just move."

He looked at his watch. 5:58.

"Where's Luis?"

SIXTY-FOUR

Airborne

33,000 feet above the St. Lawrence seaway, the passenger in seat 29C on Delta flight 2942 took out his cell phone. The command text was already entered into its display. His right thumb moved toward the send button. He looked at his watch and thought to himself. "I said I'd be there by 6:15. Perhaps five more minutes."

LOU HARRISON WAS ALSO LOOKING at his watch. It was well past 6 p.m. "Everyone accounted for? Where is your father?"

"At confession," Maria said. "It's the first time in years that he's gone."

Kojak looked through his rear-view mirror at the stunned faces that sat in the van. Behind the vehicle, three more had residents of the four houses that ringed 314 Isbell Street inside of them. He was doing 65 in a 25 mile per hour zone. Four squad cars sped ahead of the convoy with lights and sirens blaring. The detective was calculating the potential blast radius and wanted to put as much distance between the van and ground zero as he could. He was wishing there had been time to evacuate more houses.

"Maria, send your sister a text. Tell her the family is safe and sound and headed to Emilio's for dinner."

"Aren't you driving a little fast, Detective?" Maria wondered. "You're frightening Mamacita."

"I'm not frightened," her grandmother said. "You're frightened. *Tengo hambre.* I'm hungry."

LUIS RAMIREZ SAW his reflection in the glass as he opened the door to his house. The face looked much older than the birthdate on his driver's license. But at this moment, he felt young again.

Father Diego had lightened his burden. There was so much he wanted to tell Jessica now: that he was sorry he had crushed her Olympic dreams, that he was proud of the woman she was and the purpose she had found in her life, that he loved her.

Where was everybody?

He kept the cell phone Jessica had bought for him in the top drawer of the living room credenza. There it was. He picked the device up. "Just press and hold the number one if you ever want to call me, Papa." That's what she had told him to do. Luiz Ramirez was glad that he was home alone, so he could tell everything to his daughter in private. He put his index finger on the number one. The line was busy and the call went to phone mail.

A voice he knew well said, "Please leave me a message after the tone."

Always protecting her identity, he thought. Now I can help give it back to her.

"Jessi, it's Papa."

"AND WHAT WOULD you like to drink, sir?"

The flight attendant leaned into the row to hear the passenger in seat 29C's response.

"A club soda with lime, please," he said, pressing a button on his cell phone.

It was 6:19 p.m.

422 miles away 314 Isbell Street disintegrated in a mushroom cloud of fire and smoke.

SIXTY-FIVE

Flagstaff

Jess saw the voice message and recognized the number.

She checked her iWatch, calculating the time the call was placed, putting the puzzle piece into the timeline of events with a growing sense of horror. Years of self-inoculation against the macabre realities of her profession were crumbling.

"What is it?" Danny Lopez asked.

Jess's hands were shaking. She could not physically force a finger to touch the keyboard.

Her uncle gently took the phone from her, enabled the speaker and pressed the playback button.

"Jessi, it's Papa. For once, I listened to your mother. After mass, I sat in the confessional with Father Diego. I have always tried to do what was right for my family. But my decisions have not always been good ones. Father Diego helped me to understand how important your Olympic dreams were. I now realize I was wrong to deny you. I don't know where everyone has gone, but I am glad that we have these few moments alone. Things like apologies and affection do not come easy to me. But I hope that in your heart you know how proud

I am of you and how much I love you. I hope you can someday forgive me for my sins. There are so many other things I want to tell you. I will leave this telephone turned on so that I can--"

The sound that followed was nearly unintelligible. Jess could make out the explosive blast. But it was the shattering scream that she would never, ever forget. It's animal-like howl was choked off as the inferno transformed the living countenance of Luis Jose Ramirez-Sagaceta from humanity into ashes.

WHERE IS SHE?

"Mama?"

Jess barely recognized her own sobbing voice. There was no attempt to compartmentalize or control her feelings now.

"Yes, mi'ja. He's gone."

Her mother was surprisingly calm, in stark contrast to the hysterical shame Jess felt.

"It's my fault. If I had never pursued her, Papa would still be alive."

"Blaming yourself for the evil in the world only takes away your power to do something about it."

Jess's tears were flowing freely now. Tio Danny took a step closer but Jess raised a hand, signaling him to keep his distance.

"I'm coming home. I need to protect you."

"No."

Jess was stunned by the abrupt firmness of her mother's answer. The subservient Mexican spouse was gone.

"You father and I had many disagreements. We argued behind closed doors about many things. In every case, I bent to his wishes. If anyone has failed, it is I."

Confusion swirled through Jess's mind. The procession of revelations was more than she could process.

"What are you saying, Mama?"

"Your Olympic dreams. The many times you challenged Papa and I did nothing. I now understand how important it is to never surrender when you know you are right."

"You wanted me to join the team?" Jess realized her own voice had regressed to that of a child.

"I have always wanted you to be happy, mi'ja. Before your father left us to speak with Father Diego, I could see that he shared that same desire. He was so proud of you, Jessi. He loved you so much but could never express it. Our culture makes it hard for a man to show emotion. I know that if God had allowed him to talk with you, these would have been the things he would have said."

Jess realized that Rosa was unaware of the existence of the phone message. She vowed never to let her hear it. Her father's words replayed themselves inside of her head. He said all of those things. Every word. Now he was gone and she must be the protector.

"I want to come home. When it becomes known that you are all still alive, she will come for you again."

"We are in a safe place, mi'ja. You can do nothing for us here."

Jess felt lost. The clarity of purpose that was always at the center of her being had vanished. Her father's death had suddenly given her unaccustomed freedom. The moral compass she often tried to defy was spinning out of control.

"What *should* I do, Mama?"

"Find her and stop her."

The clouds of confusion slowly parted. The sobs that wracked Jess's body subsided. Her power and confidence were returning, flowing through every fiber of her being.

Jessica Ramirez knew she could never go home until she had avenged her father.

A thousand unspoken emotions filled the two words she said to her mother before she disconnected the call.

"I will."

SIXTY-SIX

Phoenix

Alexandra Clark didn't even bother to hide the request.

"Where can I find a Lesbian bar in this town?"

What happened at Isbell Street was more than she could handle. All she wanted now was alcohol and someone to hold her.

Mario punched a text message into his phone with a thumb.

"What are you doing?" Ali said.

"Getting a recommendation from a friend who knows these things."

Two words came back to him.

The Martinique.

The phone call from Jessica left Ali stunned. Her first inclination was to leave Phoenix immediately to be by her partner's side. Jessica waved it off. The singularity of purpose in her voice and the speed with which she had processed her father's death felt unreal to Ali.

The news had reopened a lifetime of wounds; how her parents had abandoned her when she came out of the closet, the whispers around the department that made her feel like a freak, the challenge of finding true love in a society with thinly veiled distaste for her preferences.

The Ramirez family welcomed her into their lives, just as she was. Ali knew that Luis was uncomfortable with her lifestyle. But he accepted it, and her, without condition.

His loss was a highly personal body blow. Ali became aware that it wasn't just Jessica who needed consoling. Waves of confusion, loneliness and despair came rushing back to the front of her consciousness.

She needed a pair of comforting arms around her. There was only one place she knew where they might be.

The Martinique was different from the other bars Ali turned to on the nights she sought companionship. This place didn't have the pounding 90s dance music, the laser lights or the DJ shilling drink specials between the tunes. It was dark, quiet and very private. Booths lined the walls, leading up to the bar, with its requisite mirror that made the place look bigger than it was. Red and black velvet wallpaper dampened the sound, a single spotlight illuminating each booth.

Only one of the twelve stools that aligned with the long walnut expanse separating the bartenders from the customers was occupied.

Ali didn't care who it was or what she looked like. So long as they shared one thing in common, it would be good enough.

"This place isn't very busy tonight," she said, pointing to the woman's drink and signaling the bartender for one just like it.

The lone customer turned from her martini. Ali could feel the woman's eyes taking her measure. She did her own self inventory: Auburn hair, blue eyes, the freckles that were remnants of too many days in the sun, a hardbody that telegraphed "gym rat," jeans, the St. Louis Cardinals T-shirt covering the sports bra and the rainbow necklace that hung loosely around her neck but conservatively above her chest.

When the inspection became uncomfortable, she spoke to break the tension.

"Ali Clark."

The outstretched hand that shook her own was confident enough.

"Jane," the woman said. "Just Jane tonight."

Ali knew the type.

"Ok, Just Jane. JJ works for me."

Just Jane looked down at her cocktail and took a dose. "What do you want to tell me about yourself? Or is this just about drinking and screwing?"

"Pretty forward tonight, aren't we?"

"Look. I've had a really shitty day and don't have time for any mating dances. What are your expectations?"

Ali thought about that. What *were* her expectations?

"I'll be straight with you," she began.

"Please don't," JJ said. "Or we'll never make it past 'hello.'"

They both laughed. The tension softened.

"I'll be *candid* with you, JJ. I just lost a loved one, a father figure. I'm in a strange town. I don't know anybody and I need someone to hold me so I can have a good cry."

"In that case, maybe we can help one another."

The drink arrived and the glasses clinked, cementing the rules of engagement.

"I'm sorry for your loss," JJ said. She sounded like she meant it.

"What brings you here?"

"To be candid right back, I swing on both sides of the fence. I've been getting too close to a guy that I know I'll have to discard. Starting to have feelings for him. Never a good thing for my screwed-up head."

"Want to tell me about him?"

"No."

"Good. Let's shift gears to other hobbies. I'm a techno nerd. Does that make you hotter or colder?"

JJ raised an eyebrow. There was the hint of a smile. Ali felt a tingle. Those lips looked inviting.

JJ gulped the last of her first drink and swirled the empty glass in the bartender's direction.

"Me, too. Fortnite or Dungeons and Dragons?"

"Dungeons and Dragons? You're not that old. Warcraft maybe. Fortnite is for kids. What's with your eyes?"

They didn't match. Ali saw that JJ needed a moment to process the question.

"There was a rock under my contact lens," she said. "One blue eye and one brown eye? Totally fits my bisexual nature." The hint of a smile revealed a row of perfect teeth. Her tongue tickled a bicuspid.

Ali was getting more interested by the minute.

"Nothing wrong with accessorizing," she said, fingering her necklace. Her cop eyes noticed JJ had one, too. The ivory dice charm was interesting. Ali would have to ask her about it later.

"How do you spend your days, JJ? Or is that beyond what we're sharing tonight."

"I work at a jewelry store. I love messing with the customer's heads and change out my eye color three times a week. And you?"

"Just passing through. Consulting assignment. I live back east. To tell you the truth, I'm damn near ready to quit the gig and go home."

"I know the feeling."

JJ slid her stool closer. Ali couldn't quite make out the aroma of her perfume. Ali saw JJ reading the tiny movements of her nostrils.

"White Shoulders. Inexpensive but effective."

The words tickled something in Ali's memory. She tried to remember what it was but gave it up. A second martini was having the desired effect. Just Jane slid a hand along Ali's back.

"You're awful tight back there. I think a back rub may be in order."

The hand slid lower. Ali had ditched the cell phone, keys,

shield and her weapon. All JJ could feel was a wallet and the firm flesh beneath it.

Ali thought she could read her mind.

"My stuff is back at the room. I didn't want to be interrupted tonight."

"Hotel?"

"Is that a question or are you asking for directions?"

Ali liked the idea of neutral ground. She could tell her prospect did, too.

JJ tipped the last of her cocktail upward, draining the glass.

"Would you like dinner first?"

Ali shook her head and finished her drink.

"Food doesn't sound good at the moment. Other things do."

JJ put thirty dollars on the bar and slid a pair of fingers into Ali's pants pocket, pulling her gently off of the stool.

"Show me the way," she said.

SIXTY-SEVEN

The Sixth Day - Flagstaff

TO: Sheriff D. Lopez

CC: Detective J. Ramirez

FR: Lorenzo Akhionbare

RE: Amore User Information

Sheriff Lopez,

Attached, please find the requested information with regard to Mahoney and Lattimer. The women involved have separate profiles and engaged from different IP addresses. Pictures are included.

Please forward the appropriate court documents at your convenience.

Let me know if I can be of any additional service.

L. Akhionbare

Amore - "Where Love Finds a Way"

Jessica Ramirez stared out the window of her uncle's office, lost in thought, looking but not seeing, unsure of what to do next. She had barely slept. Her nightmare had morphed from Michael Wright and the Grand Canyon to a visceral visual of her father being consumed by the flames of hell. The woman in the black veil was the one commonality.

"Jess?" Danny Lopez tried to break her concentration. "Jessica?"

She shook her head, trying to clear her mind.

"Yes, Tio."

"What do you want to do now? I'm ok with you heading back home if that's where you think you need to be. This is PTSD material. I'm feeling it and your family are the in-laws I'm supposed to despise."

It was an ineffective attempt at humor.

"I think Ali is right," Jess finally said. She flipped through the hard copy of the Amore information, focusing on the two pictures of the woman. The woman who was a serial killer. The woman who had slept with Michael Wright. The woman who she was sure had ordered the hit on her family.

"We must be getting too close if our perp is trying to scare me off."

"There's an entire team from four different departments focused on this now," Danny said. "NPS, Phoenix PD, the FBI and us. I called O'Brien this morning. Both of your suspensions have been commuted with no further corrective action. You and Gates are welcome back at the House whenever you want to reengage. If you feel like being with your loved ones is where you need to be, go. We can take it from here."

Jess thought about what her mother said the night before. She thought about the uncharacteristic affirmations in her father's last message. She turned her gaze again to the window. It was an exquisite morning, the type of morning that beguiled senior citizens to abandon cold weather states, trading bone-chilling winters for hellacious summer heat. Somewhere, out there, Vega was waiting for her to make the next move. The gauntlet had been thrown down. Tio Danny was testing her. Would Jess pick it up or run for cover?

"I'm staying." There was a firmness to her voice. "She's made it personal."

"If it's personal, I'm not interested in having you around," Danny said. "The only way you can be effective is if you approach the assignment as a professional. 'Personal' leads to bad judgment calls and impetuous action when careful, coordinated professionalism is required."

"Like the way you handled the Crystal Rapid thing?"

"That is apples and oranges."

"That's BS and you know it, Tio. We both are competitive and want to catch this killer as quickly as we can. Yes, it's personal now. But I intend to make it a meditation on how to do my job when someone I love has been touched. If I bail, who is to say I wouldn't bail again? That makes me useless as a cop and goes against everything I believe. I'm at a crossroads, Tio. This is a test. A test I need to know if I can pass. Please let me try."

"You just lost your father, Jessica. Nobody expects you to keep working on this thing now."

Jess noticed a manilla envelope marked "FBI" on Danny's desk. She could tell that her uncle saw the direction of her gaze.

"This wouldn't have anything to do with your FBI friend, would it?" he said.

"It has everything to do with him. I've seen so much death that I'm terrified that I will get emotionally attached to a good man and end up a basket case if something bad happens to him. Now I'm living it. It's a test I have to pass before I can ever consider letting someone else into my heart."

"Christina thinks you already are emotionally attached."

Jessica closed her eyes and exhaled. "Maybe so. If that's true then the test is already underway. I have to see if I can measure up."

DANNY LOPEZ REPLAYED his phone conversation with
O'Brien in his mind. Yes, JRam could be a wild hair. She bent the
rules when she felt she needed to, but always for the right reasons.
She was born to be a police officer. She proved her metal in the
white-hot fires of the mean streets and in the midst of a chauvinistic
culture that was always daring her to fail.

Danny thought about his own journey, how hard it was for a
Latino to be accepted decades ago when the bureaucrats were
forcing square pegs into round holes in an attempt to prove to the
politicians that there was an institutional commitment to diversity.
His peg fit perfectly and yet nearly everyone hoped he would wash
out. All except a doctor who caught a child thief and ended up
becoming the mentor who believed Danny Lopez when nobody
else would.

Perhaps this was his moment to pay it forward.

"Ok. Business as 'unusual.'" He pointed to the paperwork Jess
held in her hands. "That warrant you wanted me to get is waiting
for you at the Arizona US District Court, 123 N. San Francisco
Street." He handed her a piece of paper with the address information on it. "Go get it and fax it to this Lorenzo guy. I have a feeling
you'll be talking with him again soon."

SIXTY-EIGHT

Staten Island

Matt Orwell was the best fiberoptic splicer in the Continental Long-Lines employee portfolio. He had risen from a small-time juvenile offender to become one of the most respected members of the team. Nobody knew the ins and outs of the intricate underground network of spun glass better than this orphan from Brooklyn. Why the company had not rewarded him financially for his contributions annoyed him.

Today that would no longer matter. The devices he had surreptitiously installed for the competitor who said they wanted to monitor Continental's fiber traffic were virtually undetectable. And now he was meeting his contact to get paid more money than he had ever seen. Tomorrow he would give his notice and leave the inconveniences of The Big Apple forever.

In the pocket of his Carhartt jacket was a first-class ticket to Costa Rica. His contact promised a job in San Jose at three times his current compensation.

The splicer pulled his well-worn Toyota Corolla into what passed for a parking lot at Battery Barbour, just beneath the

Verrazano Narrows Bridge on Staten Island. He intended to demand that his contact reimburse him for the 17-dollar toll.

"Mr. Orwell?"

The man had an easy smile and looked like he could pass for a colleague. He was dressed in jeans and a plaid, collared shirt. Aside from the eccentricity of the silver dice necklace he wore, Matt concluded that this man was a collection of nondescript features that few would be able to remember. Ideal for this sort of work.

"I'm Matt Orwell," the splicer said.

"May I please see some ID." The man made the request in a genial voice. A set of perfect teeth were framed by a pair of dimples on each side of his mouth.

"I understand you have something for me," Matt said, bringing his attention from the hand that held his wallet and driver's license back to his contact.

"I do," the man said. From behind his back he produced a Volquartsen Scorpion 22LR pistol. Pointing the suppressor directly at Matt Orwell's forehead, he fired the weapon twice.

SIXTY-NINE

Phoenix

The only hints that there had been someone next to Alexandra Clark in the king-size bed was the indentation on the pillow, the lingering bouquet of JJ's perfume and a few strands of hair.

Ali was suddenly wary.

She inspected every inch of the hotel room. The wallet had gone into the safe with her gun, badge and everything else that could give away her profession when JJ stepped briefly into the bathroom to reload the contact lens. The number on the tumbler was unchanged from where she set it. The other items in her room were untouched.

She emptied the contents of the safe, inventorying each as she put them on the nightstand. Everything was there.

Exhaling, Ali flopped back onto the bed, the memories of last night still fresh. Two damaged souls, each seeking emotional release, selfishly and without commitment. There was no conversation. When it was over, both women had collapsed, exhausted. In seconds they were sound asleep.

And now, Alexandra Clark was alone.

Unanswered questions started to bubble up into Ali's mind. Who did Mario call to get the name of the bar? Was it just good fortune that JJ happened to be the only one on a stool when Ali walked in? The pick-up was easy, perhaps too easy. Did JJ have some other motivation besides getting laid?

Ali shook her head, pushing these back down into her subconscious where a lifetime of issues that surrounded her sexual preference remain submerged. There were more important things to think about.

The ID on her cellphone: It said simply, "Amore" with a Las Vegas area code.

"Alexandra Clark."

"Ms. Clark? This is Lorenzo Akhionbare from Amore. Your colleague, Detective Ramirez, told me to call you if we noticed anything that might be connected with your investigations."

"What have you got for me?"

"I correlated the list of Phoenix area names that your FBI friends gave me with our user database. It turns out that one name became active today. It's someone named Brent Foster. He had a messaging conversation with a new customer named Angela Brown. Is there an email address where I can send you the timeline?"

SEVENTY

Phoenix

"Hello, beautiful!"

April Williamson looked up from the counter where she was studying the boutique's inventory records. The man she saw was striking. He could have been an NFL fullback from the look of his well-maintained body. The smile that creased his face revealed huge dimples beneath sparkling blue eyes and dark brown hair that spilled down his forehead into a comma above his eyebrows. She figured the suit to be an Armani, perhaps 2,000 dollars' worth. The Rolex on his left hand told her he was probably right-handed. What was missing on that hand caught her attention.

There was no wedding ring.

Ann Blakely was taken by surprise. This was unexpected and she didn't like being in that position. She covered her concern with a frown.

"What are you doing here?"

She didn't seem pleased that the gentlemen had called. April deduced he was the man with the Century Club membership.

"Aren't you going to introduce me?" she asked.

Ann pursed her lips. "Michael Allen, this is my boss, April Williamson."

"Delighted to meet you, April. I'm hoping to surprise your favorite employee with a celebratory dinner tonight."

April saw that Ann was nonplussed. "What are we celebrating?"

"It looks like I will be exonerated and will be released from exile here in Phoenix."

"So this means you will be out of my life forever?" The voice was a little too upbeat.

"That's not very friendly talk for an intimate companion."

"You were a one-night stand, smart aleck, and a barely acceptable one at that."

Michael frowned. April thought it was mock surprise. "You mean I'm not your first?"

"Not that again," she answered. "When do you leave?"

"Not until you and I have finished exploring the possibilities."

"It will have to wait," Ann said. "I have some loose ends to tie up. Come back at the end of the week."

"Not even one drink tonight?"

April watched Ann pull a flashing cell phone out of her purse. The message seemed to change her mind about this tall, dark and handsome specimen.

"OK, hot stuff. I'll meet you at the Century Club at 6. Now get out of here. I'm on the clock."

Michael bowed and walked over to the counter where April was standing. He took her hand and kissed it. "It was a pleasure meeting you, ma'am."

And then he was gone.

SEVENTY-ONE

Phoenix
    Vega:
    Is it done?
    "Yes ," The man with Eastern European accent nodded at the emotionless eye of the laptop camera. "We can confirm that the packages have been deployed and all is in readiness."
    Vega:
    And your associates?
    "All have been eliminated exactly as you instructed."
    Vega:
    You have done well. Are you ready to copy my instructions and receive your final payments?
    "May we speak frankly?"
    Vega:
    Of course.
    "The Organization was willing to wire the funds to our accounts electronically. Why must we meet a courier to receive the rest in person?"
    Vega:

It is the normal procedure.

"A procedure which ended in the deaths of the men we hired. What guarantee do we have that we two will not suffer the same fate?"

It was impossible to discern emotions among the letters on the computer screen. The two men knew that the delay in Vega's response spoke volumes.

Vega:

They were mere foot soldiers. You are both trusted members of the Organization. We plan to engage your services again.

"An opportunity for which we are deeply grateful. May we respectfully ask that the final payments be electronically delivered as a show of good faith?"

Vega:

Trust is a two-way street. If one cannot trust, there can be no relationship. Ours is hereby concluded.

THE DOORS to the captain's dining room on the container ship *Spratley* burst open. A pair of assassins entered, rifles pointed in the direction of the ship's computer cubicle.

The room was empty.

One of the assassins touched his radio earpiece. "Nobody is here."

SEVENTY-TWO

Phoenix

Alexandra Clark tried to focus. In the conference room at the headquarters of the FBI in Phoenix, she and Mario McCallister sat across the table from Mike Wright and station chief Bill Roberts.

Mario was reporting.

"The statewide network is again up and running. The data backup loaded without incident. Only forty-eight hours' worth of information was lost. The team is working to reconstruct it. Apparently, there are some jurisdictions that don't trust us and have continued to maintain hard copy of their documents."

"A reasonable course of action," Roberts murmured.

"Officer Clark has helped us create a shadow network that is still visible to Vega. To an intruder, it still appears that the system is compromised. All ports on the active network are confirmed to be secure. They are alarmed in case of a breach. In that instance, the intruder should automatically be redirected to the shadow network."

"Well done," Mike Wright said. "It sounds like you two made the impossible possible."

"Just another puzzle to be solved," Ali said. "Thank you for taking us into your confidence."

"What do you make of the log we harvested from Mike's router?" Roberts asked.

"It's hard to tell," Ali said. "We know that Капитан is Russian for 'Captain.' Beyond that it's difficult to know what may be happening."

"Ten to one, Vega is your serial killer," she added. "Капитан isn't too happy about that distraction."

"Maybe this will help," Mike said. He turned on an LED projector which painted a screen shot on the conference room's white board. "Any of that code look familiar."

Ali and Mario studied it for a moment and said in unison, "That's the Phoenix code."

"The code Ali discovered in our compromised system," Mario added.

"We found that somewhere else," Mike said.

Ali felt her face flush.

"Are you gonna tell us or are we back to twenty questions?"

"It was on a computer at Delorme and Nehr, a Wall Street investment firm."

Ali rubbed her chin. It helped her think. "Do your people suspect that Vega's target is the Big Apple?"

Michael nodded. "She could be. We think that the Phoenix project may have been her proof of concept."

"Vega's a smart cookie," Mario said. "She has to have anticipated a scenario where we might crack her code. She may have a Plan B if we feed these guys Ali's sniffer. Their systems would be inoculated even before Vega pulled the trigger."

Michael's answer was cryptic. "Yes. If Ali could get in the door."

Gates was a step ahead. "There are at least three fiberoptic communication rings I know about that encircle the Financial

District. And probably a half dozen direct backup connections. The redundancy is world class."

Bill Roberts handed Ali and Mario a piece of paper with names and companies listed on it.

"See if you can guess what these guys have in common."

"From the company affiliations," Mario said, "they look like they have something to do with the fiber networks."

"Exactly. All were high-level techs who knew every mile of the fiber optic ring by heart."

"What do you mean *were*?" Ali asked.

"They are also all dead."

SEVENTY-THREE

South of Flagstaff

The Chevy Tahoe Uncle Danny provided for Jess had the feeling of home as it headed south from Flagstaff on Interstate 17. It wasn't unmarked or customized to her exact specifications, but the comfort of a familiar cockpit buoyed her spirits. She studied the special bandage arrangement Doctor Bob had created to protect her wound.

"OK to go swimming, stand in the rain or clean out the trash," he told her. "Just stay away from sharp objects."

The memories of her time with Michael Wright were still coursing through Jess's mind, a mixture of emotions that at once delighted and distressed her. She needed more time to sort them out.

Jess punched the speed dial into the hands-free display on the console.

"Michael Wright." The Agent must have clearly recognized the caller ID but kept his answer all business.

"Mike, it's Jess. I'll be in Phoenix tonight. How about I find us some authentic Mexican cuisine and associated adult beverages?"

"Can't do it, Jess. With all that's going on, I'll be working late tonight. Are you around tomorrow?"

Working late. Jess's antennae went up.

"Is Michael Allen spending time with that woman tonight?"

"Now, Jessica, you know there are some things about the assignment I'm not at liberty to talk about. We shouldn't even be saying that name on an unsecure connection."

"Thanks for the confirmation."

"It's not what you think."

"Oh, it's exactly what I think. You go ahead and chase her for the safety of our nation, or however you're rationalizing this."

"You know I can't talk about these things on a cell phone, Jessica. Why are you doing this?"

She wanted to say a lot more. Just hours earlier, Michael had been pursuing her. Now, she felt discarded at a moment where she most wanted his support. And she didn't like the secrecy. She understood that there were some things about work that two lovers couldn't discuss. But now, they were on the same team, chasing a common enemy.

"Cut the bullshit," she wanted to scream into the phone. "If you love me, prove it now."

But Jessica Ramirez couldn't say these things. The combination of culture and professional pride wouldn't let her. He would have to decode it in the way she chose to dismiss him.

"Actually, I have a lot to do tomorrow. I probably can benefit from an early night sleep. Not that you'll be getting any." She paused for effect. "Sleep, that is."

"Can we talk about this tomorrow? Meet me at the office for lunch."

"The more we talk, the less interested I am, Michael."

She had him on thin ice.

"I don't know what to tell you, Jess. I've got a job to do. You do, too. Let's talk at lunch."

"I can't do this, Michael." Jess felt anger welling up inside. She hated to cry. Tears of jealousy, betrayal and sadness felt like burning acid as they ran down her cheeks. "Good luck with life."

She disconnected the call and sent his instant return to voice mail.

SEVENTY-FOUR

Phoenix

Alexandra Clark knew the look. As much as Jess had done the body work to cover it up, Ali knew she had been crying. Gates pulled her friend into an unused office three doors down from Bill Roberts and closed the door.

"What's going on?"

"Michael. I know he's going to be with that woman tonight."

Ali tried her best poker face. She failed. "White Shoulders. Damn that bitch."

"Is it true?" Jess asked.

"They are getting close to making the connection between this Ann person and the Vega identity that crashed the network. Some geek found malicious code that's exactly like ours at a stock joint in New York. We need whatever intel we can get to see how widespread this attack might be."

"We? So it's we now?"

"Cut it out, Jessica. You know the magnitude of this thing. And why are you being such a prude about Mike? There is no understanding between you two, is there?"

Jess shook her head.

"So stop being so jealous. You're losing your edge, girlfriend."

Jess put her fists on her temples and squinted, trying to clear her mind.

"Damn it, Ali. I think I'm starting to care about that guy."

"Then let him do his fucking job."

"Did you have to use that word?"

"You know what I mean. Let's all get past this situation and then see what life has for us."

"You know," Jess said, "sometimes, I wish I were you. Having a preference for women has definite upsides."

"With just as many downsides. Imagine two people with your emotional instability and monthly hormonal hand grenades trying to navigate a relationship."

"My emotional instability?"

"I break up with people when we hit the same low points at the same time. Our goddamn periods are in sync for Christ's sake. You heterosexuals just chalk it up to the other gender's genetic imperfections. You yell and scream and then you jump back in bed and work off the tension."

"That's just it. I really want to let Michael do his thing and I'd love to work off the tension. Why does it have to be that woman? I want to be a fly on the wall tonight, but I'm afraid it would only make me more confused."

Ali thought for a moment.

"A fly on the wall, eh. I think I could make that happen."

"Ohh no. You're not putting one of your bugs in his condo."

"It would be so easy. He'd never see it and if Ann, or whatever her real name is, turns on him, we can provide backup. I bet you'd love to kick her ass."

"Would I. I'd love to throw her into that canyon, stoned to the eyeballs on that muscle drug so she can know how it feels."

"I can do this. All I need is the address. It will take me five minutes and we'll be able to see and hear everything."

"I can't condone it, Ali."

"Bill Roberts would probably thank me."

"You're not going to do it without asking permission."

"When have I ever asked for permission. Forgiveness is a gift we all should keep on giving."

"Listen to me, Ali."

"OK, OK. Tell you what. I'm having drinks with Mario after work. Come with us and drown your sorrows. You need to be with friends tonight. Now get the hell out of my office. I have another little trick to play on Miss Vega."

SEVENTY-FIVE

Phoenix

Once upon a time, every city had a bar called "The Alibi." By the turn of the century, the brand lost its luster. The few that remained had creative owners who knew how to build a loyal customer base. Such was the case in Phoenix.

Jess waded through the mid-week business crowd until she saw Mario McCallister, staking out a corner table, somewhat insulated from the pulsating conversation that permeated the place.

"You nerds always choose a table with power plugs, don't you? Where's Ali?"

Mario smiled as he gave his smart phone a quick glance. The charging cable snaked under the table to an outlet.

"She'll be here shortly." Mario glanced at the battery indicator. "Eighty-five percent. Another ten minutes and I'll have enough power for a long evening on Reddit."

What was it about men? Jess wondered. They seemed clueless about the things that really mattered, like relationships and risk.

"I don't understand you guys," she muttered. "It always feels like you are more committed to your work or your toys than you are to your women."

"If I had a woman, I would gladly toss the tech. Who would be interested in a pimple-faced guy with a questionable past who is ten times smarter than she is?"

"Oh, I think you'd be surprised. If you ever traded your Federal gig for something in Silicon Valley, I think you'd find a whole portfolio of babes who would see your self-perceived liabilities as assets."

"Maybe in a few years. I'm still learning a ton and there is enough drama in my professional life. I don't need another set of moods to contend with right now."

"So we women are reduced to a 'set of moods'?"

"You know what I mean. I heard about your phone call this afternoon. Not exactly an academy award performance on your part."

"Ali told you?"

"She said she was going to be late and it was my job to cheer you up."

"Well, you're doing a terrible job."

"Maybe. Maybe not."

Mario waved a hand at a waitress and two margaritas magically appeared.

"I believe you like yours top shelf with extra lime?"

A plate of quesadillas materialized.

"Chicken with green chile, I think it was?"

Jess leaned across the table and planted an overly passionate kiss on Mario's mouth. She held it for a good twenty seconds. He fell back against the edge of the booth, gasping for air.

Jess licked her lips. "When you find a woman who can kiss you like that, you better take damn good care of her."

Another voice rose above the crowd. "Who is making out with my partner?"

It was Ali, shouldering her way between two football player

types, with a backpack slung over a single shoulder. "Got one of those spit swaps for me, girlfriend?"

"It would be unethical to have a relationship with a colleague. You know my eleventh commandment."

Mario was still processing what had happened to him.

"I won't tell if you won't," he said. "Just let me watch."

Jess snorted. "Come see me in ten years, after you get one of those millionaire jobs in the Valley. You'll like experienced older women."

"I like experienced older women," Ali said. "Do you know any, Mario?"

"Just one," he answered, wiping his mouth with the back of his hand and looking at Jess.

Jess could tell that Ali had other things on her mind. "Enough of this TMI talk. Let me bring you guys up to date on my adventures. Mario, you ordered a margarita for my friend and didn't get anything for me?"

"You didn't tell me what your drink was. You just said, 'make Jessica feel better till I get there.'"

Jess took a long pull from the fishbowl glass. "He followed your instructions to the letter."

"Remember, girlfriend," Ali said. "No weapons allowed if you drinking."

Jess tipped the fishbowl and swallowed. "Fuck off, Alexandra."

Ali turned on her instructor's voice. "For future reference, Mario, I drink beer. The more hops the better. Pilsner Urquell if they have it."

Mario pulled a pen from the protector in his shirt pocket, wrote a note on his cocktail napkin and waved it in the air. A waitress came and went.

Ali scanned the room to make sure the noise was loud enough to cover their conversation. She leaned in and lowered her voice.

"I've got sniffers deployed at two dozen locations in the Big Apple. Thank you, Mario. We've already found the Phoenix code at six. And...I injected a little bit of magic into the JPEG profile picture of our girl's next mark on the Amore site. Every time she logs in from any device, I can track her location."

Jess couldn't help herself.

"Can you tell me where she is now?"

SEVENTY-SIX

Phoenix

"Be careful tonight."

Bill Roberts called after Michael Wright as he was heading out the door. "We know how dangerous this woman can be. Watch yourself."

Mike waved him off. "I'll be OK. I think she's breaking up with me tonight anyway. All the vibes point in that direction."

"I don't like the fact that she agreed to have drinks with you. You watch what you ingest if you two get back to that condo. I'd feel a lot better if we had some backup in the neighborhood."

"Trust me, I know what she's capable of. Give me some credit."

"Why don't I send Murphy, just in case. He can be seconds away if you need him."

"I don't want to do anything to spook her. As far as she knows, I'm just another finance guy who beat the rap."

"That's what I don't like. You're living smack dab in her victims' neighborhood."

"I'm just a distraction. She fries much bigger fish."

"You keep the panic button by that bed within reach at all times, my friend. Understood?"

"Yes, boss. I promise."

As Michael Wright stepped outside of the Phoenix FBI office and into the dry coolness of the Arizona evening, his boss dialed a number on his cell phone.

"Murphy? Bill Roberts. I need you for overtime tonight."

APRIL WILLIAMSON STUDIED HER EMPLOYEE, carefully checking her hair and makeup in the mirror behind the boutique sales counter.

"This is truly a first for you," she said. "Stringing not one, but two men along at the same time."

Ann Blakely applied the perfume that always seemed to work magic on both sides of the gender spectrum. "I'll always say yes to drinks and dinner at the Century Club, even if the guy is ninety years old."

"After working with you for five years, I'm not sure you'll ever find the man you're looking for."

"Oh, I find the men I'm looking for all the time. They always let me down."

"Perhaps you are looking for the wrong men."

Ann paused the body work and regarded her boss.

"I think you may be right, April. Neither one of these guys have a future. And Phoenix is beginning to feel like a really small pond. I may have to seek out a bigger pool of fish."

"I've always wondered why you hung around. You're way to smart, degreed and... gifted." April ran her hands seductively down her hips to accentuate the word. "I guess I should have seen this coming."

"You've been a wonderful boss, April." Ann said it with authenticity. "I've truly enjoyed our relationship."

"Where will you go?"

"That's still up in the air. For starters, I think I'll see a bit of the world. I like the idea of being an anonymous tourist. You meet the most interesting people."

Her phone vibrated. *"Looking forward to meeting you in real life tomorrow night - BF."*

"One of your losers?" April asked.

Ann nodded. "I'm really looking forward to a short, passionate encounter."

"Love him and throw him away. Just like all the others?"

Ann nodded. "Exactly."

SEVENTY-SEVEN

Phoenix

Michael concluded that anyone who had seen Ann Blakely the last time she crossed the threshold of the Century Club would never have recognized the radiant woman on Michael Allen's arm that night. Gone were the tight pants, pumps, I-shirt and blazer, replaced by black, flared, linen palazzo trousers and a transparent, white, silk blouse, revealing a tight-fitting, spaghetti-strap, cotton, camisole tank top beneath. Patent leather heels, a titanium Ebel watch, an over-the-shoulder Coach purse and the ever-present gold necklace with the silver dice rounded out the creation. The perfect companion, turning heads for all the right reasons.

Michael nodded in the direction of the other diners as the Maître D' guided them to a table. "Look at them. Now they are envious."

Ann whispered into her escort's ear. "They are all wondering how a schlub like you ended up with a catch like me."

Michael laughed. "Touche."

He studied his date as the host held her chair. The acerbic attitude just didn't fit the rest of the package. This woman could pass for anyone. He'd seen her do dress down and dress up with equanimity. She could turn the charm on and off like a light switch. He wondered how many personas Ann had in her mental Rolodex.

At the same time, the picture of a ruthless killer was hidden somewhere inside that alluring body. If the evidence were to be believed, those soft hands guided at least four men to their deaths. The perfectly manicured fingers were punching computer keys to set up a catastrophic outcome on the other side of the country.

How many more might suffer if he couldn't stop her?

Michael's cop sense was kicking in. "Why do I get the sense that this is the last time I'll be seeing you?"

"Perhaps it's because you're finally developing some grasp on reality," Ann answered. "You were an interesting one-night stand, working on an encore. The judge may have let you escape justice, but the jury is still out on what happens next."

"It sounds to me like you are playing judge and jury, Ann. There's a very thin line between reasonable intelligence and insider trading. Our job is to avoid stepping too far over it. Do you want the whole story?"

"Not really."

"Please. Hear me out and then judge me."

A Tuxedo came with their drinks without being asked. The club was that good.

"I produced the evidence, the feds wanted to hang me out to dry anyway and we had to slap them around a bit. It's really a David and Goliath thing if you think about it."

"Well, I'm glad to hear that you managed to stay on the right side of the law, this time. Let's celebrate by spending more of your company's money."

"So am I right?"

"Right about what?"

Time was running short. Michael needed to try to draw more information out of this woman. "Am I right that you're dumping me after tonight. What are the 'things you have to do' this week? As far as I know, you're just a sales rep at a jewelry store."

"That's where you men always get it wrong. There are many layers to a woman. We decide how much we reveal. For all you know, I could be a brain surgeon, working at April's place to burn off the stress of deciding who lives or dies."

Michael's alarm bells were ringing now. This person, he thought, is just like every other criminal. *She wants me to know about her crimes. But she wants me to work to figure them out.*

"I thought doctors were all about 'doing no harm.'"

"Some are. Some aren't. Medicine is just like every business. They talk about helping you get better, but in the end, it's all about the money."

"Was that your father's attitude?" Ann flinched. "From the way you talk about him, I thought you blamed him for what happened to your mother."

Ann wrapped a fist around the ivory dice that dangled at her throat.

"Oh it was totally true. He killed my mother just as if he had put a gun to her head."

She was squeezing the dice. She let go. A pair of 'ones,' snake eyes in the gambling trade, were imprinted on her palm.

"But let's just say that I've found someone more interesting." She focused on Michael's eyes. "Look. Why don't we try to enjoy this night? We're both off to bigger and better things." Ann reached under the table and massaged the top of Michael's leg. "Nobody can predict the future. We could both be dead by morning. Let's make the most of the moment."

———

TWENTY-TWO MILES AWAY, a half dozen police and FBI vehicles converged on a large brick residence in a fashionable

Phoenix suburb. Federal windbreakers and local blues aligned like a row of soldiers on the sidewalk with Bill Roberts in the lead.

He rang the doorbell, looking at the photo of the man he knew would answer it. As the door swung open, a male, six feet tall, 195 pounds, close-cropped hair and beard flecked with gray looked at the scene in disbelief.

"Can I help you, gentlemen?"

"Brent David Foster?"

"Yes."

Roberts showed his shield.

"You'll have to come with us."

"There are kids in the house. I don't have a baby sitter," Foster protested.

"We'll take care of them." The FBI man took his charge by the arm.

"Can I at least say goodbye?"

"If you play ball with me," Roberts said, "you won't have to."

Foster darkened. Roberts imagined that he knew this drill well. "Look. I've been cleared. Not guilty. There's such a thing as double jeopardy. You people ought to know about that."

"That concept doesn't cover indictments that were dropped before prosecution, my friend. We have some new evidence that you're not going to like."

"I want my lawyer."

Roberts turned Foster around and applied handcuffs.

"He's waiting at my office and I think he'll have some advice that you'll want to listen to."

SEVENTY-EIGHT

Phoenix

"We have a target!"

Jess was counting. Ali was on her third Pilsner Urquell in the corner booth at the Alibi when her phone vibrated. She pulled a laptop out of her backpack, tossing the power cord to Mario.

"Plug this baby in. It's showtime."

"What the hell did you do?" Jess asked.

Jess recognized Ali's feigned look of hurt surprise. "I asked for permission."

"You didn't."

Ali nodded. "I did."

The cameras appeared on the laptop screen. Jess could see Ann and Michael entering the condo. The woman she had grown to hate didn't waste time. Ann pushed him against the hallway wall, grabbing his head with her two hands, kissing him passionately. Off came the Armani suit coat. Ann grabbed Michael by the shirt, guiding him backward toward the bedroom and onto the king-size bed. She found the remote and pressed the button that energized the curtains, blocking out the twinkling lights of Phoenix as she unbuttoned him.

Ann gave Michael back his lips, straddling his torso, removing her own outer layers, revealing the gifts nature had given and the surgeons had so generously augmented.

"Let's make this a moment to remember."

Jess covered her eyes. "I can't believe we are watching this. If this is supposed to cheer me up..."

"It's supposed to protect his ass," Ali interrupted. She kept her thumb hovered over the send button, Bill Roberts' number already loaded and ready to fire on her cell phone. "I wish that woman would turn around so we could get a look at her face."

Jess could hear Mario processing what he saw. "Do all of you kiss your men like that?"

She knew that this would set Ali off. Mario qualified it.

"I mean do all of you kiss your *partners* like that?" He leaned toward the screen for a better view. "I wish this laptop had a bigger display."

Jess fumed. "You guys are disgusting. At least he's not kissing her back."

"Girlfriend," Ali said, shaking her head. "Give him another sixty seconds and he'll be on top of the situation, driving the train into the tunnel."

Michael rolled Ann over on her back. The last of the clothing that impeded their progress fluttered to the floor. Ann pulled him toward her, her long fingernails drawing blood as they sunk into the flesh on his back.

SEVENTY-NINE

Phoenix

Mario's eyebrows went up. "I thought people did these things under the covers."

Ali was incredulous. "Are you a virgin? Even nerd birds get laid in college."

"They look like they are enjoying it."

"She drew blood!" Jess nearly screamed it. "That bitch. I'm gonna kill her, right after I kill him for enjoying it."

"Are you in love with this guy?" Mario asked. "If not, perhaps I..."

Ali pointed to the screen. "What's that?"

It looked like a tiny bandage, a butterfly patch, most security cameras would have missed it. Jess didn't.

Jess watched Michael's rhythm slow, at first almost imperceptibly, then noticeably. Ann pulled him closer.

Ann's arms encircled Michael's back. Her fists were clinched, holding his body tightly against hers as his began to relax.

"Something's wrong," Jess said. "Call Bill now!"

Ali got her first good look at the woman's face.

"Holy shit! White Shoulders!"

"Press the button, Ali!"

"I know that woman."

"What do you mean, you know her?"

Jess could see enlightenment hitting Ali between the eyes like a two-by-four.

"I've known her 'in the biblical' sense. The bitch was in bed right next to me. Jesus am I an idiot."

Ali pressed the speed dial as the trio sprang from the booth in a dead run for the exit.

EIGHTY

Phoenix

"Are you relaxed, my love?"

Michael could feel the waves of tension leaving his body. He nodded.

Ann pushed him off of her, pulling on her clothing as she went for her purse.

He lay spread eagle on his back, not caring about anything except sleep. It didn't make any sense. A few minutes ago, he could have made love all night.

"You were right, dearest," Ann said as she buttoned her blouse. "I do have another appointment. And these are our final moments together. You see, I have resources of my own, just like you do. And I discovered you are not the man you pretend to be."

Through the haze in Michael's head, he could see Ann open her purse. She produced a breathing mask connected to a long clear tube, wide enough at one end to interface with the mouthpiece on the I-Stick.

"I'll need some time without pursuers. If I'm right, it will take them at least twenty-four hours to figure out what happened to you. That's all I require and my work will be done."

Michael felt himself slipping into darkness. Somewhere in the distance he dimly saw Ann shake a vape pen, mixing the contents inside. He could feel the mask gently covering his mouth and nose.

"Now breathe for me, baby. Just breathe."

"HE'S NOT ANSWERING," Ali said.

"Hit it again." Jess shouted it as she pounded the accelerator of the Tahoe against the firewall. She knew how fast the Bergulon could work. Time was of the essence.

Mario sat in the back seat, riveted to the laptop.

"She's put some sort of mask over his face. He's not moving."

Ali re-sent the call for a third time.

"Bill Roberts."

"Bill, it's Alexandra. Get Murphy in there now. Our perp is killing your boy. Do you understand?"

"Understood," Roberts said and rang off.

"She's leaving," Mario McCallister said. "How long until we get there?"

Ali held on to her seatbelt as the Tahoe turned a corner on two wheels. Jess was running with lights and siren on now.

"Maybe five minutes, max," Jess said, concentrating on the traffic ahead.

Ali looked at her iWatch. Everyone had read the autopsy reports by now, and knew exactly how fast the drug could do its work. "We'd better hurry. He'll be dead in ten."

EIGHTY-ONE

Phoenix

Jess heard the annoyed countenance of the Medical Examiner on the other end of the line. "Joey Price." He was probably in the middle of an autopsy and was annoyed at being disturbed

Every memory of her encounters with Michael was flashing before her eyes at light speed, her first impression at the cop shop, the kiss after the strip club bust, what it felt like to see him again in Flagstaff, and that amazing night at the hotel. All of these things and more could be memories of a dead man unless Joey Price could help her. The phone was on speaker so the others in the Tahoe could hear. "Listen to me, Joey. What do we do to keep a patient alive when they have ingested Bergulon?"

"The drug itself isn't typically deadly, unless the patient is allergic to it. In that case, a variety of bad things can happen including brain damage and death. But in most cases--"

"Cut to the chase, Joey. Our killer just dosed Michael. What do we do to keep him alive until the medics arrive?"

"CPR without the compressions. Keep him breathing. Remember, brain damage starts to happen after five minutes without oxygen. Get air into those lungs."

"That's it?"

"Yes. But get him to a hospital stat. And have them make sure he isn't allergic. It's rare, but if he is, it isn't fun."

"Thank you, Joey." There was no time to process gratitude. Jess had one goal in mind: To save Michael's life. "I hope we're in time."

At that moment, the Tahoe skidded to a stop in front of Crystal Point. The trio was in the lobby in seconds, nearly colliding with officer Jim Murphy at the elevator bay.

Jess saw the tall FBI agent pounding the up-arrow.

"The cars aren't responding. I've been here for five minutes."

She bolted for the stairs.

"That's twenty floors," Ali called after her.

"Read the elevator control display on the far wall," Jess yelled. "They are both on two."

Telling Mario to stay put, Jess, Ali and Murphy raced for the staircase.

There wasn't time for a key. Jess had her Glock in both hands, shooting a perfect circle around the door lock mechanism and kicking it open. Michael lay on the bed, exactly as they had seen him on the screen eight minutes earlier. His eyes were wide as he struggled to inhale. His diaphragm quivered. His skin was blue. As Jess approached the bed, the eyes started to roll up and backward.

Joey had given her very specific instructions. Seeing Michael in this state, Jess forgot everything. "We're losing him. What do I do?"

"You know exactly what to do, girlfriend," Ali said. "Just what you did the other night."

Jess's brain was still full of vivid memories from the night at the hotel. She bent over, interlocking her mouth with his, holding his head in her hands. She estimated his lung capacity and exhaled into his airway. His chest rose beneath her. As it naturally fell, she turned her head to refill her own lungs and repeated the procedure.

"Don't you dare die on me, Michael Wright," she said between breaths. "I was just getting comfortable with the thought of a relationship and you pull this?"

Another breath.

"That will teach you to sleep with a killer, you idiot."

Another breath.

"We were watching you."

Another breath.

"You ought to be ashamed of yourself."

Another breath. Jess was starting to feel lightheaded.

"Just shut up and give him the air," Ali said. "We don't need you passing out, too."

Jess was so focused that she didn't realize the cavalry had arrived until a paramedic gently touched her shoulder

"We can take it from here," he said, firing up a ventilator. His partner had a bag valve mask deployed in seconds.

Michael was still clearly unconscious, but Jess could see his oxygen numbers beginning to rise as the ventilator did its work. This seemed like a good thing but Jess was still worried.

"Were we here in time?"

"We won't know until we get him to the hospital," the medic said.

He was checking his patient with a stethoscope.

"He still has a strong heartbeat and his lungs are clear. What happened?"

"Nebulized administration of Bergulon," Ali said, reflexively speaking the paramedic's language.

Jess collapsed into a chair. Her own heart was racing and her head was spinning from hyperventilation.

Jess marveled at the paramedics' speed and choreography. They had Michael transferred to a gurney, covered and strapped in less than five minutes.

"Ladies and gentlemen," the medic said. "If you can give us some room, we'll get this man where he needs to go."

Jess found her voice. "I'd like to ride along," she said, tossing Ali the keys to the Tahoe.

Bill Roberts held up a hand. "I'll take those, Jessica. Change in plan."

Ali held up a hand. "No more talk in this room. Let's wait until we have a little more privacy."

"What do you mean by that?"

"We're not alone."

THREE BLOCKS AWAY, the woman who called herself Ann Blakely sat in a McDonald's parking lot. She processed Ali's statement as it whispered into the earbuds that were connected to her laptop. She snapped it shut. But not before saving screen shots of everyone in the room. She would review the recording later, especially the part where she put the mask over her victim's face. She would have her associates analyze the screen shots to tell her exactly who these rescuers were. But was it really necessary? She checked her watch. In less than twelve hours, none of this would matter. The world would be focusing its attention elsewhere.

EIGHTY-TWO

The Seventh Day - Queens, New York

LaGuardia Airport has the same rush hour problem that plagues all of New York City. The two men were annoyed that the TSA Pre-check line was almost as long as the regular queue. They found it impossible not to look over their shoulders, even though they had no idea who might be after them.

It had been a stroke of genius to make their final contact with Vega from a different location.

The pair felt lucky. They had false passports, first-class tickets to Montevideo and a safe house in rural Uruguay. All they had to do now was clear security and find a quiet corner in the airline lounge until departure.

"Traveling together, gentlemen?"

The female TSA agent barely looked up, holding out a hand for their documents.

"Yes, ma'am," the taller man said, handing over the paperwork.

The agent held the tickets over the scanner. It beeped twice, confirming their status. She studied the passports and squinted at the men. Everything seemed to be in order. Perhaps, the men thought, they were home free.

The men watched as the TSA agent closed her eyes for a moment, as if grasping for a thread of memory. She pulled a white piece of paper from underneath her podium and ran a finger across it. She beckoned two men in identical dark suits who stood near the line of baggage x-ray machines, bending her neck in the direction of the travelers.

The duo was by her side in an instant.

"Excuse us, gentlemen," one of the suits said. "Can you please come this way?"

THERE WAS a third person watching the encounter. She was exhausted after thirty hours without sleep. She landed in New York without even a carry-on bag.

"Do you recognize either of these men?" one of the suits asked.

Alexandra Clark shook her head.

EIGHTY-THREE

Phoenix

Jessica Ramirez studied the faces at the Phoenix FBI conference table. Each reflected a restless night. The way Mario McCallister was looking at her made her conclude that he was still processing the kiss. Tio Danny Lopez had the most sleep. Everyone had forgotten to call him until about an hour before. Jess scanned her own body. She could not get the visceral image of Michael Wright out of her mind. Intubated and unconscious. It was another picture she could barely compartmentalize among the dozens of dead bodies that were barely contained there. She felt spent, physically and emotionally, her facade ripped away to reveal a cocktail of raw emotions, barely contained.

And there was Ali. She should have landed in New York by now, closest to the imminent danger. Jess hoped her partner could make a difference... in time.

Dr. Joey Price was again the last to arrive. This time he had a good excuse.

"I've just left the hospital," he said. "Agent Wright will survive.

It's too soon to know if he was without oxygen long enough for any brain damage. He's not able to talk and that is...unusual. It's not a recognized side effect of Bergulon and that has the docs worried."

This news opened a crack in Jess's practiced cop stoicism. She could see Joey noting it, adding a postscript to his report.

"But not overly worried. You know how these things go. We're cautious until the patient stabilizes. I think you guys made it just in time."

With everyone in the room, Bill Roberts kicked off the proceedings.

"OK. Let's focus. Mario, the clock is ticking. Where are we?"

"We've analyzed the signatures we received from New York last night," he said. "They are definitely the Phoenix Code."

"Is Officer Clark's software deployed at every facility?" Jess could hear the tension invading Roberts' voice. "What do we know about the fiber network?"

"We're in all but two of the financial houses. Nehr and Groves wouldn't let us mess with their systems. Agent Wright's contacts at NYPD have connected the deaths of five fiber optic engineers. Same gun, same M.O., .22 caliber. Two shots to the forehead. Bodies all found in the same park in New Jersey."

"They had to be working for a handler. Do we have a sense for who that might be?"

Mario shook his head. "One of the victims had a phone number in his cell that they traced to a container vessel in New Jersey. There was gunfire there last night. There might be a connection."

"Give me your honest assessment, Mario. Will Officer Clark's countermeasures work?"

"They should. Unless our girl has changed something. She's smart enough. But you have to have a variant ready that's based on what you know about how it was compromised, that kind of thing takes time."

Jess's phone vibrated in her pocket. In her state, it felt like it was shaking her entire leg. The caller ID was a Paloma area code. "OK if I take this one?" she asked.

Roberts nodded.

EIGHTY-FOUR

Phoenix

"Detective Ramirez?"

The voice was young, eager and questioning.

"This is Jessica Ramirez. How can I help?"

"This is Andrew Milluzzi from the Engineering Department at Paloma University. Officer Clark said I should call you if I found something interesting."

Jess felt the blood circulating again as her heart rate jumped.

"What have you got for me, Andrew?"

"It may be nothing, but I found a woman with that double major that Officer Clark was looking for. Organic Chemistry and Computer Science, at MIT twelve years ago, right at the outside limit of Ms. Clark's time frame."

"And?" Jess pressed the phone closer to her ear.

"Her name is Adele Bannister, born in Detroit, Michigan. She was with a company in Europe up until about five years ago. And then... She seems to have disappeared."

More puzzle pieces were falling into place. Jess felt the noose closing around Ann Blakely's neck. She would normally compartmentalize this, keeping things professional, focused on justice. Not this time. Jess imagined her own hands choking the life out of this bad woman. It was a perverse, pleasant feeling.

"What else do you know about her?"

"Never married. Mother was a suicide about the time she graduated. Father died of a heart attack. The firm she worked for was on the UN's list of companies manufacturing chemical weapons for illegal sale to third world countries. They are still in business but have shifted to cloning knock-offs of patented drugs for medical use."

Jess suddenly felt renewed. These may be threads but she was hanging onto them for dear life.

"Andrew, you make sure to tell Officer Clark who your adviser is. You just earned your way to the dean's list. Anything else?"

"No, ma'am. Do you want me to keep digging for others?"

"I think we're good. If you have bots doing the scanning, leave them running."

"WHAT'S THIS?" Bill Roberts pointed to the contents of the plastic bag that the agent had dumped in the center of the conference table.

"We found these at the condo," the agent said.

Mario pointed to one of the devices. "That's Ali's."

Jess and Director Roberts moved in for a closer look.

The contractor gave his assessment. "It's a wireless camera, similar. But it's Russian."

Roberts looked at the agent.

"He's right," he said. "The latest in covert surveillance gear. We discovered something similar when we re-opened the Cuban embassy. It's the first time we've found one in country."

Jess wanted to share her own news about the killer. A knock on the door stopped her.

"This is getting more interesting by the minute," Danny Lopez muttered.

The door opened and an agent led a man with short grey hair and a beard into the conference room. He was handcuffed and worse for what must have been hours of interrogation.

"Ladies and gentlemen," Roberts said. "I'd like you to meet Mr. Brent David Foster."

Every cop and most of the city knew it by heart. Brent David Foster was the man who had allegedly killed three wives and walked.

Roberts stood and patted Foster on the shoulder.

"He's now working for us."

EIGHTY-FIVE

Queens, New York

"I'm Jack Poole."

The Special Agent shook Ali's hand at the LaGuardia police information booth. Why did all these FBI field guys look like ex-football players? This one wasn't in a suit though. The most formal thing about his ensemble was the button-down, cotton shirt. The jeans, the work boots and the Carhartt all said "blue collar."

"Welcome to New York."

Ali returned the masculine grip. "Alexandra Clark. What was up with those two guys at TSA?"

"We got a tip. Wondered if you had come across them in your...research."

"Never saw them before. Are they important?"

"You and I will find out shortly. I hope you don't mind getting a little dirty."

Ali considered her own outfit. It was a lot like Poole's, only wrinkled, marked with the sweat and stench of a thirty-hour day. Barely business casual in Silicon Valley. It would have to do for today's government assignment.

"Where are we headed?"

"Where five dead men used to work."

AT THE OTHER side of the terminal, the two passengers who hoped to be on their way to Montevideo and safety found themselves heading for the airport exit, a suit on each side gently but firmly gripping their upper arms to guide them.

As the doors slid open an Uber vehicle pulled in front of the line of taxis.

"Hey!" The taxi concierge called out to the driver, pointing to the sign on his right. "This is for licensed taxi cabs only. Private transportation is five hundred feet that way."

The driver got out of his vehicle. A Volquartsen Scorpion 22LR was in his right hand. He used the roof to steady his aim, the pair of ivory dice that hung from the chain around his neck swayed like the pendulum on a grandfather clock. He carefully squeezed off eight shots in the direction of the quartet that was leaving the terminal. When he was sure the slugs had hit their targets, he calmly turned in the direction of the concierge. The man raised his arms, walking backwards.

"Park wherever the hell you want, buddy. By the way, nice necklace." The Taxi attendant forgot about the curb, falling backwards as his heel hit it. That turned out to be the luck he needed. The .22 slug whistled above his head. Seconds later, the Uber was gone.

EIGHTY-SIX

Phoenix

Brent Foster felt numb. Every attorney on his team said he was in the clear, a man who got away with murder, not once but three times. He should have listened to the voice inside his head that had been whispering "blow town" ever since he was released from custody after the hung jury all but acquitted him a year ago. The new evidence was compelling. The FBI people were on a mission from God to nail him. He was sure it was all over this time.

And then came the strange offer. Help us capture this woman and the Death Penalty is off the table. You'll get life, but with the possibility of parole. What could be more important than burning someone for triple homicide in a high-profile case that made the local cops look like incompetent fools?

Sure, they had tried to sell him a story that the woman liked to kill men she thought had escaped justice, but that felt like a bluff.

Nothing made sense.

Foster needed time to think. But there wasn't any. The meeting was set for tonight. If she was a killer, why wouldn't the Feds simply let her kill him and then take her down? It would be perfect, incontrovertible evidence. And the police would be able to float their so-called allegations against Foster without him being around to defend himself.

He still had his bug-out bag in the attic at home. If they let him out, would they be watching him until tonight? Probably. The kids were with his sister. The house would be empty.

A plan began to formulate in Brent Foster's mind. Perhaps he had a few chess moves yet to make.

ANN BLAKELY WAS NO MORE. The woman who had used that name for the last five years was now Angela Brown. Gone were the blue contacts and the dishwater blonde hair. Her coloring was closer to Adele Bannister, the name she was born with. Or had that name morphed into "Vega," the mysterious hacker who sold her skills to the highest bidder?

Did she even have an identity anymore? So many names. So many lives. More lives than the luckiest house cat. Would the law of averages catch up to her now? This was the biggest project she had ever undertaken, the magnum opus of a career she hoped to jettison when the last payment hit her Swiss bank account. She didn't like the fact that she had to depend on others to help her execute. "Vega" was used to working alone. She could always count on herself. When you brought outsiders into the game, they invariably let you down.

The woman who was born Adele Bannister thought about all of these things as she packed the last remnants of her Arizona life into a carry-on suitcase. The dashboard display on her laptop showed green icons at every location where her viruses had been deployed. At the center of the screen, a digital clock counted backwards toward Noon Eastern Time. At that moment all of the puzzle pieces would fall into place. The records of billions of stock transactions would vanish. History would record this day as her own personal 9/11.

A familiar ring tone whispered from the speakers. That would be Капитан, "The Captain," making sure everything was on schedule.

Vega pressed a key to open the chat application. Капитан didn't wait for her to greet him. Nine words appeared on the screen.

"There are men in the New York fiber tunnels."

EIGHTY-SEVEN

New York

The Cortlandt subway station was the final piece of major infrastructure to be rebuilt in the wake of the 9/11 terrorist attacks. It links the disjointed parts of the World Trade Center transit plaza, connecting the PATH system to the IRT Broadway–Seventh Avenue Line. Above it, One World Trade Center points skyward, again the tallest building in the Western Hemisphere, and the sixth-tallest in the world.

Ali thought that this would be an appropriate place to begin their inspection. All five SONET fiber rings converged here. When they arrived, there were ten other men there, FBI, local police, Con Edison and representatives from the major carriers who maintained the glass spider web that connected the Financial District with the world.

Ali had done her homework. "We'll be looking for something encircling the fiber package. If we're lucky, it will be something small that will break the connection just enough to make it hard to repair. But I don't think that's what we'll find. These people killed the technicians who helped deploy these packages. My guess is that whatever is down here will make a big enough bang to take out your infrastructure, permanently."

"If you see something, say something," Poole added. "Don't touch it, just report it on the radio. Agent Watervliet here is our explosives expert. He'll do the touching."

Watervliet didn't look to Ali like the bomb squad guys back in Paloma. He was diminutive, with a head of greasy hair and cheap glasses that needed the lenses cleaned. Not unlike the skinny nerds who ran the movie projectors in her high school.

Ali led the eleven-man response team down an iron ladder that she thought must have been built when the IRT first drilled its way south in 2009. Remnants of the damage from the terrorist attacks had been wiped clean in the public areas. There was still soot and stained tile down here.

Powerful LEDs on hard hats cut beams of light out of the darkness.

"We're on the right track," Poole said. "The last visitors removed all the light bulbs to slow us down."

The vast amount of information Ali had processed over the last forty-eight hours was starting to congeal into a frightening scenario. "What are we backtiming to?"

"Backtiming?"

"When are these things supposed to detonate?"

"We thought it would be 9a.m.," Poole answered. "It's 11:40 now, so my guess is we've bought another day."

Ali shook her head. "Our girl wants to make a big splash so she wouldn't pull the trigger on a weekend. It's today. When do the most people frequent the streets down here."

One of the Con Ed men spoke up. "That would be the lunch hour. The workers are moving in and out at the start and end of the day. But they move around at lunch time. You can literally feel the rumble down here then."

That was already apparent to Ali. It was similar to the small earthquake when a train pulled into the station. Just more constant.

She thought of the precise timing needed to keep the trains properly spaced. The amount of time they had to find and disarm the explosive devices was running short.

If it was noon... Ali checked her watch.

"We've got twenty minutes," she said.

"What makes you so sure?" Poole wondered.

"Trust me. Get us the hell out of here before noon, or we'll be permanent residents."

EIGHTY-EIGHT

The Eighth Day - Phoenix

"Mr. Foster will furnish us with the time and place of his meeting with 'Angela Brown,' the name the Amore people have told us is the one that our suspect is using to lure him in," Bill Roberts told the group in the FBI conference room. "She will be wary of a police presence so ours will be minimal. No black and whites in the area, nothing that looks remotely like a cop car. I'll deploy one of my men when we know the location." He pointed to the camera gear on the table. "She probably knows what all of us look like."

Jess raised her hand. "Respectfully, Bill. This woman tried to kill my family, and one of your best agents. It's personal with me and I want to be there for the take down."

Danny Lopez shook his head. "That's precisely why it can't be you, Jessi. You're technically not even a sworn peace officer in this state and you're too emotionally involved. Let Bill's team handle this. If we pull it off, you'll have plenty of face time with her when we have her behind bars."

Jess could barely contain a professional façade. This was now highly personal. She wanted to be the one to take Ann down.

"She's hoping it will be me, Tio. If it is, she'll have to let her guard down. This is personal for her, too. If we are able to mitigate her big project, she'll blame me. If I'm the one who is there, she'll be too distracted to see the rest of you coming."

"I'm sorry, Jessica." Bill Roberts was kind but firm. "People at the highest echelons are watching this one. We have to follow the book."

Damn the book to Hell, Jess thought. Whenever we follow the book, people get killed. She would have to figure this one out on her own. Out loud she murmured, "OK, Bill. You're the boss." But her eyes were on Brent Foster. And his were on her.

Mario McCallister interrupted the debate.

"Director Roberts," he said. "Vega is online! I've decrypted her conversation!"

Капитан

"The plan is compromised."

Vega

"We solved for this eventuality. There are 27 detonation points on each of the 5 fiber rings. If anyone as much as touches one of the packages, the destruct sequence immediately activates."

Капитан

"The two men you chose to lead the assignment tried to escape. What does that tell you about your judgment? How do we know the work was done correctly?"

Vega

"It tells me that we should have wired the final payments to their accounts as they requested. They were under surveillance. We could terminate them at any time. It was your idea to save a few rubles by killing people before they got paid."

Капитан

"Be that as it may, they were in FBI custody this morning."

Vega

"Where are they now?"

Капитан

"Dead. Our man terminated them as they left the airport with two FBI agents As I have repeatedly warned, your obsession with these men in Arizona has been a disastrous distraction."

Vega

"I think not, but we'll know for sure in about 10 minutes."

EIGHTY-NINE

New York

"Over here, Officer Clark."

The voice seemed far away. Ali ran in its direction. About seventy-five yards down the tunnel, three light beams were focused on a rectangular box that encircled a thick, black thousand-count fiber bundle. A small blue light on top of the box blinked at the rate of one pulse per second.

In another instant, Watervliet was beside them. He produced a small device that looked to Ali like the infrared thermometer she used to make sure her grill was hot enough for cooking. A crowd surrounded Watervliet as he grasped the handle and adjusted the sensitivity with a thumbwheel.

"This is a Mass Spectrometer," he said. "Keep an eye on the display. If it turns red, we'll know what's inside that box."

He pulled the trigger as Ali reflexively checked her watch. It was 11:55.

The device beeped.

"Composition C RDX." Watervliet's voice sounded like he was reading his pizza order over the telephone.

Ali knew exactly what he was talking about.

"Plastic explosive. Blast radius?"

"About fifty yards."

Poole jumped in. "Anyone see anything else like this?"

A New York cop nodded. "About fifty yards that-away."

Ali turned and sprinted in the direction of the street level and safety. It was 300 yards away. A message lit up her iPhone. She read it on her watch. "12 Noon is H-Hour. Get to safety now!"

"This is all going up in five minutes, gentlemen," she yelled over her shoulder. "Last one up the ladder is a dead man."

NINETY

Phoenix

Brent Foster knew the drill. He had been through it and escaped justice before. The 2016 Dodge Charger looked like any other car. The subtle sign that it was a federal ride was a complete lack of dealer markings anywhere on the vehicle. Brent Foster watched the Phoenix scenery pass by from the back seat. Agent Murphy was next to him. Foster assumed that the outward facade of relaxation was typical FBI. Inside, the agent was coiled and ready to act, should his prisoner decide to do something stupid. The driver was following his Waze app, guiding him through the subdivision maze in the direction of home.

"I appreciate you letting me hang out at home." Foster tried to sound grateful. It was the one emotion he wasn't feeling. "I'm expecting some birthday presents today for one of the girls. They will require a signature."

"I'll be keeping you company until you hear from our subject," Murphy said. "Standard procedure."

"Come on. Is that really necessary?"

"You're now a flight risk, Mr. Foster. This is for our mutual benefit."

"This may be the last bit of privacy I have for a long time." Foster held out his hands like a magician attempting to show that there was nothing up his sleeve. "I would appreciate some solitude."

"I'm sorry, sir. You're not leaving my sight until we make an arrest tonight."

"Just what did this woman do to make you guys want to cut a deal with me?"

"You'll hopefully read all about it in twenty-four hours."

IN VEGA'S APARTMENT, the digital clock on her laptop ticked off the final sixty seconds. The scent of her perfume hung in the air. Except for the quiet beeps emanating from the computer's speakers the place was dead silent. At the five-second mark, a woman's voice took over.

"Five, four, three, two, one, showtime."

AS ALI SCRAMBLED up the ladder, the twenty-seven C4 explosive charges detonated. In search of oxygen, a fireball followed the eleven men and one woman toward the ladder.

And into the Cortland subway station. Watervliet brought up the rear, clawing his way up as the volcanic conflagration erupted. The others watched in horror as his body was consumed by concentration of fire and heat.

There was no time to mourn. They scrambled toward the exit and daylight.

Agent Poole collapsed on the pavement when the team reached the surface.

"I'll never doubt you again," he said.

THE DOOR to Vega's apartment burst open. Three assassins entered, the Crimson Trace laser beams on their AR15s sweeping the room for their target.

"*Prover' vezde*," one said in Russian. Check everywhere.

The place was small. It took only a moment to confirm that nobody was home. The three circled the laptop. The man who had given the initial order pressed his finger against an earpiece, activating the microphone.

"*Ona ne zdes'.*" She's not here.

A communications terminal opened on the laptop screen. Green letters slowly spelled a single word in English. "Goodbye."

Vega knew more about poisons than she did about plastic explosives. The charge under the kitchen table was more than enough to do the job. When it detonated, the blast vaporized the two apartments on either side. Vega liked her former neighbors. She hoped that nobody else was home.

NINETY-ONE

Phoenix

"A new delivery has arrived, for Brent."

The Amazon Echo in Brent Foster's living room alerted him that his daughter's birthday presents were arriving. Agent Murphy was unmoved. He sat across from his prisoner on a U-Shaped sectional couch.

"For Christ's sake," Foster said. "At least let me go to the bathroom alone. And can you please put the handcuffs on in front so I can aim? The hall bath has only one small window. I'm too big to get through it, and your man is sitting in the driveway facing it."

He had sold Murphy. "Okay. Turn around and I'll make the adjustment."

Foster was the soul of compliance.

"Thank you," he said. "I won't forget this."

Murphy inserted the key into the right manacle. "Let's just behave." He held tightly onto the wrist that was still cuffed.

"Turn around, slowly."

Foster did.

He saw his opening and slammed a fist as hard as he could

against Murphy's carotid artery. It had the desired effect, stunning the agent enough so he let go of Foster's left arm. The killer swung the open handcuffs through the air, connecting with Murphy's skull. The agent fell, unconscious to the floor just as the video doorbell chimed.

"A delivery for Mr. Foster?"

Foster took the measure of the UPS man on the screen of his cell phone. He was the right height and build.

Foster reached for Murphy's gun.

"I'll be right there."

NINETY-TWO

Phoenix

Bill Roberts watched Mario McCallister multitasking. The one screen, relaying the activity on Vega's computer went dark. In another window, the status of the five fiberoptic networks in New York blinked from green to red. He looked across the desk at the head of the FBI's Phoenix office.

"Something has happened in New York. We've lost the SONET rings."

Roberts leaned across his desk to look at the laptop. "What about Vega?"

"She must have disconnected. The screen said 'Goodbye.' She's gone."

"And the Phoenix Code? The brokerages?"

Mario flipped to a different window. Roberts knew that every major financial firm in the city was represented by an icon. Most still glowed green. The two firms who had rebuffed the FBI's warnings were bright red, along with one other major financial house.

"Just three down. Nehr and Groves for sure. They are the ones that wouldn't let us in. We installed at Kutzko Financial but it looks like something went wrong."

"Everyone has secure backups off site?"

"Yes. And we'll be there to help them restore, just in case our suspect changed her wipe code."

Bill Roberts felt a modicum of stress dissipate. There would still be disruptions, but it felt like his team had protected the U.S. Financial system from the worst of it.

"Where's Detective Ramirez?" Mario asked.

"At the hospital."

THE MAYO CLINIC was perennially the number one medical facility in Arizona. Like its sister institutions in Minnesota and Florida, it reflects the cultural architecture of its environment, a xeriscape of cactus, desert shrubbery and stone with an adobe feel that blends into the geography as if nature herself had helped design it.

Within its walls are some of the brightest minds in medicine. They are attracted to Mayo by the mix of challenging cases that coexist with the normal bumps and bruises of everyday medicine. There is just enough spice to keep brilliant minds limber, continually stretching the edge of the medical envelope to reveal new insights and the lifesaving treatments that come with them.

This was on Jessica Ramirez's mind as she sat at Michael Wright's bedside. He was off the ventilator. That was good. But the doctors were concerned that he still floated in and out of consciousness, eyes occasionally flickering with recognition, but silent, unwilling or unable to verbally respond to their queries.

She thought about watching him sleep as the sun rose that morning at the Grand Canyon Hotel. There was the same, peaceful half-smile, the strong, steady heartbeat thumped against her index finger as she held his hand, reflexively testing his pulse.

"I need to tell you something, Michael," she whispered. "I'm going after the woman myself."

Michael didn't react.

"Foster doesn't trust your brothers in arms. I think he'll bolt. Murphy is watching over him, but I know he'll find a way out. I'm just hoping that before he goes, he tells me where he was supposed to meet her, so I can get there first."

Jess imagined what Michael might say to all of this. *You're acting on emotion, Jessica. That's a weakness the enemy can exploit. Let the pros handle it.*

"This is something I have to do," she said, answering the silence. "She tried to destroy everything I care about." Emotion gripped her throat, choking the words as she attempted to say them. "I won't let her do that to anyone else."

Did that mean she would kill in cold blood, just as Vega had done to her victims? Would she cross into the darkness and become a murderer, too?

"I'll try to take her alive, Michael. I promise. But if she makes one wrong move, I won't hesitate to neutralize her, forever."

The door to the hospital room opened. A nurse's face appeared. "Detective Ramirez? You have a phone call."

NINETY-THREE

Phoenix

The rookie hadn't looked twice when Brent Foster emerged from the front door in the UPS driver's uniform and baseball cap. He didn't notice that Murphy's cell phone was in the man's hand instead of the electronic package scanner. The canvas backpack slung over the man's left shoulder and the bulge in the right pocket where Murphy's Glock now rested should have set off alarm bells. But they didn't.

As the brown step van pulled out of the subdivision, Foster tapped a text message into his disposable cell phone. He would use Murphy's for something else.

"'I know who you are and what you are planning. We need to talk. Call me."

THE QUIET VIBRATION of Jess's cell phone cut into the silence of Michael Wright's hospital room.

"Jess, it's Ali. Things are a royal mess here in beautiful New

York, but I think we beat your girlfriend to the punch and kept most of the stock market boys employed today."

"What happened?"

"The official line is that cause was undetermined but it has collapsed a number of tunnels, knocking out communications to much of the district. There are power outages, too. The event happened at the lunch hour. There are serious injuries."

"What's going on, girlfriend? A terrorist attack?"

"That's what it was. This woman you are after has a long reach, and associates."

"Associates?"

So this Vega wasn't working alone. The small flame of insight started to burn in Jess's mind. How far did her reach truly extend? Was there someone on the inside?

Ali continued. "She had help with the fiber thing. Seven guys are dead, five technicians and the two men the FBI believes were their handlers. It looks like whoever is pulling the strings kills the help when they don't need them anymore."

"Do you think our girl has just outlived her usefulness, too?"

"It's just a hunch, girlfriend, but if I were you, I'd be watching my back. Now that she knows we spoiled her party, she'll want some retribution. If she comes for you, there will likely be people close behind who are coming after her."

"It's tonight, Ali. She's meeting her mark tonight. I gave him a note when they took him out of the conference room this morning asking him to tell me when and where."

"Instead of telling the Feds?"

"This guy is so paranoid, he's not trusting anybody. I'm just hoping some of my Latina charm connected with him."

Ali grunted. "That's the longest of long shots. I bet my next paycheck against one of your mama's sangrias that we never hear from him again."

Jess's cell phone vibrated. The caller ID was blocked.

"Hold on a minute, Ali. I think this might be Murphy."

She punched the button to connect the call.

"Jessica Ramirez."

"Tonight at nine, The Caprice Bar. Alternate 89 South of Fredonia."

"Foster? Where's Agent Murphy?"

The line went dead.

NINETY-FOUR

Phoenix
　　Vega
　　Surprised to hear from me?
　　Капитан
　　Not surprised. Disappointed.
　　Vega
　　If this is the quality of your "Auditors," you need to raise your standards.
　　Капитан
　　No-one is irreplaceable.
　　Vega
　　Except for me, my friend. You had to know that I would create contingencies.
　　Капитан
　　What is your contingency for your utter failure in New York?
　　Vega
　　You underestimate me. This is one job where I plan to over deliver.
　　Капитан

What proof can you give me?

Vega

In another 72 hours you will have all the proof you require. The work is already done and the clock is ticking. Prepare to transmit my final payment. And don't send any other amateurs to try to eliminate me.

Капитан

Your own addictions are your undoing.

Vega

They come with the package. They are what drive me to be the professional I am.

Капитан

You have your 72 hours. Do not fail again.

Vega

Just have my money ready. And leave me alone.

———

JESSICA RAMIREZ STOOD outside of FBI Phoenix Director Bill Roberts' private office. She could hear the familiar voices of her uncle and the director in heated conversation inside. What she was about to demand was dynamite. As she knocked, Jess had the uneasy feeling she was walking into a powder keg.

"Come."

As director-level quarters went, Robert's office was Spartan. Besides a desk and a pair of chairs, there was only a small credenza and a few family pictures on the khaki-colored walls. A window provided the only color, with a panoramic view of the street below.

Jess felt bad for the director. Sheriff Lopez's digs were ostentatious by comparison.

Roberts' voice was impatient. "What is it, Detective?"

"I heard from Foster."

The cool, emotionless expression that Jess had come to recognize as standard issue for FBI agents cracked. Her uncle, sitting across from Roberts, jumped to his feet.

"Tell us, Jessica." When Tio Danny used her full name, Jess knew he was serious.

"He called me. I asked him to do it when he left the meeting and he came through. He told me where the meeting is tonight."

Now Roberts was on his feet, his fists on his desktop, leaning toward her.

"And?"

"And, I want you to let me take her down."

The director glanced at the sheriff. Technically, Jessica was in his chain of command. It should be Danny who laid down the law.

"We talked about this, Jessi. This is too big and too important. Foster put Agent Murphy into intensive care about a half hour ago. He killed a UPS driver and stole the kid's truck. He got away from us. Director Roberts has to report that misstep to Washington in about five minutes. We don't need this right now."

"She killed my father, Tio."

"All the more reason that you should not be involved. When things get personal, mistakes get made."

Roberts' patience was wearing thin.

"Tell us where the meeting is taking place, Detective. That's an order."

Jess hesitated.

"If you refuse, I'll have your badge and gun, your career in law enforcement will be over and you will spend the next ten years in a Federal prison with every perpetrator you ever arrested."

Jess had seconds to sell the plan. "She will know if you have the place staked out. This woman has been a step ahead of us the whole way. She already has an exit strategy. We have no idea what it is. And it's personal for her, too. She believes that Officer Clark and I threw a hand grenade into her plan. If it's me that she sees--"

Danny interrupted. "She'll kill you on the spot. the family has already lost a loved one, Jessica. I'm not going to risk losing another."

Roberts' private line buzzed. He activated the speaker phone, clearly annoyed at the interruption.

"What is it, Vanessa?"

The admin's voice seemed to be vibrating. "It's *Vega* on line one. No Caller ID or GPS tracking. We have the cell tower location. Agents are on the way."

Roberts held his finger over the blinking yellow button, looking back and forth between Danny and Jessica. The trio was too stunned to say anything.

The director shrugged and opened the connection.

"This is Director William Roberts. Who is speaking?"

The voice was dead calm. "Hello, Bill. We meet at last. I know who you are and you know who I am. I'm calling to dictate the terms of my surrender."

"Where are you?"

"Oh, it's not going to be that easy, Bill. We'll do things my way or no way at all. You know that I can easily disappear. I'm used to dealing with people who are much more ruthless than your little boy scouts. I know you boys had UPS track their delivery truck. It's stationary now. I've saved the State several million dollars in incarceration expense. All your kids have to do is sweep up the ashes. Are you ready to write down my directions?"

"Come in from the cold, now Vega. Tell us who you are working for and I promise to get you the best possible deal I can with the prosecution."

"I'm only going to say these things one time, Bill. So, you, Sheriff Lopez and Detective Ramirez had better take some notes."

How in the hell, Jess wondered, *did Vega know I am here?*

It was as if the woman had read her mind. "Yes, Jessica, I know you are in the room. Where else would you go once you learned about how I had planned our little date night? Your Chihuahua tenacity has been an inconvenience. The same goes for your lesbian friend. When you see her, tell that she was a lousy fuck."

Roberts intervened. "What is it that you want, Vega?"

"I want the girl whose father I killed. I want her to be the one to bring me in. Meet me for our assignation at the time and place the late Mr. Foster shared with you, Jessica. It will be single combat, Detective Ramirez. Just you and me. 'mano a mano'. Come tonight, Jessica. Alone."

Vega's calm continence turned stern. "And Bill, keep your boy scouts ten miles from the meeting place. I have people who will tell me if you don't and I will vanish. You won't know where or when I'll pop up again, but I promise you it will be connected to something that won't shed a positive light on your series of fuck-ups. Are we clear?"

Roberts showed a palm to Jessica. She was about to get her wish.

"I'll be there." Jessica nearly spat the words. "Be prepared to enjoy your last afternoon of freedom."

The cat-like calm returned to Vega's voice. "How sexy, Jessica. I wish I had time to teach you some of the moves I made in bed with Michael Wright. If the brain damage isn't too bad, perhaps he might recover enough to show you some day. Dress casual, girlfriend. Goodbye, boys and girl."

The line went dead.

Roberts had his admin on it an instant later.

"Did you get it? Did we triangulate her location?"

"Yes, sir. It's the same spot where police and fire are responding to a personal injury accident, an explosion. Perhaps ten minutes from the office."

"Have the supervisors meet me in the conference room in twenty minutes. All of them."

"There is one more thing." Vanessa paused, her voice cracking. "Agent Murphy passed away while you were on the call. I just got the call from the hospital."

Roberts slammed the phone onto its cradle with such force, Jessica thought it might break. He turned silently toward the window, contemplating the mass of humanity on the street below.

"Thousands of faces from every conceivable race, creed and color, each intent on pursuing their own definition of The American Dream. Each totally ignorant of the evil that we struggle to keep at bay."

He turned to face Jess.

"When I first became a Special Agent, the racial undertones that still manifest out there were not nearly as subtle as they are now. But I was lucky enough to have backup. That person is now the second highest ranking agent in the Bureau. He's white. But he risked his own career on several occasions to give a black man the chance to show that I do the job as good, or better than anyone else of any color."

Roberts was focused on Tio Danny now.

"We all know that this is a trap. We know that this person has resources spying on us in this very building. I'm painted into a corner. And I have no idea how to get out of it without leaving some very messy footprints on the floor."

Jess's head was spinning. She was going to get what she was demanding. She had no idea how to pull it off.

"Here's your chance, Detective. What do you propose to do?"

Jess saw a smile slowly starting to make its way across Danny Lopez's face.

"I think I have an idea."

NINETY-FIVE

70 miles north of Flagstaff

On Friday nights, the patrons are wall to wall at Caprese. Its proximity to the National Park entrance and the wide variety of liquor served attract both locals and travelers. Jessica Ramirez slipped her iPhone into her bra. The rest of her kit was in the butt pack around her waist. If things went as planned, Vega would be expecting Ben Foster and not the woman who intended to arrest her.

"How many in your party?"

The hostess was young, dressed in hiking boots, jeans and a thin flannel shirt that covered a dark green, sleeveless T-shirt. Her short brown hair and makeup-free complexion told Jess that she was probably a park service employee by day.

"I'm meeting someone," she said above the noise of a score of simultaneous conversations, not quite sure if that was the right way to put it.

"Ah, yes. She's over there. The booth under the waterfall poster."

Jess scanned the booth. A black backpack sat next to Vega

against the wall. It was zipped shut. There were no telltale handgun bulges. She wore tight-fitting cargo shorts that highlighted powerful legs. Her arms and shoulders screamed "gym rat." The T-shirt that covered her sports bra did not print a firearm that Jess could see. But there were many places to hide a weapon.

Vega had a half smile on her face. She pointed to the seat across from her.

"Jessica Ramirez, detective extraordinaire, lover of FBI agents and a fish out her depth, even in a small pond like Flagstaff."

Jess remained standing. Her tone was measured, professional.

"I'm here to arrest you for three murders and a half dozen federal charges ranging from terrorism to espionage."

"I know, I know. All in good time. Sit down. I want to get to know the woman who torpedoed my best laid plans."

"Adele Bannister," Jess said. "Also known as the international hacker, 'Vega', also known as Ann Blakely, Angela Brown, Amelia Bowen and Angelica Brewer."

"I liked that last one. It has a Hollywood feel to it."

"Seduced and murdered Christopher Stone, Harold Lattimer, Alton Mahoney, and Jacob Reily with Ben Foster on deck."

"It didn't take you long to put a name to that dirt bag, Riley. Those four are the ones you know about? There are many more."

"Graduate of the University of Oregon with a dual major in biochemistry and computer science. Worked overseas for Avarice Synthetics. Interesting name for a chemical weapons company. Hired by a dark web terrorist organization who wants to take down the New York City financial district. Killer of at least five civilians and the attempted murderer of an FBI special agent. Wanted in at least six countries. Quite a resume."

"I've always been an overachiever."

A waitress appeared. "Would you like something to drink, ma'am?"

"Nothing, thank you." Jess was annoyed by the distraction.

"Oh come on. I'm drinking," Vega said. "The least you can do is be hospitable and join me. We have all night to conclude our business."

"A club soda with lime," Jess said, shooing the server away. "Tell me something, 'Vega.' Why did you do it all? There's no money in murder and the people you work for kill their help when they are no longer helpful. I'm surprised your handler hasn't dispatched someone to toss you in the canyon after your boyfriends."

"He's tried. I always have an exit strategy."

"Not tonight you don't."

Jess was feeling confident. A small voice in her head warned that confidence without attention to detail could kill you. She knew that Vega had no intention of following anyone's plan but her own. Jess had fifteen minutes to take her down.

"Let's face it, Jessica. Men are, by and large, liars and cheats. Every one of the scum bags I killed deserved killing. You've read three of the rap sheets. Guilty as hell and the system let them walk. And what about your handsome FBI guy? Fucking me one day and you the next? How does that feel?"

That last one hurt. Jess swallowed hard and pressed on.

"Someone with your brains could have helped us lock those losers up for a long time. I don't understand the black widow mentality. Isn't it more fun if they have to stew inside the joint and think about how you beat them?"

"At forty thousand a year of my tax money? Prisons are the biggest waste of space and time on the planet. My solution costs less than a grand a piece. And nobody is building up twenty years of hate to throw at you when they get out for so called 'good behavior.'"

"Why the terrorism thing, Vega? What do you hope to gain by cratering the world economy?"

"That was just a money play. Like your friend Gates, I loved the challenge. I've always been the smartest one in my class, better than the boys and more creative in my solutions. I had the FBI scratching their heads. If it wasn't for your partner, we would be relocating an entire class of snobs into the low rent district and my holdings would triple in value."

Jess didn't like the fact that Vega seemed to know so much about her and the team. Where was she getting that information?

"Everyone owns securities these days," she said. "You're hurting a world of widows and orphans, too. Or didn't that cross your brilliant mind?"

"There's only one orphan I care about and she was going to be one of the new rich."

"How well did that one work for ya?" There was sarcasm in Jess's voice.

"If at first you don't succeed... Gates was a great beta tester for me. She taught me what adjustments to make. That has been done. In continuum of history, another twenty-four hours will mean nothing. I will still win."

The waitress appeared with Jess's soft drink. The Detective suddenly felt tired and thirsty. This had truly been a week from hell. She took a long pull through the straw.

"From what I hear, you won't be getting another chance. You're in the association's cross hairs, Vega. Your gas man who tried to kill my family probably has his sights set on you now. Your handlers don't like mistakes and you've made some pretty big ones."

Vega dismissed this. "I've vanished before. I can do it again."

"Let me ask you another thing," Jess said. "Where does a civilian get her hands on Bergulon?"

"You surprise me, Jessica. If I can take down your little electronic police playroom, I can easily get whatever I desire in the wide world of chemistry. Didn't your mother tell you that the recipe is much more important than the ingredients? That's on the first page of the migrant workers' cookbook."

Jess took a final pull off of the club soda. It was time.

"It all ends here, Vega. They let me have a few minutes with you because I wanted some private time with the woman who tried to kill my family. I don't know what happened in your past to turn you into the monster you are today, but you'll have a long time to ponder that after your trial."

"Let's not forget one thing, Jessica. I did succeed in one important way. Your father is dead."

NINETY-SIX

Grand Canyon GCN Airport

The private jet touched down right on schedule. Its sole passenger nodded to the two pilots as he deplaned, slinging a backpack over his broad shoulders.

"We were told to wait," the captain said.

"Refuel at your leisure. I'll be engaged for at least a couple of hours. I have your cell number."

A representative from the rental car company was waiting on the tarmac. He held a pair of keys in his hand for the Jeep Cherokee that was parked twenty yards away, inside the airport's security perimeter.

"You must know someone important," the rep said to the passenger. "They never let me bring a vehicle this close."

The passenger nodded and took the keys.

"Can I get your luggage?" the rep called after him.

The passenger waved him away.

The rep exchanged glances with the flight crew, pointing at the figure retreating into the darkness.

"Who is he?"

The captain shook his head.

"Won't tell?" the rep asked.

"Don't know."

NINETY-SEVEN

Caprice

Jess stood. She suddenly felt like the floor beneath her feet was rubbery and unsteady. She looked down at the glass. There was no way Vega could have spiked it. She was watching it the whole time. Grabbing for the table, she tumbled back into the booth.

Vega was smiling, dripping with scorn.

"Feeling a little unsure of yourself, Jessica?"

"How did you do it?" Jess's world was starting to spin. It felt like the time she lost a margarita drinking contest to a 300-pound linebacker in college.

"Who do you think you're dealing with?" Vega said. The casual expression had drained from her face. She looked at Jess with dead seriousness. "I like working alone. But just like you, I always make sure I have backup. My friend at the bar thought he was giving you a little white lightning with your soda pop. A surprise present for the birthday girl, I told him. That and a twenty-dollar bill was all it took."

"This isn't your killer muscle relaxant," Jess slurred. "I'd be on the floor by now."

"We'll address that bit of chemistry later. Right now, I need to help my drunken friend get safely out of this bar. You know how people like to take advantage of women who have had a little too much sangria."

Vega threw her backpack over a shoulder and pulled Jess up by her sore arm. The pain sharpened her senses and gave her back a little of the control she had lost.

The waitress appeared. "No food tonight, ladies?"

"My friend here overdid it before she even got here," Vega lied. "Can you believe that? I've left a fifty on the table for you. That should more than cover things. Make sure you share the extra with Jeffrey at the bar. He's been of inestimable value tonight."

"I sure will," the waitress said. "I hope we'll see you both again."

"Sadly, we're just passing through, my dear. You can bet I'll give you five stars on Yelp though."

The two women weaved their way through the crowded bar and out into the parking lot. Jess wanted to scream. Her vocal cords wouldn't respond.

"Let's see what we've got," Vega said, unbuckling the butt pack from Jess's waist. "Feels like the typical cop stuff. Bracelets and bang bangs."

She leaned Jess up against the side of the black pickup truck she had stolen for the occasion. It had an "NRA" bumper sticker in the back window. A citizen's band radio antenna undulated in the breeze.

Vega patted Jess down with the attention to detail of a professional.

"No wires," she said. "I would have thought someone would have wanted to hear our conversation."

She quickly found the cell phone. Reaching down Jess's shirt, she retrieved it. Off came the iWatch and Jess's Fitbit.

"I bet they are keeping an eye on your location with these babies," Vega said.

A four-wheel drive rumbled by on the road. She tossed the technology into the truck bed as it passed.

"That should give them something fun to follow," she said, opening the door to her vehicle and shoving Jess into the passenger seat. She wrapped the handcuffs around the seatbelt and secured them to Jess's wrists. "I know you usually put peoples' arms behind them. But I don't want you screaming in pain just yet."

Vega slid into the driver's seat and put the vehicle into reverse.

NINETY-EIGHT

Flagstaff Pulliam Airport

Twenty-five miles to the east, three concerned faces were reflected in the dim illumination of a pair of laptop screens. Mario McCallister, Alexandra Clark and Marty Laurent sat at a table in a corner of the Arizona Hello Hangar at the Flagstaff Airport. Outside, Danny Lopez paced a wide circle around a Robinson R3 chopper, the pilot casually counting his laps.

"She's headed east," Mario said as he watched the progress of Jessica's cell phone on his display. "Time to intervene?"

Ali looked at Marty Laurent. "What do you say?"

Marty was hunched over his own laptop. An obsolete version of the UI-View automated position reporting software, APRS for short, flickered on the screen. "Kilo Alpha Eight Tango Golf Uniform looks to be stationary," he answered. "But APRS devices don't update until there's movement. That truck is still in the same place."

"Assuming she's still taking the truck," Ali said. "Everything this woman has done has been super smart. I wouldn't put it past her to have a second vehicle we don't know about."

"Oh, we thought of that one," Marty said.

"Who's we?"

"Smitty and I. He's got the truck prepared, with a plan B in case she has another ride in the parking lot."

"I thought you said Smitty was busy tonight."

"He is. Busy paying me back for not dying on him at the Crystal Rapid."

"Our team doesn't know anything about this."

"That was the idea," Marty said. "Trust no one and prepare for all eventualities. I think someone I know gave me that advice."

Ali shook her head. "I had better tell the sheriff. He may have new orders for you."

She looked at Mario's screen. "Still eastbound?"

Mario nodded.

She put a hand on Marty's shoulder and looked at the plaster cast that held his right leg in place from hip to heel. "And Mr. Plan B?"

Marty held up a small handheld amateur radio. "We'll know in a minute."

Ali pushed the transmit button on her ROVER. "Stand by, Danny. Something's going down at Caprice."

NINETY-NINE

The Caprice Parking Lot

Kevin Smith leaned back on the saddle of his 2015 Kawasaki H2 motorcycle. Statistics said that a person was four times more likely to die on one of these crotch rockets when compared to more sedate two wheelers. Smitty was still young, single and fearless. He liked straddling a 998cc inline-four, four-valve DOHC engine and taking the machine to the edge of the envelope. He thought about the beautiful nurse he met at church and how he had better get around to popping the question before someone else did.

That could wait at least one more day. Tonight, he was just another innocuous motorcycle jockey in a circle of leather-clad bike enthusiasts. That was the idea.

He witnessed two women leaving the bar, one barely able to walk in a straight line. They went right to the pickup where a Byonics MT-AIO GPS tracker was carefully hidden. A backup unit was charged up and ready to roll in his backpack. A Yaesu FT2D handheld hung from his belt, connected to one of the network of solar powered repeaters his amateur radio club deployed to provide communications beyond the reach of cell towers.

The driver pulled carefully back out of her parking space and merged with westbound traffic. Smitty looked at the display on the Yaesu. It beeped, recording the movement of the GPS unit in the truck bed. So far, so good.

"N4FMQ," he said, articulating his ham radio call sign into the handheld. "Check UI-View. They are 'westbound and down.'"

"THE MICKEY I slipped you will start to wear off soon," Vega said. "I want your full attention for a bit longer."

Jess didn't feel like anything was wearing off. She was dizzy and nauseous. Vertigo without the altitude. Her eyes couldn't focus as she tried to look at her captor. She still couldn't speak.

Vega continued. "It's pretty good stuff. Dental variety, like nitrous on steroids. I've heard that they could pull out all four of your wisdom teeth with a pair of rusty pliers and you wouldn't feel a thing."

SMITTY PULLED the chin strap to his helmet tight around his jaw. He could hear Marty through its built-in headset.

"We've got 'em. Danny says you'll be on your own for a bit until we can get there. We don't want her knowing that we know where she's going."

"You have a great gift for rhyme," Smitty said, mimicking Inigo Montoya from Princess Bride.

"Some of the time," Marty shot back.

"I DON'T UNDERSTAND her get-away plan," Ali said. "She has to know that we'll be all over her in less than a half hour. Every exit is covered."

Mario patted Marty on the back. "We'll have them on the map until they ditch their ride. Hopefully your boy Smitty can keep close enough to point us in the right direction. "

———

VEGA PULLED the pickup off the road and into the thicket of trees she knew well. She timed her exit carefully. Not another car was in sight when she made the move.

She grabbed Jess by the chin, turning her head to get a clear look into her eyes. Vega slapped her twice. "Time to walk off that hangover."

As Vega dragged Jess out of the truck, she could hear the sound of a motorcycle in the distance.

ONE HUNDRED

West of Flagstaff

The driver of the Jeep Cherokee had no idea how his handlers could pinpoint the exact location of his targets. That was none of his concern. The US Geological Survey terrain maps were still fresh in his mind, including secluded spots where he could park his ride while he was working.

If he felt any remorse about the assignment he had been given, an outsider wouldn't have been able to spot it. The only sign of emotion was in the way he fingered the pair of small silver dice that hung around his neck. He felt a pleasurable whisper of his night with the woman who gave the bauble to him.

That was then. This was now.

He knew the wet team that had failed in Phoenix. They were very good. But not nearly as good as he was. And the notion of serving two masters didn't appeal to his sense of professional loyalty. After tonight, he would only be serving one.

The driver of the Cherokee rolled down the driver's side window. With a slight tug he broke the clasp on the silver necklace, tossing it and the pair of dice into the slipstream as his vehicle picked up speed.

ONE HUNDRED ONE

Grand Canyon National Park - West Rim

"No more movement," Marty said over the repeater. "Keep your eyes open. Even with this clear night, it will be easy to miss."

"Just like hunting foxes back in Michigan," Kevin said, remembering how he and his dad used to seek out hidden transmitters with their local ham radio club.

"Slow down a bit," Marty said. He could see the motorcycle's avatar closing on the small blue truck icon on his laptop. "You're less than a half mile away."

JESSICA RAMIREZ'S legs were working again, although her brain couldn't yet fully comprehend it. Somehow, Vega had re-cuffed her wrists behind her and was pushing her through a row of trees. Jess had no idea how long she had been walking. She decided to try out her voice.

"Where are we going?"

"Ahh. Someone is getting her faculties back."

Vega punctuated the last word with a shove. Jess stumbled forward but kept her balance.

"You're passing the test," Vega said. "Time for a talk while we walk."

"You haven't answered my question."

"We'll be there soon enough. And it won't matter as far as you're concerned. I've taken us off the grid. Nobody will find you. At least not up here."

"What's the point?" Jess felt her strength returning. "What benefit is there in killing me?"

"Let's just say that I'm a vengeful person. For someone who can easily dispose of guilty murderers, taking the next step to a woman who attempted to destroy my grand plan isn't too much of a stretch."

"Attempted? We shut your operation down."

"We'll talk about that in a moment. Right now, I want to show you where I dispense my justice."

"I read your backstory," Jess said. The vigorous walk was quickly clearing out whatever had compromised her consciousness. "Losing a parent to suicide isn't something you can easily get over. Add a disinterested father who has the psychiatric skills to screw with your head and it's not surprising you're confused."

"Confused? My dear, I've never thought more clearly in my life. It's black and white to me. You kill and you shall be killed. You steal and you shall lose your ill-gotten gains. You, young lady, have stolen my livelihood and put my life in danger. I'll need a total reinvention from ground zero. For the average person that would take a lifetime."

"But not for a genius like you?"

"Thank you for that. I've done it before as you well know. I can do it again. But you've caused me a great deal of inconvenience and you must pay the price. I understand your boyfriend didn't handle the Bergulon so well. I wonder how his recovery will be impacted when he learns he's lost his love?"

Even in the darkness, Vega could tell that this one hit home.

"You see, my dear, I know a lot more about you than you think I do. The little swimming star whose daddy wouldn't let her join the Olympic team? So you got back at him by becoming a cop. You exist in a world where you have to keep proving yourself in front of men who would just as soon see you fail. And every one of them wants to get inside those tight cargo pants. What kind of life is that, Jessica? You ought to try swinging on the other side of the fence like your friend Officer Clark."

Vega paused for effect.

"She was a disappointment."

"We reflect what we get," Jess snarled. "From what I hear, you weren't that good either."

Vega shrugged. "After tonight, it will be a forgotten paragraph in an FBI report, along with two sentences about a Mexican who spent his last hour alive crying remorsefully in a confessional."

Jessica lunged at her captor, attempting to head butt Vega in the stomach. She missed her mark and tumbled onto the hard ground.

ONE HUNDRED TWO

Grand Canyon National Park - West Rim

There was only one way they could have gone, thought Kevin Smith. With a single break in the roadside tree line, there had to be a path.

Smitty pulled a hiker's GPS unit out of his backpack and studied the topographical map. The canyon rim was less than a mile away with a nice 600-foot clearing between the forest and the rim.

He keyed his handheld.

"November Four Foxtrot Mike Quebec. Mark my location and send in the troops. I reckon they are headed due south."

DANNY LOPEZ WAS LOOKING over Marty Laurent's shoulder at the laptop screen. He scribbled the coordinates onto a piece of paper and called his pilot.

"Lennie, spin her up. I've got vectors for you. Mario, get on the horn to the office. All available units to that location."

Ali leaned back in the steel folding chair. She closed her eyes and pressed her thumb and index finger on the bridge of her nose.

Mario gave her a moment before speaking.

"What are you thinking?"

"She has to have an exit strategy."

"What do you mean?"

"She has never made a move without having the next two moves already planned out."

Ali opened her eyes and slid next to Marty.

"Show me the terrain up there."

Marty pressed a couple of keys and the UI-View application rendered the same topographical image Smitty was looking at miles away. The tree line broke into a clearing in a U-shape. There seemed to be only one way to go, toward the canyon's rim.

"What would we do if we were her?" Ali asked.

Marty ran a finger across the edge of the canyon. "She knows we are coming for her from the road, so that's out. The way I see it she has two choices: down or up."

"Explain," Mario said.

"That clearing is ideal for a chopper landing. You can bet that's where Sheriff Lopez is headed now. She's either got someone else coming to pick her up, or..."

Ali jumped in. "Or she's headed into the canyon. How far is that drop, Marty?"

"Five hundred fifty-three feet."

"And what's the longest rappelling rope they sell over the counter?"

"Six hundred feet."

"That's gotta be it. What's at the bottom of the canyon?"

"Just the river. There are no usable trails nearby. The water is her only way out. She would be about two miles from the Crystal Rapid. It's smooth sailing after that obstacle, but I sure as heck wouldn't want to run it at night."

"That's gotta be it," Ali said. "Mario, can you get us some

cavalry down to the river at the first easy take-out point after the rapids?"

Mario motioned to a female FBI agent that stood near the entrance to the hangar. He thought to himself that Bill Roberts might have had Gates in mind when he picked this agent for tonight's assignment. In many ways, she and Ali could have been twins.

———

ALI, on the other hand, was studying the woman for different reasons. The nearly invisible communication between two people who shared the same sexual preference was coming at her like a flame thrower. When this was all done, Ali thought to herself, I need to get to know this person better.

Ali shook the idea out of her head, forcing her attention back toward her colleague.

"What about backup?"

"I can get you whatever you want," Mario said, writing a note and handing it to the agent.

"But unless they are very lucky," Marty added, "it will be a recovery operation and not a rescue."

ONE HUNDRED THREE

Flagstaff Pulliam Airport

The chopper carrying Sheriff Danny Lopez lifted slowly off the tarmac and ascended into the darkness. Danny noted that there wasn't much traffic on the roads at this hour. All he could make out was what looked like a black Jeep Cherokee pulling into the executive aviation lot.

He turned his attention to the panorama ahead. With a full moon and a carpet of stars illuminating the scenery, one could almost navigate as if it were daylight.

THE FBI AGENT stepped into the open air outside of the hangar. A soft breeze encircled her with a confluence of scents, a memory of the heat of the day and the cool promise of an Arizona evening. She had just finished dialing Bill Roberts' cell number when she heard the voice.

"Officer Clark?"

There was a resemblance, she thought. An easy mistake that

was especially possible at night. The agent looked up, and was about to speak when the muffled report of a silenced Volquartsen Scorpion 22LR bit into the silence of the evening.

THE SHOOTER FIRED a second headshot as the agent's crumpled form sprawled on the concrete parking lot.

"Nice to have met you."

He returned to his vehicle, pointing the Cherokee toward the receding drone of the police helicopter.

ONE HUNDRED FOUR

Grand Canyon National Park - West Rim

Jess and Vega broke free of the trees. The same brilliant sky that Vega used to illuminate her coital activities painted the gentle transition from green grasses to sedimentary rock with a silver glow. She twisted the handcuffs that held Jessica's arms fast behind her torso, forcing her victim to the ground.

"Ok, sister. Time for some final goodbyes."

Jess was grateful to be on her back, even though the steel from the cuffs cut into her wrists from the weight of her body pressing against the hard turf. Vega would expect her to fight, but Jess needed time and cover to execute her plan.

Her opponent was wearing a mountaineer's harness which Jess thought might be her ticket to a helicopter extraction.

"It doesn't have to be this way," Jess said. "With your knowledge and experience, there may be other options. Have you ever thought about a job with the Feds? They could learn a lot from a smart person like you."

Vega leaned her head back and laughed.

"You see those stars up there?" she said. "That's probably the number of people in the organization who are chomping at the bit to earn a payday by killing me. And you think prison will keep them away? Jesus, half of their guys are probably already inmates."

"It could be done." Jess was selling it. She rolled over on one side to look Vega in the eyes as she moved a hand into her right rear pants pocket. "You write the ticket. Tell us where you want to be incarcerated. We'll vet everyone who has access. You're smart enough to help us identify them. Knock out enough of the team and there isn't a judge in the land who won't look kindly on your situation."

"You're making one error, sweetheart. You're assuming I'm going to get caught. That's not going to happen."

Vega turned to her backpack, carefully unzipping it. She retrieved a face mask connected to a small plastic tube. She slid one end of the tube over the mouthpiece of her vape pen.

Vega rolled Jess on to her back, pinning her shoulders to the ground with Vega's knees. She hovered the mask over Jess's face, shaking the contents of the vaporizer to make sure the mixture would be fast and effective.

"That little project in New York you think you stopped? The truth is, I've been watching your every move. The little worm your friend Gates thought she was deploying to stop me? I modified it. When it's done its work in the Big Apple, Alexandra's creation will clone itself in every major stock exchange around the globe. If she was really that smart, she would have figured that one out."

The handcuff key was almost where it needed to be. But this news stopped Jess cold.

"How?"

"Do you think I work alone? I deployed my own Trojan Horse and none of you even thought to question it."

Vega bent down until Jess could feel the singe of her hot breath.

"Anything you want me to say to your FBI friend? I'll be stopping by to see him on my way out of town."

Jess reddened.

"Oh, I'm not going to fuck him. I'm going to kill him."

Vega pressed the face mask against Jess's mouth.

"If there's an afterlife, I'll just be making sure you two lovers get to share it together, starting now. Just breathe for me, Jessica. It will all be over in a few minutes."

The cuffs were off of one of Jess's wrists. That was enough.

She put every ounce of her anger into the blow. A throat punch knocked Vega off balance. A hip thrust, rolled her adversary onto the ground.

Both women were instantly on their feet. Jess kicked the face mask and vaporizer away from the field of battle.

Vega ran at her, trying to grab Jess around the waist. The detective side-stepped the move, throwing her perp closer to the canyon's rim. As Vega crouched to regain her balance, Jess leveled a front kick under her chin.

KEVIN SMITH STOOD at the edge of the tree line. The GPS he planted in the pickup truck had done its job. Now the raft driver turned volunteer cop was providing a play-by-play via his handheld amateur radio.

"I don't know how she did it but Detective Ramirez got out of the cuffs. They are now kicking the crap out of one another. Where is everybody?"

Sheriff Danny Lopez's voice broke in. Kevin could hear the roar of the helicopter turbines in the background. "We're three minutes out, Smitty. If you've got a flashlight, give us a sense for a landing zone."

THE TWO WOMEN were both experts in the martial arts. Punches, kicks and throws intermingled into an ugly ballet of violence. Jess kept the location of Adele's backpack in her mind's eye. Her Glock was in there.

Vega grabbed Jess's right arm, trying to rip away the bandage that Dr. Bob had secured over the knife wound she had received during the abortive meth lab incident. It wouldn't budge. Jess landed a right-hand chop to the side of Adele's neck and she went down. The Detective sprinted for the backpack as she saw a flashlight snap on near the tree line.

Vega was faster, grabbing Jess by the legs. The two crashed to the ground, Jess squirming out of the hold and planting a kick in Adele's solar plexus. She swung her handcuffed right hand at Adele's face. The sharp steel hasp sliced open a gaping wound on her right cheek.

"There's a gun in the backpack," Jess yelled in the direction of the light. For a moment she wondered if she was sharing the information with friend or foe. There wasn't time to make sure.

Vega was again on her feet. Only she wasn't running in the direction of the backpack. Overhead Danny's helicopter bathed the ground with an unhealthy white light.

"She's headed for the rim." Danny's voice boomed above the noise of the rotors on the chopper's PA system.

Jess recognized Kevin's voice. "I'm with the good guys, Detective, do you want this?"

The area was bathed in the luminance of the chopper's spotlight. Jess could see a large coil of rope at the canyon's rim. Vega kicked it into the darkness and snapped her harness into a rappelling position. She was over the edge in an instant.

Jess called to Smitty in her commanding voice.

"Is there another harness in that bag?"

"Nope. But there is a pair of gloves."

She met Kevin halfway, putting the gloves on and shoving the pistol down the back of her jeans.

"Tell Gates that we have a traitor on the team. Tell only her and nobody else. Do you understand?"

Kevin nodded. He would need time to get somewhere where there was a cell signal to transmit the text message.

"Nothing is ever easy," Jess muttered as she ran for the canyon's edge.

The helo followed with its spotlight.

Vertigo or not, she said to herself, I'm bagging this bitch.

Rappelling was part of the training protocol for undercover cops. Carefully concealing her fear of heights, Jess had done the minimum necessary to qualify. That didn't include a trip almost six hundred feet down into the darkness with someone below who wanted you dead.

The wound on her right arm was talking back at her with a vengeance. With her brake hand on the rope, she began the ride, fighting the throbbing pain. Adele's weight made the process difficult. But the pursuer was motivated. With her legs perpendicular to the wall and her torso leaning slightly outward Jess scampered after her prey. She was surprised that the vertigo wasn't an issue.

"Get mad at anyone or anything who wants to hurt you," her father said, all those years ago. "You'll forget everything else."

Normally, a rappel down the sheer face of a canyon was something to be savored. The natural force of gravity offset by the gentle friction of gloves against rope made for a scenic ride. Jess would remember little of it. Danny had the chopper pilot covering the scene with the spotlight. She could see Vega touch bottom and run in the direction of the river. There was an S-Rig waiting.

In the time it took Jess to reach the ground, Vega dragged the boat toward the rushing water, firing up the outboard the moment it was afloat.

The raft shot into the current with Jess running parallel to the river. There wasn't much space or time to get where she wanted to be. She ran up the side of a small boulder launching her body as best as she could in the direction of the dark apparition.

"You were right, Gates," Danny said into the chopper's radio. "They are heading straight for the Crystal Rapid."

ONE HUNDRED FIVE

Flagstaff Pulliam Airport

Mario McCallister paced back and forth in front of the computer monitor in the airport hangar. The GPS dots remained stationary. With flight operations done for the evening, the entire airport felt abandoned.

"It's driving me crazy not knowing what's going on."

He realized that Marty Laurent had hobbled outside to see if he could get a better signal on his handheld radio. Alexandra Clark was deep in thought, her steel folding chair leaning backwards against the hangar wall.

Ali seemed to be talking to herself.

"Our girl obviously thought of a Plan B to try to ditch us. What if she also has a Plan B in New York?"

Mario stopped in mid-stride. This girl's brain was always working.

"Bring up the schematic of our virus. Let's see if it has a Trojan Horse hidden in there somewhere."

Mario complied, but his impatience was evident.

"That could take hours."

"Maybe, but it's a good way to keep our minds focused on something we have a better chance of controlling. Let's..."

ALI STOPPED IN MID-SENTENCE. Her practiced eye noticed a single, tiny flicker in the interlaced scan on Mario's laptop screen.

"Let's what, Ali?"

Gates pulled a thumb drive out of her pocket.

"Let's run some quick diagnostics on your toy there, Mario. I'm getting an uneasy feeling."

She popped the USB device into a slot on Mario's laptop, opened a terminal window and typed a command.

Marty Laurent stuck his head around the edge of the hangar door.

"Hey, guys! Your FBI babysitter has been shot."

With a single vibration, Ali could tell that she had just received a text message.

It was from Smitty.

ONE HUNDRED SIX

The Colorado River

    The S-Rig river raft dipped and bounced amid the white froth of the Colorado, its thundering turbulence amplified in echoes off of the canyon walls. Vega Bannister knew this most dangerous section of the river well enough to have a false sense of confidence in her ability to navigate it in the darkness.

    She felt grateful for the bright beam from the helicopter's spotlight, seemingly guiding her towards mile 99.

    An apparition materialized out of the ink, landing hard in the bow of the craft.

YEARS OF HORSE-PLAYING around the Paloma YMCA Pool were imprinted into every fiber of Jessica Ramirez's body. The leap from the rock was almost reflexive.

    But now she was on her knees, off balance. The soft underbelly of the raft made it impossible to gain a footing.

Jess had the Glock in her hands, trying, unsuccessfully to aim it at her quarry.

"Give it up, Vega. Point the raft toward the shore before the rocks ahead kill us both."

"A fitting end to a pair of high-functioning psychopaths," Vega yelled over the roar of the rapids.

"It will be a short conversation with the department shrink if you make me pull this trigger. "

"I've saved the state a ton of money, Jessica. You and I both know that every one of the people I killed deserved to die."

"I'm not playing with you, Vega. Turn us toward the shore now."

Her eyes said it all. "Nothing will stop me from getting what I want. God help you if you get in my way."

The killer could decode the meaning in Jess's iron stare.

"We're not that much different, Detective. We both want retribution. You have to wait for a broken justice system to render judgment. I don't."

VEGA WAS surprised at the icy calm in Jessica's voice.

"You have two choices, Vega. You can let me put these bracelets on your wrists and take your chances with the justice system you so despise. Or you can die, right here, right now. Which will it be?"

Vega slammed the outboard motors to port. A gunshot echoed though the canyon. The bullet passed through Adele's right forearm, shredding the steel cables that controlled the direction of the propellers.

She looked upward in the direction of the sound.

She couldn't see a thing.

A second explosion echoed across the canyon walls. A projectile pierced the edge of Adele's shoulder, nicking the bone and shredding her right bursa sac. Even in the darkness, Vega could see the blood spurting from the wound.

FIVE HUNDRED FEET ABOVE, Danny Lopez could see the pinpoint flashes erupting from the Canyon's edge. He raised an AR15 Rifle into firing position, motioning to the pilot to refocus the light toward what he knew were gunshots.

The sheriff cinched his seatbelt tight around his waist and aimed his AR15 toward the gunfire.

"We'll only get one chance," he yelled. "Get me as good a view as you can."

WITHOUT THE SPOTLIGHT, it took a moment for Jess's eyes to adjust. As the scene came into focus, she could see Vega trying to stem the blood flow from her shoulder with her left hand. The S-Rig now without the powerful outboard motors spun and twisted in the swirling vortices of water.

They were entering the Crystal Rapid, out of control and in complete darkness.

ON THE UPPER CANYON RIM, a man with a high-powered rifle was caught in the piercing beam of the chopper's spotlight. He squinted to block it out as he turned his weapon in its direction. A single shot to the gas tank should bring it down.

Above the wail of the helicopter's turbines he could hear the AR15's unmistakable signature. He knew enough about helicopters to feel confident that the gunshots he was hearing would be impacted by the powerful downdraft of the aircraft's rotors.

But Danny Lopez had shot a half dozen errant bears who insisted on encroaching on campsites from choppers like this one. He know how to adjust his aim.

And sometimes fate intervenes.

A Federal Hollow Point round ripped into his neck, severing his right carotid artery, shattering the third cervical vertebrae as it exited his body.

The assassin responsible for the deaths of five fiber technicians and the explosion that killed Jessica Ramirez's father fell headlong toward the churning rapids, thinking it ironic that Vega had indirectly snuffed out another killer who nearly got away.

ONE HUNDRED SEVEN

Flagstaff Pulliam Airport

"Is this a company laptop, Mario?"

Mario McCallister was clearly perplexed by Ali's question. "Of course, it is."

"What I mean is, does this machine belong to the FBI?"

"No, ma'am. Remember? I'm a contractor. This machine was given to me by The Maitland Corporation."

Alexandra Clark picked up the computer and smashed it onto the concrete hangar floor.

She drew her own service weapon and pointed it at Mario's chest with one hand while showing him the message on her smart phone's tiny screen with the other.

"It's been phoning home, Mario. And something tells me our bad girl may have fucked me in more ways than one."

Ali jerked her head in Marty Laurent's direction. "Take my cell and press 9. Time to let Director Roberts know how the bad guys have been one step ahead of us."

Marty was confused, but in no mood to question a woman with

a gun. All he could muster was, "What do you want me to tell him?"

"Tell him that the contractor DC sent us has been sending our every move to a company with Russian connections. I'm not quite sure yet if Mario here knew about it, but until we're certain, it's best to keep him away from his technology. Grab the boy's cell, too, while you're at it, will ya?"

Mario was stunned. His voice trembled as he tried to sell his innocence. "I swear I had no idea my computer was sharing information with Maitland. I didn't even consider the possibility."

Ali's eyes narrowed. "That could be so. In fact, I really want to believe that you're telling me the truth. That friend who recommended the gay bar in Phoenix. Was she the one who ended up in my bed?"

The expression on the contractor's face spoke volumes.

"Director Roberts will have to sort out whether you go to jail for stupidity or walk the Green Mile for treason. For now, turn around for me so I can add some extra jewelry to your wrists."

The dawning realization was more than Mario McCallister could handle. Even if he could sell the story that he knew nothing about the hidden countermeasures, his career was over. There were darker secrets in his past that were sure to come to light now. He could feel the truth closing in on him.

The young Maitland contractor quickly weighed his options. There was only one. He felt for the extended filling that capped his right third maxillary molar. He bit down hard. The vicelike pressure from the mandibular molar below broke the cap, releasing the cyanide capsule within it into his mouth.

"I'm sorry I let you down, Gates," he said, just before the poison did its work.

ONE HUNDRED EIGHT

The Crystal Rapid

Jess saw the assassin fall into the canyon. Even in the darkness, she could see recognition on Adele's face.

"God damn the Captain."

Jessica heard Adele's words but couldn't make a connection. Keeping her weapon pointed at its target was the goal. Inside of her head, a raging argument was under way.

One voice was commanding her to pull the trigger. The moment of retribution was at hand.

The other voice was Tio Danny's. "We swore an oath to serve the cause of justice, not to dispatch it."

The Colorado River asserted its dominance, tossing the S-Rig into the air. The raft slammed back into the current on its side, launching Jess into the water.

The full moon revealed Adele's form, bobbing above the tiny mirrors of light that reflected off of the modulating currents.

A lifetime of competitive aquatics took hold. With strong, confident strokes, Jess clawed her way through the turbulent vortices toward her prey. She was surprised to see Adele's equally powerful arms pulling her in Jess's direction.

The two women collided as they shot over the top of a rock and into a tornadic hydraulic. Hands found clumps of hair. Fists tried to land punches, slowed by the density of the water. Jess felt a leg, intertwining her own around it.

Powerful fingers gripped her throat.

The pair ejected out of the hydraulic and slammed into the side of a huge boulder. Incredibly, Adele didn't release her grip, forcing Jess's head to remain below the surface. Pressure on the arteries that pumped blood to her brain began to darken her consciousness.

The currents pounded Jess against the unyielding granite, dredging up a long-forgotten memory in her mind.

She was eleven, at the pool like always. Theo was a fifteen-year-old white kid, a bully who exerted privilege with his muscles, even though, in her barrio, it was he who was the minority. An argument over a beach ball devolved into a grappling match. Theo held Jess's head underwater. She could hear muffled laughter above her as she flailed away, consuming the oxygen in her system. Somehow, she was able to get a hand above the surface and slammed Theo's head into the side of the pool. He released his grip and began to sink to the bottom, thoroughly concussed and unconscious. It was Jessica's junior lifeguard training that saved the little punk.

He never bothered her again.

All of this raced through Jess's mind in the space of a nanosecond. Following Adele's arms with her own, she was able find the woman's head and set her hands on each side.

Pressing her thumbs firmly into Adele's eye sockets, Jess expended the last of her strength slamming the woman's skull against the wall of rock.

The hands that gripped Jess's windpipe released. Her mouth broke above the surface and she gulped some air. The oxygen recharged her muscles and she again smashed Adele's cranium against the sleeper, this time with greater force.

Even in the swirling blender of the rapids, Jess could taste the blood. Her eyes focused. Her antagonist was now limp, pressed against the boulder by the steadfast water pressure.

Jess could hear her uncle's voice. "You have neutralized the threat. Let it go."

"For my father," she said to herself, watching the puppet-like waving of hands and legs in time with the uneven flow of the water. Jess released Adele's inert body, allowing it to slip away from the sleeper and back into the most dangerous section of the Crystal Rapid.

Now, her only thought was self-preservation.

In the darkness, Jess had no idea where more sleeper rocks might lie or what fresh turbulence might smash her body to bits. She assumed the survival position, floating on her back, trying to keep her head and legs above the water.

Jess closed her eyes. She did not think about Vega, nor the closure that killing the killer might bring. Her fury was directed at the river. She was completely at its mercy. For once in her life, she felt totally helpless. There was nothing to do but ride it out.

She let go of the rage, allowing her body to go as limp as possible, while maintaining a survival posture. As her mind started to clear, her father's face appeared before her.

He was smiling.

"You can do this, Jessi. *Tu puedes.*"

ONE HUNDRED NINE

Colorado River Mile 99

Stephen Morris stood with a dozen park rangers and several FBI agents at the take-out point, just below the Crystal Rapids. Several powerful floodlights bathed the river in artificial noonday sunlight. Five hundred feet above, Danny Lopez scanned the water for any sign of life. There was already a report that the S-Rig was lodged against a boulder a half mile upstream. The body of a male had been seen nearby, broken and lifeless on a jagged outcropping at the river's edge.

Binoculars swept the surface. Everyone realized they were holding their collective breath.

"There!"

One of the rangers pointed toward the confluence where the white water mellowed into a strong, steady current. A human form bobbed out of the foam, undulating unnaturally amid the eddies.

Strong arms lifted it out of the water as it came within reach, gently depositing the broken mass on the ground where two paramedics immediately began their work. It was clear that something had shattered the skull. Morris could see what looked like gray gelatin on the rubber gloves of one of the first responders.

"Brain matter," the medic said, shaking his head. "Note the time of death."

The head ranger shined a flashlight on the face, comparing it to a pair of photographs in his free hand. He nodded to an associate who pressed the transmit button on his radio.

"We have your suspect, Sheriff. She's dead."

A two-word response echoed back.

"Where's Jessi?"

There was another shout. The binoculars turned back toward the edge of the rapids. The battered and bruised figure appeared at the edge of the boiling vortex. A hand slowly raised, waving weakly but confidently in the direction of the rescuers.

The ranger with the radio didn't wait for an order.

"It's Detective Ramirez, Sheriff. She's alive."

ONE HUNDRED TEN

The Ninth Day - The Mayo Clinic

They wanted Jess to stay in a wheelchair. She wasn't having any of it.

She did agree to take the one recliner that sat next to Michael Wright's bed in room 314 at The Mayo Clinic. She was a mass of contusions, abrasions and bruises. But miraculously no broken bones.

Alexandra Clark sat next to her in the uncomfortable class-room-type chair that motivated family members to keep visits short.

Michael was breathing on his own but still slept. The scans were negative, but the docs were first to admit that they weren't sure how or if he might recover.

Jess thought Ali looked exhausted. They were all going on forty-eight hours without rest.

"I'm sorry about Mario."

"Me, too. If I hadn't been so focused on his technical genius, I might have been able to figure him out earlier." Ali sighed. "Men. A single gender responsible for the sum total of the world's problems."

For the first time since their encounter in the river, Jess thought about Vega, but not about her murders, her plot to destroy a good portion of the world's financial system or about how this woman had nearly killed her.

"What about Vega? Michael won't ever tell me, so maybe you will. What was she like?"

"In bed? A lot like I was that night. Desperate, sad, and I think, lonely."

"I guess in the end, we all want affirmation...and love."

The mood in the room was getting a little too serious for Ali's sensibilities. "Vega was smarter than I thought she was. The bitch modified my code."

"So that was what she was telling me at the canyon?"

"But I'm smarter than *she* thought. I had the guys at Paloma U run a scenario like this two days ago. Wouldn't you know, those little shits already had it worked out? Their scanner caught the bug and smashed it."

Jess's tone bordered on sarcasm. "Our financial system remains safe and the envy of the world."

Ali brushed a hair away from the Paloma Police shield she again wore on her belt. "And we're still underpaid and overworked."

"Why did that perp shoot the poor FBI girl at the airport?"

"Because she looked enough like me in the dark to make him think that's who he was killing. Our bad girl wanted to send both you and me to hell and her associate blew the identification. I thought the girl was attractive. Kind of a compliment in a perverse sort of way."

Jess put a hand on her partner's shoulder. "Are you OK, girlfriend?"

"Yeah. I just need to sleep in my own bed, with a good book, or someone who's read one."

Jess knew the humor and bravado masked a complicated soul, trying to exist in a world where conventional wisdom about who you should love singled Ali out for scorn. She could imagine the loneliness and pain her partner must feel.

But cops didn't express emotion to one another. She simply said, "One crazy way to spend a suspension."

Ali and Jess touched foreheads They said nothing, but their eyes spoke volumes. Their bond was unbreakable. Their friendship a treasure. Jess felt overwhelmed with gratitude. She could see it in her partner's face.

Ali finally broke the spell. "Tell you what. The next time I suggest coming with you on a vacation, talk me out of it."

Alexandra Clark slowly stood up and walked toward the exit. She stopped in the doorway, the smart grin was back on her face.

"Oh... And when that son of a bitch wakes up, slap him around for sleeping with my conquest."

The only sounds in the room were the soft, rhythmic chirps of the heart rate monitor and the regularity of Michael Wright's breathing.

It took effort, but Jess was able to get to her feet and lean over the edge of the bed so she could whisper in his ear. The warmth of her breath reflected Michael's masculine scent back to her nostrils. The memories of their first meeting in the squad room at Paloma, the night at the hotel and the nightmare at the condominium rushed back into her consciousness.

Jess thought she detected the slightest flicker in the catatonic eyelids. She gently twisted Michael's expressionless face toward hers.

"Wake up, Michael Wright. Cut out this unconsciousness bullshit and show me that you are as tough as I think you are."

The rhythm of Michael's breathing broke. The FBI agent inhaled slowly, as if he were tasting the clear Arizona air for the first time. His eyes opened, corneas contracting in response to the sunlight that was streaming in through the windows.

"Jessica." Michael's voice was just above a whisper. "Did we get her?"

He was alive!

"We got her."

"Is she dead?"

"Yes."

"And the virus."

"Destroyed. Your world is again safe for democracy."

"Jess, there's something I want to tell you..."

Jess pressed the red button that alerted the nurses' station.

"Shut up, Michael. I'm getting the doctors."

ONE HUNDRED ELEVEN

The Mayo Clinic

Three familiar faces greeted Jess as she entered the waiting room: Tio Danny, Dr. Bob and Dr. Price.

Ali was absent. Jess knew that goodbye moments were not among her best friend's most favorite things. She caught Danny's attention by typing on an imaginary keyboard.

"Yes, she's already gone," he said. "Bolted for the airport right before you got here."

Danny asked the question that was on everyone's mind.

"How is our boy doing?"

"He just woke up. Babbling like an idiot. The docs are with him now."

"How are *you* doing?" he said.

She looked at the two doctors, holding out her hands as if to say, "What do you guys think?"

"She'll be OK," Joey Price said.

"Only the good die young," Dr. Bob added.

Jess felt her own energy starting to wane. She found a chair and did her best not to look like she was collapsing onto it.

"On one hand, I feel like I should thank you all. You made sure that this good girl didn't die this week. On the other hand, I want to have a talk with my grandmother for even suggesting that I come out here. It's been an experience I could have definitely lived without."

"You had plenty of chances to back off," Danny said. "And it's pretty clear that we would not have caught up with our perp nearly as quickly without you and Alexandra."

"Most of us never get a 'save the world' moment, Jessica," Dr. Bob said. "Even though few people outside of this room will ever realize it, you had yours this week."

"More importantly," Danny added, "I think you answered that question."

"Which one?" Jess asked.

"Did you have what it takes to be a good cop? I think you've had it all along."

It was the key question of Jess's life. If this experience had taught her anything, it was that she would have to pass that test every day. She thought again of how the thundering power of the Colorado River nearly killed her. No matter how good or bad you were at the life you intended to lead, the game was ultimately a crap-shoot. You rolled the dice and dealt with the consequences. Why not expect that your dreams might come true? Why not take the risks to follow your passions?

As these things churned inside her mind, Jess expected to see Michael Wright's face appear. Even with his flaws, Michael was about as close to the perfect man as she had ever encountered. She was surprised to see a different face appear. Dara Torres.

The swimmer was exactly the age Jess was now when she competed in her final Olympiad. What might it take for Jess to rebuild her aquatic skill set to follow in her role model's footsteps?

She pushed herself up from the chair and stood.

"Dr. Price, are Margaritas indicated for pain relief?"

"I can prescribe something much stronger," Joey said. "It looks like you need it."

"Nothing doing," Jess said. "Which one of you boys knows a good bar where we can all go and self-medicate?"

ONE HUNDRED TWELVE

48 Hours Later - The Last Day -The Mayo Clinic

Jess could tell that Michael Wright was getting stronger. Would he be strong enough to say goodbye?

Her bags were packed. Tio Danny was outside, waiting to take her to the airport. The Family was what was important now.

Jess felt impatient as she stood next to Michael. He was sitting upright, his FBI agent eyes scanning the room. That was a good sign. When he turned to focus on Jess, his fingers gently caressed her cheek.

"You did good, Jess. I should have been more up front with you from the start."

"About a lot of things, you *pendejo*."

Michael grinned. Jess saw the dimples emerge at the corners of his mouth. She liked those dimples.

"Wow. That experience at the condo," he said. "Talk about unsafe sex. By the way, that mouth to mouth you gave me was superb."

"You're gonna be all right, Agent Wright. The docs say there is no permanent damage. Although I'm not sure I agree with them."

The intensity of Michael's gaze made Jess feel uncomfortable. She could have predicted what came next.

"I need to tell you something," he said.

"Please don't."

"I love you, Jess. I think I have since that moment I saw you arguing with that idiot Batavia."

Jess gently removed the fingers that were drawing circles on her cheek from her face. She placed Michael's hand over his heart.

"Be careful about that, Michael. We come from two different worlds. You may never understand mine unless I decide to let you in. My family is number one and anybody who wants to share my journey would have to accept that. And my career is in Paloma, not Washington or Phoenix or Flagstaff. In that river, when it was between me and mother nature, I wasn't thinking about retribution, or that woman, or you. I was thinking about how much there is still left to do. You'll have to work a lot harder to convince me that loving you is worth the sacrifice."

Michael was positively glowing. Jess wondered if he heard anything she had said.

"When you talk like that it only makes me want you more, Jessica. You are an extraordinary woman with a huge, sensitive heart. No amount of swagger can disguise that. In many ways, we share the same dream. You don't have to walk the path alone, Jess. Our relationship doesn't have to be about sacrifice. We don't have to share a home. We don't even have to live in the same town. I'll give you all the space you want. But I will be there for you when- ever you need someone to hold you, someone to wake up to in the morning, an ear to listen to your troubles and a partner to help you fight to create the world you dream about."

Michael flipped the hand that Jess had pressed against his chest, gripping hers, firmly but gently.

"Marry me, Jessica Ramirez. Let's share the adventure together, in good times and in bad, in sickness and in health, for as long as we both shall live."

Jess felt her cop skepticism kicking into high gear. The last week had changed her life in a profound, fundamental way. She needed time to process it all, to rediscover her own reality, to recalibrate who and what she wanted to become. The addition of another set of moods to this blurry picture was the last thing she needed.

Jess put Michael's hand back on his chest and touched his nose with an index finger.

"You have some *cojones, huevón*. Whatever drugs they gave you are warping your brain."

She could see Michael's strength returning. He raised his arms, taking her face in his powerful hands. She felt the tenderness in his touch as he gently pulled her toward him. She didn't resist it.

Her lips were inches from his. His breath smelled like peppermint and rubbing alcohol.

"You don't have to answer in this moment, Jessica. I just wanted you to know what *my* life's goal is now. Can we at least explore the possibility that two driven, independent spirits might just make pretty good soulmates?"

"Sounds like the drugs talking," Jess whispered.

He raised his head from the pillow, kissing her deeply, tenderly, lovingly.

Kissing, Jess decided, had a different meaning when there was something beyond blind animal passion behind it. She felt that same attraction the first day they met and had been wrestling her simmering desire for Michael Wright to the ground ever since. There was still so much they did not know about one another.

Jess wondered what this stranger was made of. This was one prize he would have to earn. Did he have the balls to pass the test?

Michael finished the kiss by running his tongue across her upper lip.

"What do you say, Jess? I don't know where this may ultimately take us. But can we at least try to see if what we feel right now might grow into something more?"

Jessica Ramirez smiled.

AFTERWORD

Shelley Appelbaum gave me Alexandra Clark, Jess's sidekick.

Eric Eggenberger taught me about poisons, asking me to blur real names where they might influence bad people to misbehave. Graham Hetrick's "I Speak For The Dead" opened my eyes to the world of the Medical Examiner. Joey Price's skills are patterned after Graham's gifts.

Lee Goldberg keeps telling me to "keep it short."

I try to emulate his style and sensibilities. Dan Brown, James Patterson, Megan Abbott and Alison Leotta all inspired and encouraged me at just the right moments, for which I am forever grateful.

Bruce Sokolove has been incredibly supportive of every endeavor of mine, since the day he called me to tell me what was wrong with Michigan State University in 2010. He's given me a number of behind-the-scenes experiences that taught me just how important and brave our men and women of law enforcement truly are.

Like many authors, I base some of my characters on real people and sometimes inject real cops into Jess's adventures. If you recog-

nize yourself herein, thank you for your selfless service to a popu-
lace that doesn't always understand the magnitude of your sacrifice.

Thanks to Bonnie Knutson for allowing me to bring her
wonderful husband, Bob, back to life. His penchant for Manhattans
and his deep love for his amazing wife are the whole truth and
nothing but the truth.

Mary Sutton turned me on to Dawn Alexander. Anyone who
hopes to learn the craft needs coaches and Dawn has been one of
the best. Thank you for helping me refine an art that is a constant
exercise in reinvention.

Authors often cringe when they get feedback from their editors.
Joan Turner's sensibilities were right on the money. A dozen roses
to Louise Dawn for bringing us together.

Each of us who take up The Craft had someone who encouraged us at just the right moment. For me, that person was Dr. Roy
Davis, my high school English teacher. He taught us about Ray
Bradbury through the music of Elton John and was the first to tell
me that I had what it took to grow into a good writer. Dr. Davis
passed away just as "Chasing Vega" was going to press. This story
would likely never have been written if our paths had not crossed.
Godspeed.

One can't undertake the solitary journey of a writer without
support at home. My kids and grandkids help me compartmentalize the daily grind, put up with me reading rough drafts and
always give me helpful and candid feedback.

My sister, Judy, honed her own editor's chops over years in the
publishing industry and a librarian's eye for an audience. Her sense
for what did and did't work was essential to my evolution as a
writer. We lost her just as the book was coming into the home
stretch. It is dedicated to her memory.

And then there's my wife. How I ever lucked out to get her to
marry me over four decades ago is still a mystery. She is my soulmate, my light and my true love. We treasure every day we are
given together.

Any inaccuracies or errors in these tales are completely my fault. I hope you suspended belief when necessary and enjoyed the ride.

Jessica has her own Twitter handle: @DetJessRamirez. I'm @TheTShepherd. You can get to know both of us better at TerryShepherd.com.

ABOUT THE AUTHOR

After too many years in corporate life, Terry Shepherd decided to reinvent himself and study the craft of Detective Fiction. He created his protagonist, Jessica Ramirez, in December of 2018 and has been putting her in peril ever since.

Terry and his wife live in Jacksonville, Florida, just minutes from their children and grandchildren. Terry also writes kids books about the, "Waterford Detectives", so his grandson can always have a starring role.

 facebook.com/the.terry.shepherd

 twitter.com/TheTShepherd

 instagram.com/The.Terry.Shepherd

EXCERPT FROM "CHASING THE CAPTAIN"

"Damn, that hurt," Jess muttered to herself. "Remind me never to fire an RSH-12 revolver with one hand ever again."

And what was wrong with her? Jumping onto a moving helicopter at the edge of a damn skyscraper? Jess's mind was in full fear-of-heights terror. Dropping 557 feet with a rappelling rope felt like an elementary school playground compared to this insanity.

But the man who ordered her father's murder and the man who contributed to Vincent Culpado's death were inside that cabin.

Jess intended to make them pay.

Her shooting hand was still numb but managed to slide the cannon back into her pants. She intertwined her arms and legs around the skid, holding on for dear life.

It occurred to Jess at this moment that putting a bullet into the engine of the only thing keeping her from falling to her death might not have been the wisest move. She didn't like the sounds of shattering metal and the black smoke that vomited out of the back of the enclosure.

And what if the bad guys knew she was right below them? Jess was a sitting duck.

One poor decision after another, Jess. When you make it
personal, you make mistakes.

As the terror swirled around Jess's insides, the outside world
snapped into focus and she beheld the sight below.

London at night was a picture postcard on its worst days. A
carpet of stars painted a ceiling above the city lights. The full moon
cast the dark concrete silhouettes below into stark relief. It was
breathtaking. Whatever building Jess had been in was perched on
the edge of the Thames. She didn't know enough of the city yet to
pick out landmarks, except one.

The London Eye was dead ahead.

"Don't call it a 'Ferris wheel,'" Lee had warned her. "You'll
make the locals think you're a tourist for sure."

The gargantuan trademark stopped taking passengers at 9pm.
LED lighting covered its spokes in blinking dot matrix, painting
pixilated scenes throughout the night that resolve into pictures at a
distance.

Jess could see a colorful depiction of the Union Jack as the
aircraft approached it.

They were losing altitude.

Jess's consciousness flipped back to survival mode. The distraction of the scenery vanished into what she tried to imagine were
possible landing sights.

Jess didn't like any of the options.

The uppermost gondola pods of the London Eye drew ever
closer. There was some question in her mind if the chopper could
clear them. Above the piercing whine of the turbines, she heard a
door swinging open above her. Voices were yelling.

"She's here. She's right below."

A fist appeared with an AK47 in it. The prop wash caught the
shower of bullets, throwing them back behind Jess as she clung to
the skid below. She knew the shooter would adjust for the slipstream the next time.

An idea came to her, and Jess calculated the odds. They weren't good, but she couldn't think of anything else to do.

The hand with the rifle appeared again, and Jess made her decision.

A pod loomed large directly below. It was now or never.

Jess unhooked her legs. A single appendage was all that separated her from a five hundred foot plunge to the unforgiving concrete below. Jess's right hand gripped the landing skid. The cannon was in her left.

The helio cleared the London Eye with ten feet to spare. Jess fired a single shot at one of the pod's skylight windows. It shattered into a million safety glass shards that littered the floor of the gondola.

Jess let go of the chopper and thought of her father.

"Chasing the Captain" - Book Two in the Jessica Ramirez Thriller Series - Available at Amazon.com

Made in the USA
Middletown, DE
04 September 2021

47589062R00205